Sand Castle

To Whitney,
With Best Wishes,
Joe Palmer
June 26, 2005

By

Joe Palmer

Library of Congress Cataloging-in-Publication Data
Palmer, Joe, 1951-
Sand Castle : a novel / by Joe Palmer.
p.cm.
ISBN 0-9715402-3-3 (alk. Paper)
1. Construction industry—Fiction. 2. Italian American families—Fiction.
3. Family-owned business enterprises—Fiction. I. Title.

PS3616.A339S26 2005
813′.6—dc22
2004046387

Printed in the United States of America
First Trade Publication 2005

Barnhardt & Ashe Publishing, Inc.
Miami, Florida
www.barnhardtashepublishing.com

For my wife, Vickie, whose love and encouragement made this book possible and my life worthwhile.

Prologue

The yacht was rocking gently to and fro, creaking as a boat often does in the water. It was anchored out in the deep Atlantic, miles from the Delaware shore. The sun bounced off the top deck, reflecting beams of light from the railing.

As the Coast Guard cutter gently pulled along the starboard side of the yacht, nothing seemed amiss, except that this 50-foot boat seemed to be deserted. Initially, Commander Jefferson Matthews had thought that Shannon Mahoney, young daughter of the vessel's owner, was overreacting because her father had not returned for the night. Perhaps he was out on the water, enjoying sailing time since his wife was visiting her family on Cape Cod. But now the commander and the entire crew sensed danger with the eerie quiet and apparent abandonment of the boat.

The commander ordered the boarding seamen to be cautious. They quietly boarded the boat, holding their weapons, ready to use them. There was soon a call for the commander to come down to the cabin. He jumped aboard and descended the stairs into the large cabin. There was John Mahoney and his assistant; hands tied behind their backs, kneeling in a slumped position. Both had been shot in the head, execution style. This seemed to be a professional hit.

Matthews was frozen in the moment. He knew now that the daughter had a right to be concerned. Matthews radioed the news of the murders back to shore. The daughter and the absent wife would be informed and an investigation would ensue.

Matthews instinctively knew that this was big news. Mahoney was the CEO of a national, high-profile construction company, whose roots were once reputed to be in organized crime. His Italian American wife, Teresa, was part owner of that company and member of the family that was liable for those roots. These murders were big news.

1

She had arrived! Judging from the flurry of the household staff assembled outside the main entrance of the house, this was an important occasion. Riggs, the butler and household manager, gave instructions to the maids about the receiving line. The household staff was so excited and happy about the arrival. Their line stretched from the main entrance down to the drive, eight staff members all in a row.

As the long black limousine wound its way around the circular drive, Teresa Viscomi Blake Mahoney leaned forward and gazed up at the summer mansion. She sighed as she contemplated the dreaded meeting about to take place. She reached down to calm three-year-old Sarah Ann Mahoney by placing a hand on her knee. Teresa then pointed the way to Craigville Beach to her sons, Robert Blake Jr., 13, and Anthony Blake, 11. The children were happy to be at their late grandfather's home on Cape Cod.

What did this Osterville, Massachusetts estate mean to her? What should she do with the home when she became its owner? Teresa honestly didn't know the answers to the questions and she was unsure that her husband, John Mahoney, would allow her the time to explore her thoughts.

This was the home that Papa had prized. Papa's purchase of this house was an announcement to the world that an Italian immigrant had made it. This was the home in which she spent many magical summers taking caravans of friends down to the Association Beach at Craigville. This was a place where family gathered and meals were shared. Here is where Robert had proposed and she had accepted.

Teresa returned from her memories to observe that the house and grounds seemed to be in utter chaos. Workmen were everywhere erecting tents for the grand reception that would take place tomorrow. The servants knew that Teresa would, and should be, their priority. The workmen would be gone in two days. By Sunday they would have dismantled the tents, chairs, and tables; but Teresa would remain. At least the staff was hoping she would.

Subdued in her thoughts, Teresa had little time to be embarrassed by the formality of the servants' reception until the limousine pulled up to the main entrance and stopped. Before the driver could get out to run over to the other side of the limousine, Riggs reached down and opened the door. "Welcome home, Miss Teresa, Master Robert, Master Anthony, Miss Sarah." The children scurried away to the kitchen, Robert holding Sarah's hand as he guided her through the house.

Teresa thanked Riggs for the reception in her usual friendly way and greeted each of the household staff by name. Teresa then asked Riggs which family members were present for the dreaded meeting. Riggs explained that Madame was awaiting her arrival in the library, along with Madame's attorney, John Swartz; Teresa's attorney, Joe Cutruzzula; and Teresa's brothers, Frank and Anthony Viscomi.

Riggs ushered Teresa through the foyer into the mahogany-paneled library. As they entered the library, Riggs announced "Mrs. Mahoney" and closed the double doors behind her as he exited. Madame rose from the sofa in the center of the room to greet Teresa. Madame Claudia Viscomi, Papa's widow and second wife, swished through the room as she greeted Teresa. "Welcome, welcome, Teresa. I'm so glad that you have decided to attend my wedding tomorrow. I was hoping to wrap up these negotiations with you or John on the phone so that you would not be inconvenienced. I'm hoping that you and John are seriously considering my offer."

Teresa took a deep breath before addressing Claudia. Her eyes swept the room and noted that there was nothing in the room that was indicative of the fact that her parents, Angelo and Catherine Viscomi, ever lived in this home. Claudia had completely and gaudily redecorated the room in an Italian provincial style. Where were the comfortable sofas and chairs that had made this home a summer haven for the family? "Hello, Claudia! I decided to come to your wedding because family means everything to the Viscomis. I am truly grateful that you have found happiness."

Teresa then greeted each person in the room until her eyes met Joe Cutruzzula's. "Joe, thank you so much for coming on my behalf today! It is so good to see you."

Joe moved quickly to the center of the room and hugged Teresa. "I couldn't resist your request, Ter. I'm glad to be of help to you and I'm glad to visit with your family. You know how much this family has meant to me through the years."

Joe Cutruzzula hardly looked as though he were the son of an immigrant Calabrese shoemaker from the North End of Boston. Joe, in his Italian-made, pinstriped, double-breasted suit, had the look of success. His swarthy complexion, combined with the wavy black hair, made him the object of much feminine attention. But Joe, though he had some brief relationships, didn't seem interested in a long-term, committed situation.

Joe was truly dedicated to the Viscomi family. His father, Vincent, journeyed with Angelo Viscomi to the United States from a small, hillside village by the sea in Calabria, Monte Paone. Vincent's destination was the North End of Boston and Angelo Viscomi's was Youngstown, Ohio, where he started a construction company and earned the millions that built a family empire.

Joe was eager to renew his old friendships and suggested that he, Teresa, and Anthony get together for drinks at his place on Craigville Beach Road in West Hyannisport. Anthony and Teresa agreed that they would like to get together in the near future since Teresa hoped to stay at the Cape for a short period of time.

"Let's get down to business," interjected John Swartz, Claudia's attorney. "Teresa, your husband, John Mahoney, informed us that you would be interested in receiving a cash settlement in exchange for the deed to this summer home. As you know, your father's will stipulates that upon any remarriage of Mrs. Claudia Viscomi, the ownership of this house, Sand Castle, and its contents pass to you. Mrs. Viscomi is willing to make a generous offer for the house and will negotiate on any of its contents."

Claudia interjected, "Because you and John own a large summer home near Bethany Beach on the Delaware Shore, I was hoping that you would consider a settlement on the house. I so love it here and the house contains special memories that can never be erased. I know how John dislikes the Cape and that you rarely get to visit your other summer home that you shared with Robert in Hyannisport. I hope we can be amicable about this house."

Teresa had prepared herself all day for the barrage and decided to speak up. "I'm not prepared to give Sand Castle up because Papa wanted me to have it. John Mahoney is my husband but he will not make this decision for me. Please don't try to coerce me; I'm determined to abide by my father's will at this time." Teresa then pleaded but stopped abruptly, "Joe?"

To spare Teresa from further confrontation with the formidable Claudia, Joe quickly interjected, "Please give us the papers to sign for transfer of ownership. We will be in touch at a later date if we decide to sell. Mr. and Mrs. Mahoney will need time to discuss this issue in private and sort out their thoughts."

John Swartz and Joe reviewed the papers and Claudia reluctantly signed them. Claudia's demeanor had visibly changed and it was reflected in her tone. "I've asked Riggs to prepare your house in Hyannisport for your arrival because we don't have room in this house for you and your family during the wedding festivities. You may select a vehicle to use for the next few days from the list that Riggs will provide. I'm not vacating the house until you and John come to a decision and force me out! Somehow, I think John will change your mind and we will be having a short chat in the very near future."

Claudia opened the double doors and called Riggs. "Riggs, show Mrs. Mahoney the vehicle list and get a member of the staff to help her unpack at the Hyannisport house. Then, please contact John Mahoney for me immediately."

Joe and the Viscomi brothers stepped out of the room and waited for Teresa. Teresa stopped as she reached the foyer, turned back, and addressed Claudia. "I'm not prepared to give the house up yet and John's persuasion or demands will not sway me at this time. I'm prepared to allow you use of the house, which we will negotiate later. However, don't try to manipulate me. I decide what I want for myself and my children."

At that, Teresa left with Riggs to review the vehicle list in the formal sitting room on the other side of the foyer. As her eyes glanced over the list, she saw that Robert's former Jeep Wrangler was still on the list. For a moment she considered asking for it, but she knew that John would be irate. She selected a blue 2001 Jeep Grand Cherokee. Riggs informed her that it would be delivered to Hyannisport that evening.

Teresa exited the house and met her brothers and Joe at the front entrance of the mansion. The group had made arrangements to meet for a 7:00 P.M. dinner at The Chowder House near the Hyannis Airport. Teresa agreed readily. Perhaps, she could avoid a call from John if she were at dinner. Joe then offered Teresa and the children a lift, but the limousine was already waiting to drive them to the other house.

As Riggs ushered the children back into the limousine, Teresa wondered what she would say to John about them staying in the Hyannisport house. Teresa realized that Claudia's maneuver in living arrangements had set her up for a terrible argument with her husband.

2

As the limousine pulled out of the driveway of the mansion, Teresa pointed to the gate's granite sign, "Sand Castle." She requested that the driver swing around to Craigville Beach on the way to the Hyannisport house. Teresa noticed that Joe was driving in the little Saab convertible ahead of the limousine and Anthony was behind her in his BMW. Anthony soon turned right to his house on Long Beach Road and then the other two vehicles turned left to drive the length of Craigville Beach.

The little cottages and motel across the street from the beach had yet to be filled with guests since this was the early part of May. The Barnacle, a small food concession stand that faced the beach, had yet to be unboarded for summer business. Teresa thought about the Barnacle, Robert, her brother Anthony, and those crazy, warm days at the beach. She tried not to think too much about Robert because she still missed him, but she couldn't help it now in these familiar surroundings. Would anyone believe that she still yearned for him after seven years and a new four-year marriage to John Mahoney, in addition to having a little girl to bring up.

Perhaps John knew her feelings about Robert. He certainly resented her attachment to the Hyannisport house. Claudia had indeed set her up for a fall with John. He would be in a rage when he found out that she would be staying in Hyannisport and with his daughter.

As the car rounded the bend on Craigville Beach Road, the beach became less visible. Joe approached his home, a blue Dutch colonial on the left side of the road. After he turned into his drive and got out of the car, he waved to Teresa and the children as they drove toward Hyannisport. Teresa was soon lost in her memories and anticipation in seeing the cottage. She had not stayed at the house since she married John four years ago. Papa saw to it that the house was maintained and he sometimes used it as a guesthouse when too many of the Youngstown relatives visited at once. Teresa and the children always stayed with Papa at Sand Castle until he passed away.

Teresa acted as a tour guide for the children. The car passed newly-built townhouses. Teresa pointed to them as she explained that the new houses sat where there was once the old candle factory. She then pointed to the tall fence as they reached the intersection of Scudder Lane and Irving Avenue, the location of the Kennedy Compound, home of the late Jacqueline Onassis.

The car turned right onto Irving and started up the hill toward St. Andrew's By the Sea. Teresa's home was halfway up the hill between St. Andrew's and the Kennedy Compound, a small, full Cape. There it was in all of its simplicity. The only major change made in the last seven years was a replacement of its white clapboard with now-weathering, cedar shingles.

When the car stopped, Teresa couldn't contain herself any longer, and she jumped from the vehicle. A voice from the door screeched, "Mrs. B! You're home!" Maggie ran out from the center door and wrapped her arms around Teresa. "Mrs. B, Mrs.B, how I've waited for you to come home."

By this time, little Sarah had run over to her mother and asked, "Mommy, why is she calling you Mrs. B? Everyone calls you Mrs. Mahoney."

"Hush, Sarah," replied Teresa. "Maggie knew me when I had a different name, Teresa Blake. You know Sarah, just like Robert and Anthony's last name."

"Maggie, I am so glad to see you!" shrieked Teresa. "It's been too long. Thank you so much for coming here to help us out."

Maggie hugged Teresa so tightly that it seemed that she would never let her go. Maggie was sobbing loudly. "Mrs. B, how could I miss the chance to see you and the boys and little Miss Sarah. Boys, give me a hug. I haven't seen you since last year when you came to stay with your grandfather in Centerville."

Maggie Sullivan had been an old Blake family retainer. She left the older Blakes on Nantucket when Robert had married Teresa. She lived with them on the Cape and in their Youngstown house. She left Teresa's employment soon after the marriage to John Mahoney four years earlier. It was incomprehensible for her to understand Teresa's remarriage. Mahoney's presence was very difficult for Maggie to abide.

Maggie would come to the Cape to stay at the big house whenever Teresa came to visit her father, without John. The Blake Trust paid for her wages and her supervision of the vacant Hyannisport house.

Teresa pulled Sarah up to Maggie and said, "Maggie, this is our Sarah. I finally have my girl!"

Maggie stepped forward and enveloped Sarah into her arms. "Miss Sarah, you are such a welcome sight," cried Maggie. Maggie would not allow her feelings toward the father hurt the child. Maggie stood and ushered Teresa into the house. Teresa held tightly to young Robert's hand as she entered the small center hall. Her eyes swept the hall and the joining rooms on either side.

Nothing had changed since she and Robert lived here. Dark, hardwood floors with braided rugs were beneath her feet. The furniture was the same. Colonial wing chairs in the living room flanked the Chippendale, camel-backed sofa. Pine occasional tables sat on either end of the sofa with brass lamps. The dining room sat to the right of the foyer. A large, dark-pine, oval table sat in the center of the mauve, oval-braided rug. Windsor chairs were placed around the table and a matching large hutch sat along the opposite wall. This house was a tasteful and homey retreat.

Teresa's eyes searched the rooms once more as tears filled them. Here is the home that she shared with Robert. Here so many happy days passed with him and the boys. How she missed this home; for that is what it truly was, home. John refused to come to this house. It was Robert's, and he wanted none of that. Although he was good to the boys, he would not tolerate anything around that would remind him of the late Robert Blake.

"Mommy, why are you crying? Don't cry, please," pleaded young Sarah.

"It's okay, honey. I'm just happy to be in this house after so many years. The boys spent their childhood summers here and we were so happy," explained Teresa. The boys took Sarah by the hand and showed her the upstairs rooms. Maggie promised the children that she would take them back to Craigville Beach to fly a kite if they hurried to change into their jeans. Maggie knew that Teresa needed to be alone with her thoughts.

Teresa sank into the comfortable wing chair in the living room. The tea that Maggie had served her was cooling. Teresa took a bite out of the chocolate chip cookies that Maggie had baked in anticipation of their arrival. Teresa was lost in thought. She understood why John would be so uncomfortable in this house. It breathed Robert. Its very essence held Robert's memory, even though there was only one photograph of Robert in the whole house, in the master bedroom. She sat with her memories, as Maggie ushered the children out of the house and into her car. Teresa called to them that they must come back in a few hours in order to meet the family and Joe Cutruzzula for dinner.

Teresa wondered what it would mean to her family to own the big house in Osterville and what would she do with this home? She and Robert had always planned on moving to Nantucket, either to his family's home still occupied by his parents, or nearer to the beach. All those plans had changed when Robert died. And John disliked the Cape. He kept urging Teresa to place the Hyannisport house on the market and sell the big house to Claudia. How could she let Claudia take over the big house forever? Papa tried to make sure that it would go to her and eventually to one of the children. But will the children want it, or will one of the boys choose their Blake grandparents' Nantucket home? The large beach house in Delaware, so modern and so unlike Teresa, was where John wanted to relax. The yacht was there, as were his children from his first marriage. John would never leave Bethany and definitely not for the Cape.

Ringing as though it were a shrill call to reality, the telephone interrupted Teresa's thoughts. "What in the hell are you doing there?" demanded John.

"Hello, honey," calmed Teresa. "The big house was in such an uproar that Claudia insisted that I stay here." John was clearly irritated. "There is no way in hell that I'm staying there," John stated emphatically. "I'll meet you at the wedding and leave directly for a rest for three days in Bethany. I hope you can wrap up this mess and get rid of those Cape Cod properties. Let's make a break with the past and move on to a bright future," John commanded.

"I'll talk with you tomorrow at the wedding, but I can't make a quick decision, Johnny. I just can't," Teresa gently responded.

Teresa hung up the phone and sank into her chair. How could she give up either of these homes and be buried alive in Delaware with John's friends and his children? That was not a clean break for her. Teresa knew that it would be difficult before anyone would be satisfied with her decision on the properties. Whatever was decided would bring controversy and derision. One or all would be very unhappy, whatever the outcome.

3

The dining room of The Chowder House was alive with chatter as Teresa ushered the kids into the non-smoking area. Anthony and his wife, Betty, came into the restaurant with their son, Joey, a short and chubby thirteen-year-old, who was anxious to see his cousin, Robert Jr.

The cousins chummed around together every summer during Robert's brief visits to his grandfather's summer home. Joey was often invited to visit Robert Jr. at his Uncle John's and Aunt Teresa's summer home in Bethany, Delaware. Sometimes Joey was invited to accompany Robert Jr. and Anthony when they visited their Grandpa and Gramma Blake on Nantucket. Both Robert Jr. and Joey missed the days when they spent summers in Hyannisport with Teresa.

The members of the family commandeered a large table in the dining room. All were dressed casually and Teresa's air of relaxation and warmth quickly enveloped the family. As they looked at the menus, Joe Cutruzzula sauntered in, wearing khaki shorts, a Cape Cod tee shirt, and boat shoes.

"Pushing the season a little, Joe?" inquired Teresa.

If Italians could blush, Joe may have. But he beamed. It was difficult for him to hide his obvious affection for Teresa. Joe had spent every childhood summer with Teresa. He had idolized Robert Blake when he ruled the beach at Craigville during his high school years. All the girls ran after Robert, who remained sincere and unaffected by the attention. Not Joe though, he preened and primped his hair and molded his fine, bronze body until the girls literally chased him down. Joe craved the girls' attention, perhaps as a ploy for Teresa to notice him. But Teresa had eyes only for Robert.

Joe had become fast friends with Robert and Teresa. He liked family occasions with the Viscomi family. He enjoyed Anthony Viscomi's companionship.. He looked up to Anthony and Robert. They were his heroes. This relationship lasted through college and even after Teresa's and Robert's wedding. He loved the Viscomi family and

Robert. But all that ended with Robert's untimely death. The car accident had been such a tragic surprise.

After the accident, Joe and Teresa became closer. They shared the grief and the longing for a loved one who is lost forever. After two years, Joe tried to share his deep feelings with Teresa. He was in love. But Teresa had recoiled. Not because of Joe, but because of her love for Robert. To fall in love with a close friend of Robert's was unthinkable to her. It was too close for comfort. Joe knew all of her past and all of her emotions. She was too vulnerable with Joe. No, it was not right, not possible.

On the other hand, Joe and Anthony became like brothers. Joe replaced Robert in Anthony's life. Anthony could not turn away from Joe. He wanted that warm male relationship, something he could never have with his younger brother, Frank. Joe and Anthony began to sail together out on the warm waters of Nantucket Sound. Sometimes they would sail over to Nantucket, taking Teresa and the boys to visit Robert's parents, the elderly Blakes. And that ended, too, when Teresa married John Mahoney.

Anthony rose from his place to embrace Joe. Joe, in turn, bent to kiss Betty and Teresa on the cheek. He greeted each of the children, separately acknowledging each by name.

Anthony joked, "Guess we outlaws weren't invited to the rehearsal dinner tonight!" Joe bellowed out that it was no loss to anyone at The Chowder House. Teresa and Betty decided not to comment in front of the children.

Anthony cursed his brother Frank and wife Sarah who were at the dinner kissing up to Claudia. "Frank will give his eyeteeth to remain in Claudia's good graces. He wants to be mentioned in the will. He covets the big house and he is confident that Claudia will win her tug of war with my awesome sister! Hey, Sis, did you know he has been talking daily with that husband of yours?"

Anthony did not mince words when Claudia and John Mahoney were concerned. He was disturbed that Claudia had a large part in administering the family's fortune. Frank had given in and John Mahoney was a usurper. Life had been so much better before Papa married Claudia. Anthony was known to rail on for hours about the family business and the interference of Claudia and John Mahoney. No one could silence Anthony but Teresa.

"Enough, enough, Anthony! Let's bury the hatchet tonight and forget about this horrid family business," pleaded Teresa. "I am so weary of this! Are houses, companies, and inheritances worth being miserable for the rest of our lives? Is this what Papa would have wanted?"

Anthony responded that Papa should have never married Claudia. That wedding forever disrupted the peace. But Teresa pleaded to stop the conversation since she would soon be debating the house issue with John. She wanted a lively, fun-filled family dinner tonight. But Anthony was on a roll. "Enough is enough, Ter. Especially since you married that jerk, John Mahoney." Teresa looked wounded and glanced at little Sarah who had not heard the remark. Betty quickly rebuked her husband as Joe shot Anthony a dark, disapproving look.

"I am sorry, Sis, truly I am. I would never hurt you. I just get carried away. Please forgive me, Ter," pleaded Anthony. Teresa immediately absolved her repentant brother. They called for the waitress and ordered dinner. Teresa would not allow anything to spoil this evening since much discomfort would come by attending the wedding and dealing with Claudia. Teresa adored The Chowder House and nothing was going to prevent her enjoyment of the baked stuffed lobster.

Across town at the Hilton resort, the rehearsal dinner was getting into full swing. Glasses of champagne were raised in homage to the wedding couple. Frank Viscomi was very pleased to offer a toast in honor of the couple. "To Claudia and Carlo, may they be happy for at least 100 years. May they know the love of the entire Viscomi family. God bless both of you."

Cheers erupted from the crowd and Sarah Viscomi beamed with pride for her husband, Frank. Claudia and Carlo embraced and kissed. The three-piece orchestra began to play as Carlo ushered Claudia to the floor, her pink chiffon dress bellowing as if in a gentle breeze.

This was not a true Viscomi gathering. Frank was the only stepchild present. The guests were distant relatives or business associates of the late Angelo Viscomi. All were afraid to snub the bride because of her obvious power in the company. It was better to risk Teresa's feelings. Claudia, Frank, and John Mahoney certainly formed a triumvirate that ran the company, despite Anthony's views. Teresa usually stayed in the background allowing her husband to attend to the business.

The glasses clinked all evening with toasts. The prime rib dinner certainly showed no vestiges of the Viscomi family's immigrant background. No, this event was a societal happening. Anyone who was anyone, in Youngstown, Ohio, was here. Several of John Mahoney's managers were here from the York, Pennsylvania Branch of Viscomi Construction. Cape Cod society stayed away; after all, this was New England. Even though this was a moneyed event, it was an event with Italians.

Frank Viscomi cut in on Carlo to dance with the bride-to-be. Frank's wife, Sarah, who was always the family's live wire, danced with Carlo. All seemed to be having the time of their lives. The evening stretched into the wee hours of the morning, long after Teresa and her children had settled into their beds in Hyannisport.

4

The morning of the wedding was glorious. The sun beamed brightly through the trees in Hyannisport. Teresa woke to the smell of coffee brewing in the kitchen. She jumped from the bed, dressed in slacks and a sweatshirt, and bounded downstairs to the kitchen. Maggie, ever alert to the sound of Teresa's feet on the stairs, poured Teresa a cup of coffee. Teresa and Maggie sat at the dining room table. Both thanked the good Lord for the weather and the strong coffee. Teresa ate a blueberry muffin and drank her coffee swiftly. If she hurried, she could take a stroll around Hyannisport, to the special spots she had shared with Robert.

Teresa was going on a sentimental journey this morning. She was venturing out to meet Robert's spirit and to reminisce about times gone by. Teresa tied her shoulder length dark brown hair back into a ponytail. Sunglasses hid her dark brown eyes. The bulky sweatshirt did not accentuate her trim, feminine figure. Her five foot five inch frame, typical of an Italian heritage, did not indicate the strong character that lay within. Teresa had resolve and was fiercely protective of both her family and of Robert's memory.

Teresa exited the door and walked down the hill and straight down the road to the dock. Approaching the dock, she eyed the sleek sailboats anchored there. She turned and walked back up the street to the corner of Irving and Scudder and turned down to Nantucket Sound. She passed the homes of the Kennedy Compound and gained access to the beach through the Hyannisport Beach Association. There she walked on the beach in bare feet while holding her shoes in her hand. She so loved it here. There was much less traffic at this time of the year and it certainly was different than when the late Jacqueline Kennedy Onassis came to her home. In the past, police were stationed here to direct the traffic. Now, only a sign directing traffic past a stockade fence indicated that this was once a president's summer home.

Teresa walked over to the private road to Squaw Island and circled back to the house. It was still early and she needed to prepare for the onslaught that would come from family pressure at the wedding. She was not looking forward to seeing Claudia wed or facing the ire of John over the house.

John wanted to be free and clear of the Cape. He was tied to it as long as Papa lived because of loyalty and the business. Now, he resented coming here and being faced with Robert's memory, Robert's house, and Robert's grave in the nearby St. Francis Xavier Cemetery. Robert was not buried with his Bostonian ancestors, but was given a plot at the Cape. His widow wanted him to be buried close to where she wanted to live, where they were happy together. Owning the Osterville mansion and estate certainly complicated matters now. John would not be tied to the Cape and John demanded loyalty, complete loyalty, and wifely obedience.

Teresa expected a major altercation over the house. *Was John right?* she asked herself. After all, she owned several homes. She owned a house in Hyannisport that was maintained by the Blake Trust. She and John built a modern summer home in Bethany, Delaware. Bethany was the place John loved the best. She sold the home she had shared with Robert in Youngstown after the remarriage and relocated to York, Pennsylvania. In York, Teresa and John built a thirty-five-room home. Teresa managed the home as John expanded the Viscomi Construction Company. Bethany was a short drive from York and the family could unwind there in the beauty of the ocean and blue skies.

How life had changed. Summers spent here on the Cape and winters in Youngstown were the norm through her childhood and her marriage to Robert. Life with John revolved around York and Bethany. Life had changed and so must her habits and traditions. She had chosen John; now she must honor that choice. But did that choice demand her turning over the family heritage to Claudia for money?

Teresa was lost in her thoughts as she arrived back at her house. If she chose to keep Sand Castle in Osterville, what would she do with this house in Hyannisport? Dreading the showdown with John and Claudia, she did not realize that Joe was seated in the dining room with Maggie and the children. Joe was here for her. Dear Joe, he was always there when she needed him.

Joe rose from the chair and embraced Teresa. Wishing her good morning, he settled back in the chair. "Maggie, I have forgotten what a great cook you are. This breakfast is simply wonderful and you did it for me." Joe gushed over Maggie; he always did.

Maggie beamed because of the praise. "You always could get me to cook for you, Joseph! I'd do almost anything for that praise." Joe quickly answered her, "Come away with me, Maggie, my love. Teresa wouldn't have me, what about you?"

23

"I'm twenty-five years older than you, Joseph Cutruzzula. Stop your nonsense so that I can clean this place up before you all go to the wedding." Joe could always charm her. In fact, he was charm personified.

"Ter, I've come to see if I may escort you to the wedding." Joe smirked at Teresa as she grinned and thanked him for his thoughtfulness.

"Thanks so much, Joey. John is coming up from York and should be here. I don't want his bad mood, because of Sand Castle, extended to you. It would be much easier if we kept it between the two of us and you were on the sidelines," answered Teresa. "I can certainly take care of myself."

"I took care of you when we were kids, let me help!" retorted Joe. Teresa seemed lost in her thoughts and really didn't want distraction. "Joe, I'll need you later. I want the house, I want my children to know the happiness that I knew at Sand Castle; to feel the warmth of family. I'll try to pacify my husband. You keep Claudia and her lawyers off my back. Deal?"

Joe quickly replied that it was a deal. "Guess I'll go home and dress in my finest for this shindig. I'll see you there! I know this is difficult for you but it'll be over soon and Claudia will be on her way to the Chesapeake to get on that yacht and go down to the Caribbean."

Joe was trying to be supportive because he knew the dynamics of the situation. The relationships were almost too much for Teresa—the marriage of a rich stepmother, whose wealth came from the Viscomi family fortune, to a former flame from the old country.

Claudia disliked her stepdaughter, Teresa, the most because she was the apple of her father's eye. As the second wife, she simply resented the father-daughter relationship.

Anthony, Teresa's brother, disliked both Claudia and John Mahoney, Teresa's second husband. Anthony resented Claudia's and John's interference in the business, even though it had never been more successful. He allied himself with old family friends who were not part of the construction business. Rumors had it that these friends of Papa were involved in organized crime.

And then there was Frank, the brother who supported Claudia and worked well with John. He was always loyal to his brother-in-law, no matter what the issue. Frank loved Teresa, but he was determined to stay within the power of the family and the construction company. Thus, he remained on the best terms with Claudia.

Carlo was Frank's friend and a retainer of the late Angelo Viscomi. He had romanced Claudia in the old country before she met and married Angelo Viscomi. Complicated relationships produced complicated situations during social occasions.

The family relationships and dynamics were complex. John worked with Claudia and kept her involved in the business even though Teresa, Anthony, and Frank owned equal shares. Teresa knew that John had great business sense and left the matters to her husband, even though she sometimes differed with his decisions. John aligned Teresa's shares of the company with Frank's and Claudia's. Anthony was always outvoted. Teresa's head was pounding, a terrible migraine had suddenly appeared. "My God," she cried out in desperation. "How will I ever get through this?"

Maggie grasped her hand and pulled her close, rocking her. "Hush, child; remember, everything works out in the end," soothed Maggie. "God's will be done; so seek it."

Teresa sobbed and choked back her tears. After hugging Maggie, she slowly moved up the stairs to prepare for the wedding.

5

The afternoon was sunny and the sun peaked through the leaves of the trees that covered the streets of Hyannisport. Teresa prepared to leave the house with the children. The boys were dressed in pinstriped suits, with long red ties. Little Sarah Mahoney was dressed in her best finery.

When Teresa descended the stairs, the children loudly applauded her beautiful appearance. Teresa was dressed in a very becoming navy blue and teal suit. It spoke of elegance and simple sophistication. She wore gold earrings that had been given to her by Robert, a simple gold crucifix that was a gift from her father, and a diamond and emerald encrusted wedding band. She had felt that the ring was a bit gaudy and impractical. It represented John's success, much as Sand Castle was Papa Viscomi's statement of achievement. She had accepted his selection of the ring and provided him with a white gold ring with diamonds around the front. Pleasing John had been and continued to be her priority. He had taken her, loved her, and protected her from a dark, cruel world. That world was an unfriendly place that left her husbandless and her children fatherless.

Teresa took Sarah's hand and called to Maggie, "We're off, wish us luck and pray for me."

Maggie rushed to the door, kissed Teresa, and straightened the boys' hair, pushing the bangs away from their eyes. "God will bless you, Mrs. B. It will be all right. Trust in God." Teresa squeezed Maggie's hand as she exited the foyer with her children. The chauffeur of the awaiting limousine stepped forward to open the door for Teresa and the children.

The car wound around Craigville Beach Road. Joe's house looked empty and dark. Teresa was consoled that she'd at least see his smiling face at the wedding. The traffic was backing up at the entrance to Sand Castle on the Osterville end of Main Street. The sun was bright and there was a gentle breeze coming from Nantucket Sound.

As Teresa's limo entered the grounds through the grand, wrought-iron gates, she leaned over to peer at all the elegant tents displayed on the lawn. Champagne fountains and strolling violinists were the precursors of the event. The orchestra was beginning to set its music in order and guests were ushered out onto the chairs that were arranged upon the lawn. The lawn was overflowing with guests. Teresa greeted old family friends and family retainers, especially the longtime associates of her late father, Angelo Viscomi. These were the associates that didn't quite fit into the construction business.

Mario Testa had brought his twenty-five-year-old son with him to present the young man to the Viscomis. Tony Foccata was well on his way to feeling no pain as he sipped his tenth glass of champagne. Tony was rough looking; he had hardness in his soul. He moved through the crowds with his obese wife. What a pair! He had an uncouth appearance and she wore a size 26 paisley dress. Teresa couldn't believe that Claudia had invited them as she was always condescending to the old retainers. Looking past Tony Foccata and Mario Testa, Teresa focused in on a very handsome Joe Cutruzzula, who was talking to her brother and sister-in-law, Frank and Sarah.

Riggs greeted Teresa, as John Mahoney stepped forward to roughly grab his wife's arm. "Get inside this minute," spewed John. "I have had quite enough of your memories and their interference in my life. Enough is enough!" John was rough in his manner and curt in his language. He had nothing to lose in being direct.

Anthony, upon observing John's roughness, began to walk toward his brother-in-law. Joe quickly stepped in front of Anthony and stared him down. "Anthony, now is not the time. Teresa is expecting inappropriate behavior. Let her take care of this today," Joe pleaded.

Anthony groaned loudly and shook off Joe's hand. "All right, but I'm gonna make him pay and he'll know it is from me when it happens," answered Anthony.

Betty came over and led Anthony and Joe away to retrieve a champagne cocktail. Teresa's children followed young Joey Viscomi, while his parents entered the house through the marble-floored, front hall. Joe watched the couple enter the home and pleaded with God to protect Teresa.

John was much rougher with Teresa than ever before. His grasp on her wrist had left a red mark and he pushed her roughly into a chair. "I want to be rid of this place and this sick, God-forsaken, family enclave," bellowed John.

Teresa gathered her composure and stood, shaking inside. "John, calm down and give me a chance to discuss this with you. Let's put on our best faces for the family and the associates. We can come to an agreement about everything in the next few weeks. You know that this is difficult for me. I want to do the best thing for all of us."

John responded that he was not staying at the Cape more than an hour after the start of the reception. He wanted to stand by Teresa's side and represent the power of both the family and the company when the old man's widow wed. Appearance was everything to him. He was in charge and he wanted all to know his power.

Relenting, but only for the present, John offered Teresa his arm and they descended the front steps of the mansion. Teresa quickly gathered her composure from the rough treatment. John escorted Teresa to the chairs reserved for the bride's family. Shortly thereafter, Anthony and Betty, along with Sarah and Frank Viscomi, joined them. All of the children were to march down the green aisle of the lawn before the bride. Joe Cutruzzula sat closer to the back, behind the company officers and the dreaded family associates.

As the music began, Claudia followed the children down the aisle. Her petite, knee-length dress was very flashy in its stark black and off-white colors. Carlo waited for her at the end of the temporary aisle. The judge invoked God's name and all responded in a great Amen. The service was short and sweet. It ended with the bride and groom standing in a receiving line.

Teresa and the children wished Claudia well and congratulated Carlo. Claudia received Teresa's good wishes with misgivings. However, Claudia warmly greeted John, throwing her arms around him. "John, my savior, you are here and will straighten things out before my honeymoon is over." John whispered that everything would be resolved within the next week and that Claudia would be able to return home to Sand Castle once more.

Teresa winced at the conversation. How could she withstand such pressure? John's behavior was becoming abusive. How could she escape his wrath and hold the marriage together? John demanded obedience and loyalty. She knew she would talk with Joe as soon as possible and ask his advice. It certainly seemed that keeping the estate would be impossible.

The orchestra tuned and began playing, while the prime rib dinner was served. Teresa mused that this was a fine show, staged with her father's money. *How different was this display from the traditional Italian fare of my first wedding to Robert,* she thought. The family was losing its traditions and cohesiveness. The loss was made evident in the little things—music and food. Was she the only one who longed for the tradition? *Where was the heritage of an Italian family? Where was the history?* she silently questioned.

After a tedious, two-hour stay, John had had enough and told Teresa he would see her in a few days at Bethany. He and Teresa moved to bid farewell to each member of the family and the old company associates. He moved around to work the crowd before leaving.

"I'm sorry Teresa, I just want us to simplify our lives. We don't need more homes in distant areas of the country. I must attend to the business in the East as Frank and Anthony do in Youngstown. I want you close to me in Bethany where we can be together and my girls can visit." John then bent and kissed her on the cheek.

Teresa had almost forgotten about her erstwhile stepdaughters, Kara and Shannon, who were very stubborn. Her relationship with them was fragile and always tedious. The only bridge between her and John's daughters was the love each had for little Sarah Mahoney. Living on the Cape would be impossible for them, given their reluctance to move away from Bethany Beach.

"John, there's a lot to talk about; but you should know that I am dedicated to preserving our family and making a wonderful life for all of us, including your girls," responded Teresa.

John kissed Teresa's hand as he and his assistant moved toward the driveway to leave for York. John turned to say goodbye to Frank Viscomi when he noticed Anthony by the champagne fountain with Mario Testa and Tony Foccata. They were huddled together in a Machiavellian pose. John kissed little Sarah goodbye as he entered the waiting limousine.

Joe Cutruzzula walked over to Teresa's side as John's car headed out the gates toward the Hyannis airport. Joe put his arm around Teresa's shoulders and suggested that she take the day off tomorrow to sail to Nantucket to visit her in-laws, the Blakes. Teresa responded with enthusiasm that the kids would want to go, as would Anthony and Betty. "Let's do it, Joe; let's do it."

At that moment, Claudia departed the house with her new husband. She grinned at Teresa and waved goodbye. She called loudly to Riggs, "Have the decorator awaiting me upon my return. I intend to redo the rest of the house."

6

Anthony and Betty arrived with little Joey at 6:30 A.M. The wind was brisk and the ocean rough. Fog was settling in and visibility was very poor. Teresa and the boys had awakened early to greet the Viscomis. Teresa offered breakfast pastries, juice, and coffee to the group as they awaited Joe. Teresa was very anxious about sailing in this weather. While loving the wind in her face, she really wanted the sun also. Poor visibility was not something that she could brave. This one issue was the only thing that caused major differences in the past with Robert, who had been so carefree and fearless. It was so ironic to Teresa that he lost both his life and a major part of hers in an unfortunate automobile accident.

Joe arrived to greet the assembled family. He readily accepted a cup of coffee and a glass of juice. He was dressed in sailing attire and his olive skin already looked slightly tanned. "Ter, what do you say about scrapping the sailing trip and taking the Hy-Line Cruise to Nantucket? I'm not comfortable with the weather."

Teresa smiled, knowing that Joe was keenly aware of her phobia. He had no intention of ruining the day for her. "Thanks, Joe, I would really appreciate relaxing aboard a larger ship. Grandpa Tom and Grandma won't want us to cancel." Anthony and Betty quickly agreed. Young Anthony, Robert, and little Sarah piled into Uncle Anthony's van with thirteen-year-old Joey. Teresa and Joe boarded his red Saab. Joe called out that he would follow Anthony to the docks in Hyannis.

As Teresa rode to the docks, she pondered the recent events with John, who expressed his strong feelings about her need to break with the past. It was easier said than done. She felt no attachment to Bethany, although the beach was wide and beautiful. The surf there could be ferocious, unlike the calmer waters of Nantucket Sound. The house there was modern, built on stilts to withstand hurricanes and the resulting floods. It was beautiful but never really the charming home that the Hyannisport home and Sand Castle were. Besides, John's girls visited there. Sometimes they were very disagreeable and they resented her invasion of their father's life. They truly disliked Teresa for her presence in their lives. The only thing they had in common with Teresa was their love for young Sarah Mahoney.

Teresa had lain awake most of the night, debating with herself about keeping her father's wishes and living part-time at Sand Castle. She just couldn't see how to make it work with John on this issue. Her only conclusion was that she must sacrifice the Osterville mansion to smooth the waves of her troubled marriage. Perhaps she could sign over her ownership of the Hyannisport cottage to the boys. The Blake Trust continued to pay for the expenses of the home and the boys visited there from time to time. John couldn't possibly complain about that house. After all, there were no financial obligations and it would eventually go to the boys. Teresa resolved that she would endure future summers in the modern beach house in Bethany.

As Joe drove pass Saint Francis Xavier Church, Teresa told him of her thoughts. "Joe, I must ask you to prepare papers to sell Sand Castle to Claudia. It's the only solution. I've contemplated it over and over. I must do this to save my marriage and family."

Joe was somewhat surprised but admired Teresa for her determination and sacrifice. "Okay, Ter, I'm so sorry that it had to come about in this way. No problem, I'll draw up the papers for the sale tomorrow." Joe wouldn't even try to dissuade Teresa because he knew about the terrible stress of the situation. He hoped that she would not be remorseful about selling the estate after all was said and done.

Following in his Saab, Joe pulled up behind Anthony's vehicle in the parking lot of the Hyannis docks. Teresa and Joe emerged and met the others at the ticket booth. Joe and Betty ushered the kids onto the boat as Teresa asked Anthony to stay on the dock for a few private words with him. Joe carried little Sarah on his shoulders, as young Anthony and Robert Jr. followed with Joey Viscomi.

"Anthony, I've made an important decision. You should be among the first to know. I am going to sign Sand Castle over to Claudia. I can't fight John over this issue. I must keep my family together. The past surrounds me here, in Hyannisport. I'm overwhelmed by Robert's memory. In Osterville, Papa is still alive and doting on us. It's just too much for John to deal with and it's not fair to him or the children. He needs to be his own man without shadows from the past, whether it be a late husband or a dead father-in-law."

Anthony listened tensely, holding his jaw muscles together. Anger was visible on his face and his eyes grew dark. "That bastard, that Mic bastard. You marry Irish and this is what you get. Our whole family loses its heritage and birthright. If you don't want it, then Sand Castle should be Frankie's or mine. Claudia ruined the family when Papa married her and you just finished us off with John! Damn both of them!"

31

Teresa looked as though mortally wounded. Yet, she understood. "Oh, Anthony. You have a beautiful home right here on the beach and Frankie is a block away on Craigville Beach Road. I must save my marriage and try to make our family more cohesive. John promised Claudia the house. Right or wrong, he promised it. I just don't need any additional issues between us; his daughters certainly are enough for me to handle. I need to make this marriage work, for the boys and for Sarah."

Anthony softened somewhat for his sister. His face showed affection and he embraced her. "Ter, it's all right. I'll even suffer this one for you, but listen to me. I'm gonna make that bastard husband of yours pay. When I do, he'll know that I'm the one who did it. I promise you this!"

Teresa turned and boarded the boat. Looking toward Joe, she smiled and suggested that they ride up on the open deck, despite the fog, mist, and chill. Joe asked Betty to get refreshments for the kids and he waved for Anthony to board since they would soon be underway. But Anthony was using the pay phone at the dock. He appeared to be having a very heated conversation. He glanced toward Joe and waved. "I'll be up in a moment."

As the ship sailed for Nantucket, Joe and Teresa sat arm in arm on the deck. Teresa rested her head on his shoulder. Betty and Anthony ministered to the children's needs, serving hot chocolate and snacks from the ship's snack bar.

The voyage was uneventful. Before long, Anthony joined Teresa on the deck. "Ter, I love you and I will not let this come between us. We must support each other because we are all that's left." Tears were streaming down Teresa's face, as she hugged Anthony. "Thanks, kid, I need you more than ever. This is truly difficult for me, but you must understand, I mean to do it."

As the ship sailed into Nantucket, it passed Brant Point Light. The lighthouse foghorn sounded loud, the wind was blustery, and the sky was an overcast gray. After leaving the boat, the group made its way up to Tom and Naomi Blake's mansion. A former captain's home, its white clapboard shouted out to passersby that this is New England, this is Nantucket, this is old money, and social success.

Teresa, her arm through Joe's, gazed up at the widow's walk where she and Robert spent so much time sunning themselves, reading books from the Athenaeum, and cuddling while sharing their innermost and deepest thoughts. What happy times both of them had spent here. This would have been her home someday, if Robert had lived.

Tom Blake opened the door and ushered his guests into the large foyer. The mansion was decorated in eighteenth-century period. The papered walls reflected a warm informality. Tom embraced Teresa. This tall, gray-haired man, who was so culturally and socially skilled, had immediately accepted Teresa into his family long ago. He loved her deeply as if she were his own daughter. Robert's death and her subsequent remarriage did not in the least change his affection for her. Teresa was now and would always be a Blake to him.

Naomi Blake came rushing to the door, without her usual decorum. Her hair was drawn up in a bun, giving her a sophisticated New England, yet grandmotherly, appearance. She also embraced Teresa, before Tom ushered the entire group into the dining room. Naomi continued to hold tightly on to Teresa, with tears streaming down her cheeks. "Love, it is so good to see and hold you. You have been away too long. Come in, come in. Cook has prepared your favorite dinner. We all want to make this homecoming very special."

Naomi hugged the boys and young Sarah. Neither she nor Tom indicated any preference for the boys over little Sarah, even though she was not their granddaughter. They loved Teresa and they would love her child. They tried hard to forge a relationship with John, especially during their visits to York to see the boys. John, on the surface, seemed to tolerate the Blakes, at least in their presence. After their visits to his home, he always complained about their old-style ways and their fussiness.

Naomi and Tom presided over their guests at the long dining room table. The children chattered eagerly about a post lunch exploration of Nantucket Town. Roger Cook, the Blake family's longtime chef, fussed over Teresa who, in turn, fussed over his boiled New England dinner and special bread pudding dessert. Teresa felt warm and safe here. She adored both of Robert's parents and appreciated their affection for her. After being orphaned by the death of her father, she considered these good people her second parents.

Near the end of the lunch, the telephone rang. Tom Blake rose to go into his library to answer the phone. After an audible gasp, he demanded Naomi's presence in the library. Naomi could be heard sobbing and the room, full of adults, grew silent. With the children chattering away in the background, Tom called Anthony to the phone.

Teresa's mind was in a blur. *What could possibly be wrong?* Joe and Betty anticipated what could only be bad news. Teresa sat calmly and quietly, awaiting some kind of announcement.

Anthony called Teresa into the library where a weeping Naomi was leaning against Tom. "Teresa, it's Frankie. John has been murdered on the boat offshore from Bethany!"

7

Teresa felt like she was in a trance as she listened to her brother Frankie relay the news. Surely this was a terrible nightmare. She felt as though it was an out of body experience. She repeated each of Frankie's phrases for the group huddled around her.

"It was an execution style hit. John and his assistant were found with bullets in the back of their heads. Both were bound and gagged. No one else was on board. The Coast Guard observed the yacht drifting several miles out from Bethany, Delaware. They boarded the fifty-foot boat, where John and his assistant were found below in the cabin."

Teresa took in a deep breath and exhaled slowly. She could barely take it in, yet she immediately decided to make some snap decisions on details for the next three days. The details of arrangements buffered her from the reality and shock.

"Frankie, please make arrangements for a funeral in Youngstown after official inquiries are over. Anthony, we can use Papa's house, I mean, your house there. Can't we? No, on the other hand, we must go to York where John was well known. Frankie, I'll be in touch. Please select a funeral director and arrange for the wake to be held at our home. Thanks, brother!" Teresa operated best in a crisis. She always seemed to deny her personal feelings until everything was organized. Then and only then could she give into grief. It had been the same when Robert died. Grief and unbelief came quickly this time.

Anthony was overwrought. How could Ter be so calm? "Honey, sit down! Teresa, let me get you a drink," consoled Anthony. Tom rushed in with a glass of red wine.

Teresa burst into tears. "What is happening, why oh why? And we parted on such bad terms. My God, why, why, why?" Teresa wailed loudly and seemed as though in shock. "This cannot be happening, just can't be happening, this is a bad dream! Someone, wake me up, please!" pleaded Teresa.

Joe moved to her side and grabbed her hand, pulling her to her feet. "Ter, come on, let's go, come on, let's go now. Joe ushered her up the stairs to the ladder and up to the widow's walk where all of Nantucket Town lay before her. He comforted her, holding her close, letting her cry. "Ter, take this slow, very slow. You must think of the boys and little Sarah. Calm down, take a deep breath."

Teresa sobbed and sobbed, her head resting on the lawyer's shoulder. "John was not perfect, but he didn't deserve this! Now my children are fatherless again. My God, how can this have happened?" Joe didn't respond but held her tightly until she was more composed. "Joe, send the boys up here to me. I'll talk to them first. Please make sure that little Sarah is occupied until I can talk with her."

Joe went for the boys, who were just coming back from the ice-cream parlor. They were practically dragging little Sarah behind them. "Boys, your mom wants you to go up and see her on the widow's walk. Sarah, come with me. We will go get some Nantucket Nectars at the store."

The boys eagerly climbed the ladder to the widow's walk. Their mother was sitting on the flat roof. She asked them to sit down and told them about their stepfather. Little Anthony sobbed but Robert Jr., so much like his father, promised to take care of his mother and to protect her.

The three descended from the walk. The boys went outside to be with their grandparents, who were in the garden. Teresa took Sarah to the upstairs study and tried to explain death to the little one. Sarah was too young to comprehend the tide of events. She could little understand what changes would occur in her life. She sighed and asked her mom when they would be able to go to the beach again. "Soon my child, soon," calmed Teresa cuddling her child.

Teresa decided to stay on the island and fly the next morning to Harrisburg, where she would get a limo to take her to York. The boys and Sarah would stay behind for two days with Naomi and Tom. The Blakes would bring the children home the night before the funeral. Teresa didn't see the necessity for the children to attend the wake. She had to protect them. She requested that Anthony and Betty tell Maggie about the news and then ask her to come to help organize the household in York and prepare for guests.

Anthony and Betty flew back to Hyannis. They needed to pack for York and the burial in Youngstown. Joe wound his way back to the Hy-line dock and caught the last available ship back to Hyannis. He needed time to think, to understand what had happened, how it happened, and why.

Joe wanted to comfort and protect Teresa, but she had her family. It was true that he was in love with her. He only admitted the fact to himself after Robert's death. Joe would have never betrayed Robert, who was his one true friend. Joe hated to see Teresa in pain; and he hated seeing the children so hurt. He agonized over several questions.

Who hated John so much? Was he into anything illegal? Did anyone benefit from his death?

Joe let his thoughts wander further. *Why didn't Teresa take his love seriously before she married John?* He asked that question over and over to himself. He wanted her so, even after being chased by a bevy of beautiful women. Some of the women were difficult to escape. He indulged in playful relationships often, but not seriously. The fact remained, Teresa was the only one for him. He knew it. He believed it. He ached over it. Yet, nothing could come of this love while John lived, but now he was gone. *Oh, come on Joe,* he said to himself. *Stop this nonsense and just be there for Ter.*

8

Joe Cutruzzula sat at the rear of Saint Columba Cathedral in Youngstown, Ohio, as the body of John Mahoney was brought into the church. Teresa and her children, John's daughters, his mother, and brother Sean followed the casket. The family sat in the front pews. The large church was packed with Viscomi family retainers, public officials, and many former business associates of the late Angelo Viscomi.

As the priest began to intone the Mass of the Resurrection, Joe was lost in thought, recounting the events of the last few days. John had been murdered along with an assistant in execution style. Teresa, along with her family and in-laws, held a quiet wake at the house in Wyndom Hills, York, Pennsylvania.

Much discussion and derision with John's family, including his mother, came about the decision to hold the wake in York, away from the many family friends and distant relatives in Youngstown. Teresa could not bear the antics of the family in their traditional Irish wakes. It would be too much for her to bear. Just in case there would be trouble with the family, she arranged for Tom and Naomi to take the children directly to Anthony's house in Youngstown. They would join her and the rest of the family for the funeral Mass.

John's daughters, Kara and Shannon, were completely indignant over Sarah's absence from the wake. How could this interloper keep her from their father's wake? Open hostility flared in private, but Teresa remained calm and endured several slights. Anthony, Betty, Sarah, and Frankie were there to support her. Joe tried to help arrange details, while staying as unobtrusive as possible.

John's mother, Molly Mahoney, had never really cared for Teresa; but she tried to offer some solace and comfort. Claudia Viscomi De-Roches swooped into the York mansion with her usual flair and love of acting. Her new husband, Carlo DeRoches, did not feel out of place in the least. Claudia tried to manage the event by directing the house staff and then continued to pester Joe about Sand Castle's sale. Joe politely let her know that this was neither the time nor the place to continue the discussion. In Teresa's state of mind, Claudia would definitely lose any hope of securing the mansion.

Joe was lost in thought as the priest prayed during the Offertory. *No explanation for the killing, but it was definitely an execution style hit. What caused it? How could it be that John was unaware of danger? Could this have come from within the old Angelo Viscomi organization? Who could have been close enough to arrange such a hit and be successful, without giving warning signals to John?*

The priest intoned "This is the Lamb of God who takes away the sins of the world. Happy are we who are called to His supper." Joe realized that he was on his knees and that communion time had come. He watched as Teresa, the children, the older daughters and the rest filed in line next to John's coffin to receive the Eucharist. After the Eucharist distribution, the priest began the blessing of John's body and recited the prayer to the angels to lead John's soul into Paradise. Joe mused, *it will be a difficult journey for the angels.*

The body was carried outside of the church and placed inside the hearse. Family, friends, and associates followed. John's mother entered the second limousine with Kara, Shannon, and an unidentified woman. *It must be John's first wife and mother of the girls, Kelly Mahoney,* Joe thought. Kelly Mahoney did not look like her daughters, but she reminded Joe of someone he had met before. *Who?* She had an earthy appearance, ruddy, but attractive.

John was buried next to his father at Calvary Catholic Cemetery. A large, marble monument marked the family graves. Teresa calmly placed a rose on the coffin and departed with little Sarah and the boys. Kara and Shannon wept openly with their grandmother. Their mother, Kelly, tried to console them.

The Mahoney family was incensed that the reception was held at Paone, Anthony Viscomi's mansion. Here the widow and the young children could control the behavior of the Irish clan. As Teresa's limousine wound the bend into the circular drive, she burst into tears. She was home, with her siblings and with memories of Mama and Papa. It comforted her to be there.

Paone was Teresa's childhood home, her haven from the storm of the real world. This is where Papa shielded them from the evils of the world and his questionable business activities. Anthony and Betty had made few changes to this house; and Claudia had no interest in redecorating this house or, in fact, living here. Sand Castle was her love, her home, and her stage for acting out the play that is life.

Anthony and Betty acted as gracious hosts for the reception. Teresa steeled herself against the brusque behavior of John's mother and daughters. They were clearly put out over the location for the reception. Claudia swept into the house with her usual flair, commenting on the old decor and her dislike of the house. She approached Teresa to give some unwanted advice.

"Teresa, I'm so sorry that you have experienced this twice in your life. Losing your father was very difficult for me, but I have learned to live and love again. Don't shut yourself out with memories, learn to live, experience life, and get a new start in a completely different environment. You must make a break. You have been too surrounded in sadness and grief for your young age."

"Thank you, Claudia, for the advice," responded Teresa in a trance-like, proper tone. Teresa had no intention of making decisions at this stage of the game, and it would be against her nature to respond inappropriately in public. She had made decisions three years after Robert's death and that was too soon. "I will be taking my time by putting my life in order and consulting with my attorney about financial obligations and responsibilities," she concluded.

As the flurry continued, Joe watched the group of attendees, observing their interactions. Anthony Viscomi disappeared behind closed doors of his study with Mario Testa and Tony Foccata. *What could that be about?* Joe wondered. Frankie and Sarah Viscomi were talking in an animated fashion with Carlo and Claudia. The Mahoneys were grouped together in the formal salon. Sean Mahoney, John's brother, sat with his mother and nieces. Kara and Shannon were dissolved in tears, as their mother sat nearby smoking a cigarette.

Teresa entered the salon to speak with the girls. "Kara, Shannon, we must make arrangements to get together to talk things over and plan for the future. We must pull together now, because our loss is great and we can never be the same."

Kara shouted angrily, "How dare you pretend to care for us after destroying our family and tearing our mother from our father's heart!"

Teresa, calmly and lovingly, replied that John and their mother had divorced long before she and their father dated. Teresa would have never looked at a married man. Surely the girls knew that.

Kelly Mahoney swiftly came to her girls' side as did their grandmother, Mollie. Kelly was blatantly rude. "Little Miss Teresa; you, with all your money. How could you know what was in John's mind and heart? You, who were so wrapped up in that dead Robert of yours! You couldn't have possibly loved John. But he pursued you! Yes, all the while he was telling me that he wanted to reconcile and remarry. He wooed me and seduced me and then married you! Yes, Ms. Teresa! You haven't begun to hurt. Your little Sarah, the one who you took into your home and raised as your own, the one who was given up by a distant Irish relative, well surprise, she is my child, mine and John's. I was pregnant with her while you were leaving for your wedding night and honeymoon. He insisted on taking her, and I had to agree or lose all financial support. I was strong-armed; but I can assure you, that period is over. It's my turn now, and I want what's mine!"

Teresa felt as though she had been ripped apart. She was totally surprised and devastated at the same time. This was a blast that totally disintegrated her inner strength and she broke down in sobs. Joe, who had discretely followed her and heard the whole thing, led her from the room. Mollie followed them out and tried to help comfort the grief-stricken widow. "I begged John to tell you about Sarah. Even with our differences, I didn't want you to find out this way. I am sorry."

9

Teresa sat in the living room of her Hyannisport cottage early in the morning. The mist and fog had rolled in from Nantucket Sound. It was going to be a cloudy, rainy, overcast day. The temperature was very cool for this time in June. A fire was in the fireplace, above which sat a beautiful antique clock that was just striking 8:00 A.M.

Teresa sat on the comfortable, overstuffed-sofa, looking up at the clock and remembering when she and Robert found it in an antique shop in Wellfleet. How he fell in love with that clock and she talked him into leaving it. She told him that it didn't match the decor she had in mind for the house. Then she asked Maggie to go and purchase it. After decorating the room, she asked him to go into the pantry and bring out the crowning touch for the mantel. He was so excited as he raced back into the room. Almost dropping the clock, he had begun to cover her face with his kisses. That seemed so long ago, but yet almost like yesterday.

Teresa was at home alone in this house with all of her memories. Robert Jr., Anthony, little Sarah, and cousin Joey were at Tom's and Naomi's home on Nantucket. There, the kids would spend a couple of weeks exploring the island and swimming at deserted beaches. Tom would show them adventures and Naomi would spoil them. Teresa was so happy that she could depend on her in-laws. Little Sarah Mahoney needed some distraction and a safe haven from the uproar that continued since the funeral. Kelly Mahoney's attorney had contacted Joe to indicate Ms. Mahoney's wish to gain custody of young Sarah.

Joe was not surprised by this strategy. He had already taken charge as soon as they had left Youngstown for the Cape. He arranged to have DNA tests on Sarah to disprove the accusation of John's ex-wife, Kelly Mahoney. John's will was to be read in York and Teresa decided not to attend. Perhaps it would be a key to learning about Sarah's parentage. A copy of the will would be delivered the next day to Teresa in Hyannisport. Joe hoped that it would give them the details.

The police investigation into the murder was going slowly because Bethany rarely ever had a murder. The state police were being called in. The crime scene had been stark and devoid of any evidence. Not even a hair could be found from an outsider.

Teresa had been up and about for hours. She had welcomed the coffee and pastries prepared by Maggie. She loved to sit in this room by herself and drink in the warmth of the home and its memories. This morning she was filled with memories and grief. But it wasn't the husband, whom she had just lost, that permeated her memories. It was Robert for whom she was grieving, even now, only three weeks after John's death.

She did not even understand her own thoughts at this time because of all that was going on around her. She only knew that John had caused unbearable grief to her and to the children by keeping his terrible secret about Sarah's parentage. Loss of love and of her husband's life produced little emotion but anger. Teresa's total psychological state was affected by the tragedy of circumstances as described by Kelly Mahoney. How much evil could lie within a soul to cause such anguish and pain at a very difficult time?

Earlier in the day, she had been sipping the strong coffee from a giant mug, while curled up on the sofa. She examined her wedding ring. She stared at it and twisted it on her finger, looking at each diamond and emerald, remembering how beautiful it was and how pleased John was to buy it for her. Then Teresa slowly took the ring off of her finger and placed it on the coffee table. She reached for the box on the table and opened it. Inside was her plain gold wedding band from her marriage to Robert. She placed it on her wedding finger on the left hand and held the ring tightly. After a few moments, she placed the diamond and emerald encrusted ring in the box. She called to her trusted housekeeper. "Maggie, please take this box over to Sand Castle. Ask Riggs to place it in my father's safe, the one in the library." She had decided to keep the ring for Sarah.

Teresa played with the gold band on her finger for several minutes. She held her hand out to look at it, and then she buffed it against her slacks. She was lost in thought about Robert, dismissing the thought of the total mess surrounding Sarah's parentage.

Teresa began to think of Sand Castle. Since the funeral, three weeks ago, Teresa immersed herself in planning the house's restoration and redecoration. It helped to keep her from breaking down. This was her crutch to remain stable and in control of her emotions. The only glitch was her failure to tell Claudia.

Riggs was invaluable to her in supervising every detail of the renovation. He remembered the informal and comfortable decor that existed in all but two of the rooms. He worked with Teresa to recreate the same feeling but with new colors. The formal living and dining rooms were to be in the Chippendale and Queen Anne styles. Angelo had stored much of the former furniture for future use. These pieces would be reused and refurbished with updated colors. The foyer would retain the same decor as the formal rooms. The rest of the home would be redecorated with large comfortable sofas, chairs, pine, and wicker. The informality of the late Catherine Viscomi, Teresa's mother, would once again reign in the house.

Teresa was thoughtful enough to arrange for storage of the furniture that Claudia had purchased. Teresa did not feel that it was appropriate for the architecture of the house and gladly determined that the articles be given to Claudia, who would be returning from her honeymoon soon. *Where would she go?* Teresa pondered. Carlo and Claudia had every intention of coming back to Sand Castle. But now Sand Castle was completely disassembled. Dust was everywhere, wallpaper was being stripped from the walls, and the original hardwood floors were being refinished.

Teresa wanted the restoration to be completed by Labor Day weekend. She intended to host the traditional end of the summer picnic at the house. She could already envision her boys, little Sarah, her brothers, their wives, and Joe around the picnic tables. Kids would be flying around everywhere, enjoying the last hurrah of summer. Riggs would be busy in organizing a perfect family affair and Maggie would certainly be objecting to little decisions that he would make.

Lost in thought, Teresa was caught off guard when the telephone rang. She wondered what life would have been like without the phone. She answered it to hear a greeting from Riggs, "Miss Teresa, Maggie and I placed the box in the safe as you requested. No one knew about the secret compartment in the rear of the safe except you and myself. Nothing has been touched in it since Mr. Angelo's death. There are papers inside that Maggie looked through. She is very distraught and asks that you come here immediately with Mr. Cutruzzula. Please hurry, I am very concerned."

10

After calling Joe, Teresa darted for the Jeep and sped around Craigville Beach Road to Main Street and on to Sand Castle. Joe exited his Saab as Teresa jumped from her vehicle, leaving the door wide open. She leapt and bound up the stairs two at a time. Riggs opened the door for her and Joe ran in behind her. The place was literally a disaster of a construction site. Riggs led her to the only completed room, the mahogany-paneled library. In the center of the room, on the floor before the fireplace sat Maggie. She was trying to gain composure and was sobbing. Riggs had brought some coffee but she seemed to be on the verge of hysteria.

Teresa bent to comfort her. "Maggie, please, take a deep breath. Are you all right? Please take it easy." Maggie shuttered, her whole body shaking. "Oh, Mrs. B; Oh, Mrs. B. Nothing seems as it really is." With that, she broke down in sobs.

Maggie slowly rose to her feet and handed Joe a fist full of papers. She burst into sobs again and was uncontrollable. "Riggs, send for Dr. Rhodes, we must get help to calm Maggie down." Teresa cradled Maggie, who had sunk back onto the floor.

Teresa rocked her and tried to comfort her until Dr. Rhodes came and examined her. He looked Maggie over and gave her an injection to calm her. "Mrs. Mahoney, what could have possibly upset Maggie like this?" inquired the physician.

"Well, Doctor, I'm not quite sure about that," responded Teresa. "She discovered some…"

Joe quickly cut Teresa off and interjected, "Maggie has had a lot of strain with the death of John Mahoney, her care for little Sarah, and the restoration of the house.

She has discovered her limits in bearing all this responsibility; she is overwhelmed with stress and emotion." Joe's explanation seemed to convince the physician.

Dr. Rhodes looked about the restored room. It seemed to call Angelo and Catherine back to life. He remembered the gracious home and his many visits to treat Catherine in her last years. "Seems Maggie and

Riggs have done a great job so far." His eyes perused the room, taking in every detail, every piece of furniture, and the restored mahogany-paneled walls. "I will be at home all day. Please call me if Maggie should have more trouble."

Riggs ushered the doctor out through the front door before coming back to Teresa, Joe, and Maggie. Maggie and Teresa were seated on the comfortable overstuffed sofa. Teresa was still comforting Maggie while Joe, in a chair next to the fireplace, reviewed the papers given to him by Maggie.

Joe's face was ashen, his facial expression was grim. "Joe, what could this possibly be, what is it?" Teresa was becoming more and more concerned.

"Ter, let me assimilate this for a few moments. This is really difficult. I can hardly believe it. Joe was clearly registering pain as was Maggie. Teresa reached for the papers. Joe grabbed them from her. "Ter, sit down and we will discuss this new information. It just couldn't have been discovered at a worse time."

Joe began slowly, enunciating each word. He wanted each syllable to be heard and no misinterpretation to occur. "Maggie has found an interim report from the Palmieri Private Detective Agency in Boston. To be specific, it is a report issued by Vincent Palmieri, owner of the agency."

"But, Joe, what could possibly be so traumatic?" interjected Teresa. Maggie sobbed as Joe asked Teresa to be patient and not interrupt.

Joe continued, "The second set of papers is an unsigned will as requested by your father. It is dated the day of his death." Maggie sobbed, "Oh, my God! Oh, no!" Joe responded curtly, "Maggie, this is difficult enough. Shut up!" Teresa angrily told Joe to get on with it, while she cradled Maggie.

Joe continued his verbal review of the documents. "Ter, this investigation was initiated to investigate Robert's accident." Teresa turned a shade of pale.

"Who did this and why?" asked Teresa.

"Ter, be patient, I will try to carefully interpret the contents, then you can read them over yourself. Your father, Angelo Viscomi, hired Vincent Palmieri to investigate the suspected murder of Robert Blake. This seems to have taken place a year after your remarriage to John. The interim report was submitted a week before the death of your father. Mr. Palmieri states that the word on the street then indicated that Robert was hit in execution style."

Teresa looked at Joe in disbelief, trying to comprehend the words she was hearing. "The whole accident was a cover-up so that the world and your father would not suspect foul play." Teresa sobbed but tried to steel herself to accept the words and drink in this new information.

Joe moved toward Teresa and put his arm around her. Maggie began sobbing again. "Ter, you need to be really strong now, for everyone, especially the kids. The report discloses names of the alleged conspirators and murderers. Ter, John Mahoney is named as the key figure in the alleged conspiracy. It alleges that John chose renegade Viscomi retainers to carry out Robert's murder. John's role is not questioned. Palmieri seems definite that John was the main conspirator. Palmieri reports that he believes that either Mario Testa or Tony Foccata, or both, were involved in Robert's actual murder. He is not sure that all of this information about the accomplices is correct. However, there is one disturbing fact in the report. Palmieri has indicated that all evidence points to an unnamed member of the Viscomi family as a co-conspirator. It is possible that it could have been a trusted family associate, but Palmieri thinks it is a family member."

Teresa tried to take it all in, running it over and over in her head. "My God, my life has been a lie these last five years. Could John have really taken Robert from me? Why?" Teresa continued to think out loud as Joe once again interrupted. Maggie had calmed down somewhat and Riggs stood quietly in the corner. Teresa was as though in a trance.

"Ter, the unsigned will is dated the day your father passed away. It changes the inheritance significantly. You were to receive Sand Castle immediately instead of waiting until Claudia remarried. Provisions were also made to eliminate John's participation in the Viscomi Construction Corporation. You were to have control of the company, but you were to share the profits equally with Anthony and Frank. Neither was allowed participation in the business and Claudia was completely disinherited. She was to receive nothing." Joe continued to explain that provisions in the will protected Anthony and Frank from financial ruin.

Teresa could not focus. The words were running together. Everything was a blur. Maggie, having regained minimal composure, asked Riggs to bring some coffee for everyone. Joe pondered the meaning of the unsigned will and report. He was suspicious that Angelo Viscomi died on the day he was to sign that will. Deciding not to mention these thoughts to Teresa at this point, he secretly vowed to look up Investigator Vincent Palmieri. Joe asked himself frightening questions. *Could this all be more of a labyrinth than anyone could have guessed? Did John really kill Robert? Why was John murdered and did someone kill Angelo Viscomi? Was it to protect his or her inheritance?*

As Riggs began serving the coffee, Joe cautioned everyone present to not breathe a word about these matters to anyone outside of the room. Teresa immediately understood the necessity of Joe's request. All took a vow of silence. After all, could a family member be involved and would that person continue with his or her ruthless bloodshed?

11

Later in the afternoon, Teresa and Maggie sat together in the house in Hyannisport. The unpleasant weather coincided with the sordid information that was revealed earlier through Maggie's discovery of the papers. Teresa was numb. She was in deep thought, afraid to allow her emotions to surface. She struggled to retain control and not dissolve in tears. Fidgeting with her gold wedding band, she rang it around her finger over and over again.

Maggie had regained her composure and sought to be supportive of Teresa. Bringing her iced tea and a smoked turkey sandwich, she tried to comfort her with little physical gestures, fluffing the pillows, and pulling the ottoman over for her to rest her feet and legs. Maggie just sat with Teresa, neither looking at each other nor saying a word. Both were lost in thought. Teresa was in silent agony. The man she grew to love and married was someone she didn't know. Could it really be that this man, her second husband, ordered the murder of Robert, the love of her life? How could she have married such a corrupt individual and why didn't she recognize his brutal nature?

Over and over Teresa agonized, holding in her tears, thinking of Robert and his untimely end. Over and over she heard the words, execution style hit on Robert. *No, no, it can't be; it was a hit on John, not Robert. Robert died in an accident on Route 6.*

Teresa continued to review everything in her mind. *Who could have played the part with John? It couldn't have been Anthony, he has been so supportive. What about Frank? The family member, was it Claudia?* Claudia was completely disinherited by the new will. Frank and Anthony were not disinherited but completely set aside in deference to her. *And, although Papa loved Robert, it wouldn't be in his nature to disinherit a child. Which retainer could have done this, Foccata or Testa?* Teresa knew, as did her siblings, that all of the Viscomi business ventures were not quite above board. Her father attempted to turn everything into a legal enterprise but some loyal retainers clung to their old ways.

Teresa never felt more alone. There was no one, other than Joe, in whom she could now confide. She knew Maggie was trustworthy. Riggs would be the soul of discretion, but he would not want to participate in a family matter. Neither Anthony and Frank and their wives nor Claudia and Carlo would be briefed. And then it hit her like a ton of bricks and tears began to run down her cheeks. *Papa died before he could sign his new will. Could he have been, no, surely it couldn't be? Was it even possible that Papa was murdered?* Teresa's thoughts shocked her. "Oh my God, Papa?" she muttered. Maggie was paying close attention and responded, "I know, I know!"

Teresa's mind raced over more questions. *How could these papers have remained secret in the past four years? Claudia certainly did not know about them because they were still in the safe. If she had known, surely she would have destroyed them. What about John Swartz? Was he a party to anything? He was Papa's attorney, the one who drafted the will.* Other names came to mind. *Carlo DeRoches had worked as an accountant in the company and was friendly with Frank. He married Claudia, who had allied herself with John in the running of the company. How does all of this fit? And then there is Tony Foccata or Mario Testa, or both. They are very close to Anthony at this time. They always seem to be in conference with him. Why? What part does that play in this mess? And was Robert's death a cover-up by the physician, Dr. Rhodes?*

A gentle rapping at the door interrupted Teresa's thoughts. Anthony Viscomi and Tony Foccata were ushered into the living room by Maggie. Teresa looked up at the two, somewhat startled.

"Sis, what is going on around here? Maggie, are you okay? Heard that there was quite a stir at Sand Castle today and that you had to call the doctor. Is everything okay; what happened?" questioned Anthony.

Teresa was stunned. Maggie quickly interjected that the world finally tumbled in on her and she just had a breakdown. "The realization of all that has happened to the family suddenly hit me, and I feel a great responsibility to help Mrs. B and the children through it all."

Anthony responded that he understood but that this was a greater burden on Teresa. "Maggie, you need to gain self-control. Teresa does not need you to give into emotions and this type of behavior."

12

Joe Cutruzzula, while driving to Boston in his Saab convertible, with the top down, seemed unaware of the afternoon chill. He enjoyed the brisk wind blowing in his face and dark hair. Joe was on automatic pilot. The car seemed to direct itself along Route 6, over the Bourne Bridge to Route 3. He didn't notice passing the exit for Plimouth Plantation in Plymouth. Neither did he remember the promise he had made to the young Blake boys about taking them to the working museum to experience a wonderful part of America's history. He was headed to Boston to find Vincent Palmieri.

Emotions were running high in his attempt to support Teresa. How entangled was the web that they had begun to uncover? Who could he trust? Joe, in his heart, could not think that Anthony was a key player in Robert's murder. Robert was his friend, his true blue brother in spirit. So great was Robert's love for Anthony that he named his second son after Anthony. But then, Anthony's actions toward John were not explainable. He had made threats against John. John was murdered shortly thereafter. Anthony had been associating with Tony Foccata and Mario Testa. They were talking at Claudia's wedding and were seen at his house on Long Beach Road. One of them, perhaps both, was implicated in Robert's murder. And then...Angelo dies mysteriously the day he was to sign a will disinheriting Claudia and taking all power away from Anthony and Frank. Did the old man die naturally or did someone, the same someone who killed Robert, hasten his death? The five hundred million dollar estate was well worth killing for, at least for someone greedy.

Joe was afraid that he would uncover more information that would further devastate Teresa. She had to be very fragile at this time, believing that her second husband might have killed her first husband. To make matters worse, she realized that a close relative or family associate was implicated in her husband's murder and that her father's death might have been the result of changing his will. The second husband is then murdered in gangland-execution style years later.

Somehow someone had to benefit by all these machinations. Joe was particularly concerned about unraveling information about the not so legal side of Angelo Viscomi's organization.

As Joe drove through the North End of Boston, he pondered about what to say to Private Investigator Vincent Palmieri. He drove to the office of the Palmieri Agency, a narrow row house not far from Old North Church. He looked around and saw a small Italian cafe. Ducking into the shop, he picked up a couple cups of cappuccino and two cannoli. Joe reasoned to himself that a good Italian pastry would serve as an oblation.

Running up the stairs to the second floor office, he burst in, demanding to see Vincent Palmieri. The office had the air of old style Italy. The decor resembled a Mediterranean setting with a touch of early Vatican thrown in for good measure. In two opposite corners sat statues of the Madonna and St. Anthony.

Palmieri's old prig of a secretary sat there looking like the stereotypical old maid librarian, bun in her hair with little wisps flowing freely and little spectacles perched on the end of her nose. She was about to shield her boss when Mr. Palmieri waved her aside.

"What is the meaning of this? Who are you?" bellowed the dark, thin Italian with black eyes. Palmieri was about five feet two inches tall, slender, dark, and exotic looking. He appeared to be in his early forties, with slight graying around his temples. His dark and heavy, but trimmed, beard gave him a manly look. Based on first impressions, one would not want to meet him in an alley at night.

"Excuse me, Mr. Palmieri, my name is Joe Cutruzzula. I am the attorney for Teresa Viscomi Mahoney and a close family friend. We recently reviewed a preliminary report that you gave to Mr. Angelo Viscomi two years ago. It has been stored in Mr. Viscomi's safe in the house on Cape Cod. Neither Mrs. Mahoney nor I knew of the existence of this report or of the preceding investigation. We are interested in..."

Vincent Palmieri cut Joe short. "Come into my office, let's not allow those refreshments to go to waste. Please sit down. I'll close the door so that we can have a private chat."

"First, Mr. Cut—, what did you say your name was?"

"Joe Cutruzzula, but call me Joe."

"Okay, Joe. Please call me Vinnie. How can I help you?"

Joe began to discuss the last month's events and the discovery of the papers in Sand Castle's safe. Vinnie listened closely, taking notes.

"First of all, Joe, I need to verify your association with the family and Teresa Viscomi. I know that this information must be confidential, but I must investigate your background and identity before I can be confident that you are who you say you are." Palmieri leveled with Joe.

"Fair enough," Joe responded. "But we need to move quickly. I don't know if Teresa is in danger. We certainly don't know who to trust."

"Joe, this is the deal. I will do some background checks. You return to the Cape and I will notify you when I deem it is safe for me to be involved with you. I'll be in touch soon."

Joe was reluctant to leave without answers, but he knew nothing short of a physical confrontation with Vinnie would make him divulge the needed information. And Joe wasn't so sure that he could get the best of Vinnie Palmieri. He was bewildered that this man had bested him. Here he was, an educated man, second generation Italian American. He prided himself on the success that he had achieved. He had made something of himself and his opponents in court called him eloquent. He wielded power with his vivid rhetoric. Now, he had allowed his emotions to rule his actions. Above all, he needed to remain calm for Teresa's sake. Joe needed Vincent Palmieri on his side.

"Well, Vinnie, I'm not usually so abrupt. In fact, I'm somewhat embarrassed by my overtures to you. Please check into the background of anyone that will make you feel comfortable. But please do it ASAP, since Mrs. Mahoney seems to be in a terrible dilemma." Joe left after giving Palmieri his business card, writing his Cape home phone number on the back. "Please call me soon!"

On the drive back to West Hyannisport, Joe had to stop to put up the convertible's top. The sky had turned gray and foggy with scattered showers. As the windshield wipers moved back and forth over the windows, Joe realized something that should have been apparent to him all along. This was truly a very dangerous situation and Vincent Palmieri was not about to divulge information without verifying Joe's own role. Vinnie was cautious and might be afraid that he was being set up.

Joe decided to report the day's events, including his interaction with Vinnie, to Teresa the first thing in the morning. He needed a good night's sleep and time to think. But he was not prepared to wait long for Palmieri. He'd wait three days and no more.

13

Joe awoke slowly in his king size bed. He squinted at the sunlight coming through the window and stretched his lean muscular body against the sheets. He always loved the feel of cool sheets against his skin. Stretching again, he yawned and groaned loudly. Slowly his eyes fixated on the digital clock by the bedside. *Eight A.M.,* he said to himself. *Bet Teresa is already sipping her morning coffee on her sofa. I better get moving.*

He roused himself and slipped on a pair of boxers. Washing his face and brushing his teeth was a must before going downstairs. He needed more sleep because he had found it difficult last night. Tossing and turning, he had dreamed of Robert and murder. Descending the hardwood stairs in his bare feet, he moved toward the kitchen and filled the teapot with water and set it to boil. He filled the coffee maker with three rounded scoops. He poured the boiling water into the coffee press and plunged the grounds down. *Voila, a nice strong cup of coffee!*

Joe stood next to the kitchen counter and sipped his coffee. He continued to review the entire mess over and over again in his mind. All thoughts of anything but Teresa's welfare had left his head. He must help her get through this and sort out what really had happened. Taking a pad, he began jotting down the names of the key players.

Robert, Teresa, John, Angelo, Claudia, Carlo, Anthony, and Frank. Who had what to gain? Or, who had what to lose?

Joe decided to give Teresa a call to see if he could come over to relate yesterday's events to her. He needed to tell her that he was going to put his practice aside and work on her behalf until the whole thing was satisfactorily resolved.

"Joe, of course, come on over. Maggie has made cinnamon rolls and good strong coffee. We have orange juice, too."

Joe dressed in khaki shorts and left the house. He put the top down on the car and started the ignition. Perhaps he could take Teresa on a drive to Truro. He remembered that she liked to go to the Cape Cod Highland Light and gaze out over the ocean. He decided to suggest it.

When he arrived at Teresa's Hyannisport house, she was standing in the door, waiting for him. She waved as he pulled up. He jumped out of the car onto the driveway and greeted her with a hug. Teresa grabbed his arm and ushered him into the comfortable living room. Maggie was waiting to serve him the rolls, juice, and coffee.

"Teresa, take a ride with me to Truro. Bet it's been a couple of years since you've been to the lighthouse! We can talk privately on the way."

"That would be great, Joe," Teresa whispered as her arm settled through his. She squeezed him, telling him that she really needed some time in the great outdoors—time when she could think and meditate.

The Saab turned onto Scudder Lane and they drove through Hyannis to Route 132 and eventually Route 6 East. The car sped along the highway and Teresa's dark brown hair blew in the wind. She was so glad to have worn her sunglasses since this was one of those bright and glorious Cape mornings. "No fog today, Joe. Perhaps all of these events were just a bad dream!"

Joe responded, "For your sake, I wish they were a bad dream. But they are real enough."

They drove straight up the Mid-Cape Highway, Route 6, through Eastham and Wellfleet. Turning down the road to the Highland Light, Joe asked her when she had last been here. "About a year after Robert's death. He loved this area and I loved to spend time with him here."

"Well, Ter, Robert and I had that in common too. I don't believe there is a more beautiful spot on the Cape!" Robert parked in the small parking lot on the right and ushered Teresa toward the lighthouse. The beauty of the restored lighthouse astounded Teresa. "I wish I had been able to see them move this baby," she quipped.

"It's unbelievable!"

"Ter, I'm taking you up to the top." She gasped that she didn't realize that it had been possible. Joe paid the fee of three dollars per person and climbed the circular stairs to the top of the lighthouse. Looking out, they could see the ocean and the Cape Cod Bay. A sign at the top pointed toward Portugal, five thousand miles away.

Descending slowly, Teresa savored every moment. She and Joe strolled out onto the observation deck, behind the lighthouse, overlooking the Atlantic. They stood for several minutes when Teresa finally addressed the issues. "Joe, thanks so much for this trip. I've enjoyed it so much. And you were considerate enough not to talk about my troubles. I do know that you have much to tell me, and I've had just enough of a breather."

As they wandered back to the Saab, Joe told her of his visit with Vinnie Palmieri. He told her he was worried about her safety and suggested that she hire some security guards. She balked at the idea, but

Joe continued to press her. "Think of your children. They need their mother more than ever. And think of little Sarah, you don't want her with Kelly Mahoney if something happens to you!" Teresa told him she would think it over, but only when the children returned.

"Either way, Ter, you must be safe; and I'm not confident about alerting Vincent Palmieri either. We will just have to let things play themselves out," Changing the subject for the moment, Joe suggested they stop for lunch at the Lighthouse Restaurant in Wellfleet.

Teresa readily agreed. "Perhaps, we could stop in a little antique shop also."

After Joe and Teresa each downed a plate of fried clams and a draft beer, they went to the little antique shop down the street. Teresa eyed a Cape Cod cranberry glass pitcher. Joe recognized Teresa's admiration for the pitcher. "It will be my housewarming present for you when you move into Sand Castle," he said with a beaming smile.

"Oh, Joe, I'll treasure it forever; and it will always be a reminder of our lovely day in Truro."

The drive home was slow and delightful. The sun beat down upon their heads and the warmth filled their bodies. The drive through Hyannisport's tree covered lanes around the shore was magical. This place was truly paradise.

Pulling up to her cottage, Teresa noticed a car parked in the front with Maryland license plates. As they entered the house, Maggie's greeting was interrupted by a familiar voice.

"Hello, Teresa, I see you haven't taken much time to mourn my father. I've come to discuss the will and arrangements," declared twenty-year-old Kara Mahoney.

"But Kara, I've not received a copy of the will yet," acknowledged Teresa.

Kara looked puzzled and explained that it should have been sent next day delivery. "We will discuss Sarah's living arrangements, the disposition of the houses, and the money as soon as you receive your copy," announced Kara as though she had the upper hand.

Teresa stared blankly at her stepdaughter. She then focused on another person in the living room. Kara, noticing Teresa's quizzical look, made an introduction. "Mario Testa Jr., say hello to my stepmother, Teresa Mahoney." Then to Teresa, she explained, "Mario was good enough to drive me here. We will be staying in Hyannis."

14

Teresa sat in the living room of her Hyannisport home. Staring into the fireplace's blazing logs, she tried to prepare herself for the impending meeting with Joe and John Swartz. They had agreed to meet with her to discuss John's will and the disposition of various properties to John's daughters. Teresa really had no idea what to expect. She really wasn't worried about property or the homes in York and Bethany. After all, she had the house here in Hyannisport and she had decided to keep Sand Castle. That reality had to be evident to all since a major restoration was being carried on by Riggs.

Claudia probably had no inkling about Teresa's decision to keep Sand Castle, since she returned to her honeymoon cruise after the funeral. In fact, Teresa really hadn't discussed Sand Castle with anyone. After John's funeral, she just dug in and immersed herself in the details. The restoration helped her to forget all of the bad things about little Sarah's birth and John's murder until the discovery of the papers in Papa's safe. Life seemed to change then for good. Nothing would ever, could ever, be the same.

Teresa drew her knees up to her chin, as she sat on her overstuffed sofa, sipping coffee, and munching on the wonderful sticky buns that Maggie had so lovingly and thoughtfully prepared for her. Maggie was buzzing around her, hovering, mothering. Teresa was grateful for the care and the love. Maggie was family. The quiet was reassuring in the house, so calming, so wonderful. The property and the money did not concern Teresa. She was concerned about what surprise could be within the will that could wreck lives or impact living arrangements for John's family, especially Sarah. Their lives were in a legal limbo.

The doorbell rang and Maggie greeted Betty, who came over early to see if she could be of some moral support to Teresa. "Ter, good morning. Just dropped by early for some sticky buns and coffee. I knew Maggie would be up and spoiling you with some good food. I felt like some spoiling myself."

"Oh, Mrs. Betty," feigned Maggie.

"Betts, you're always welcome to be spoiled here by Maggie and me. Besides, that no good brother of mine is always working too hard and never spends enough time with you. Get him to take some time off and take you on a vacation!" Teresa suggested.

"I'm afraid with John gone now, that will never happen." Betty retorted. Betty was very supportive of her husband in his work with the company. He tried so hard to do the things that were needed. He always seemed to be outvoted by the others, Claudia, Frank, and John (with Teresa's proxy).

"Ter, your brother adores you, please support him. Help him to pull this company together! Oh, my, I am so sorry!" Betty wept, then brushed her auburn hair back from her freckled face. "Oh, Ter, here I am going on about Anthony when I came over to help you and support you! I am so devastated to know that I've done this to you!" She collapsed in tears onto the sofa. Teresa leaned over and gathered her into her arms and held her.

"Betts, we are family. We love each other. We are here for each other. You and Anthony helped me survive when I lost Robert. Stop this now! We are famiglia—true Famiglia Italiana and we will not allow others to bring us down. Nothing is as important to us." Teresa tried to reassure her.

Maggie brought more coffee and buns; and the women sat silently in the room, sipping coffee, listening to the crackling fire, and holding each other's hands firmly— just waiting.

At 10:15 A.M., the doorbell rang and Maggie greeted Joe at the door. He came into the living room and saw Teresa and her sister-in-law hand-in-hand.

"So guys, are we off to see the wizard?" Teresa and Betty giggled at Joe's question.

Teresa told Joe, "Yes, of course, so that we can get Betty some courage, Teresa a brain, and Joe a heart." They giggled more. Joe smirked. If Teresa only realized how much of his heart he already had to keep under wraps.

At 10:30 A.M., a quick succession of people came to the house, starting with John Swartz, Claudia's attorney, who also drafted Papa's unsigned will, and John's attorney. Kara arrived escorted by Mario Testa Jr. She quickly announced that her sister Shannon could not stand to be in this house and decided to remain in Maryland.

John Swartz quickly got down to business when everyone was seated in Teresa's living room. He handed some papers to Joe and began to read the will. John left his homes, in York, Pennsylvania and Bethany, Delaware, in four equal shares to his three daughters and his wife Teresa. However, Sarah's shares were to be controlled by his daughter Kara. His money was to be divided among his daughters with control of Sarah's also going to Kara. Teresa was to have a small trust fund allowance. He asked that Teresa remain in York and Bethany to raise Sarah. His shares of Viscomi Construction were to go to his daughters also. The estate was valued at thirty million dollars.

At the conclusion of the reading, Teresa and Kara were asked to sign papers to put the property in their names. Joe advised Teresa not to sign based on Kara's control of Sarah's assets. Teresa told Joe that her portion of the assets of Angelo Viscomi's estate equaled about one hundred twenty-five million dollars. The stipulations in John's will would not stop her from doing the things she needed to do. However, based on Joe's recommendation, she would wait for further discussion.

Kara became indignant at Teresa's decision not to sign and vowed to invalidate Teresa's share in the will.

"Kara, this is not a time for emotions; let's just sit back and think. I'm sure things will work themselves out and we will be able to move on. I just want to be sure everything is in order."

Teresa tried to reason with Kara, but to no avail. The girl's hatred for her stepmother was based on issues Teresa never knew existed.

Joe escorted Kara to the door. He addressed Mario Jr. "Take her to your room at the Ramada," he suggested. "Get her calmed down. This sort of display doesn't help anyone to work through the issues." Joe couldn't believe he was hearing himself being so practical and rational when Teresa was involved.

Maggie handed their jackets to them at the door. John Swartz was behind them; he handed Joe a small sealed envelope and told him that he would be in touch about these matters and the Viscomi property. Then he promptly left.

Even John Swartz was feeling uncomfortable since he had originally been a retainer of Angelo Viscomi. He furthered the malice by representing Teresa's stepmother in a negotiation to take the family home. Just now, he was involved in reading the less than favorable will of Teresa's manipulative husband. Even though there was really no loyalty on his part to Teresa, there was a little sympathy.

As noon approached, Maggie announced that she was serving New England Clam Chowder and a garden salad in the dining room. Teresa, Joe, and Betty went into the room and gathered around the table. Joe pulled out a Windsor armchair for Teresa to sit in. He then did the same for Betty, after which Teresa asked Maggie to join them. They sat around the table and discussed the weather, the surf, the beach, and the fog—everything except the morning events.

After lunch, Joe rose and offered to drive Betty back to her home on Long Beach Road. They both embraced Maggie and graciously praised her chowder. Joe handed Teresa the sealed envelope that had been given to him by John Swartz. Teresa saw them to the door and watched them walk to Joe's little Saab through the foggy mist. She waved to them as they drove down Scudder and headed toward Craigville Beach.

Teresa went back into her living room and drew a blanket over her legs as she sank into the sofa. Being alone with the crackling of the fire was a solace to her after the morning's surprises. She fingered her plain gold wedding band from Robert, thinking no one mentioned or noticed it. She played with the envelope, rubbing it over and over and over—afraid to open it.

15

As the sun went down, the cool June weather made Teresa appreciate her bedroom fireplace at the Cape. She sat propped up in her bed, while looking around the room. This room was an authentic New England bedroom. In fact, the entire house was authentic historic New England. Teresa decorated it this way to please Robert. This was Robert's home. You could feel him here. You could almost expect to turn around and see him, even after all of these years. No wonder John really didn't want to ever be in this house. He never spent a night in the house. After her marriage to John, they always stayed at Sand Castle or with Frank and Sarah on Craigville Beach Road.

The bedroom here in the Hyannisport house was very feminine. It was Teresa, all Teresa. Robert told Teresa that she should make it all hers, that way she will want to spend a lot of time in it and with him. He was romantic and full of love. Teresa was full of thoughts about Robert. She gathered the down quilt and pulled it up over her upright knees, while grabbing the envelope that Joe had given her earlier in the day. She stared at it; she was uneasy. On the outside it read:

To be opened in the event of my death—
John Mahoney

What else could be waiting to ensnare her, the family, and little Sarah? How much more could she deal with or have to handle? Teresa took a deep breath and used her finger to open the envelope. She began to read the text…

Dear Teresa,

If you are reading this letter, I am no longer living and you are surviving me. By this time you may have learned that I have kept a few secrets from you. You may not learn all of these secrets. The disposition of

my property has been made so that you and Sarah will be tied to them. The Blake family has made provision for your boys. In addition, after your demise, all three children will be able to live wherever they desire, with a decent inheritance. For your own safety, I encourage you to divest yourself of any Cape Cod home that you may now own.

My daughter, Kara, will have sole authority over Sarah's inheritance from me. My family will have the ability to fight you, should you not abide by my wishes. There are ways by which Sarah's adoption can be challenged, if you disregard the terms of my will. John Swartz will serve as the family attorney. Kara will be advised by her mother, Kelly Mahoney.

I know that much of this may be difficult for you; but please know that, despite what it looks like, I truly loved you, even to my death.

John

In astonishment, Teresa laid the letter down, her mouth open. There were no tears in her eyes now, not for John. There would never again be tears for John. She twirled her wedding band over and over and grew more resolved that no one would ever again make her feel this way. She had to find out the extent of the conspiracy within the family and the company. She needed to know if Robert and her father were murdered. And if they were murdered, she wanted to know if John took part in it. Then, she needed to know why John was murdered. She had to uncover the truth for the safety of her sons and the security of little Sarah. Finally, she wanted justice for Robert and her father.

The only way to uncover these mysteries was to take charge—to take charge of her life, to take charge of her homes, and to take charge of Viscomi Construction. Teresa reached for the phone and called Tom Blake in Nantucket. "Hello, Grandpa, I really need your help! Could you get in touch with Tina, Robert's former secretary, and ask her to come to the Cape as soon as possible? I really need her and I'll make it worth her while. Also, I'm going to need you and Grandma to help me organize a new home. Further, I need help in getting the boys and Sarah settled into a new school."

"Okay," Tom responded in a positive manner.

"Oh, Grandpa, you are a true doll. I love you and Grandma more than I could ever express!" Teresa was overwhelmed with love for her in-laws and needed to draw on their support more than ever before.

After her conversation with Tom Blake, Teresa called Joe. "Joe, can you come over at 9:00 A.M. sharp? We've a lot to do and I want you to start some negotiating with Kara over some terms in John's will. I'll go into more detail tomorrow, but I have some ideas that will make the negotiations proceed in a smooth manner. After that, I'm going to make you an offer you will not be able to refuse. Good night."

She smiled as she hung up the phone. That Joe, what a wonder and a dear! How could she ever live without him? Teresa then took a pen and tablet and made a list of negotiation points on which Joe could work. She also listed a few things that she needed Riggs to arrange. The first was to rent a house for Claudia and Carlo for a month, upon their return in two weeks. Sand Castle was definitely not inhabitable and it would never be given back to them. Teresa was restoring it to its former glory and she was going to live in it. It was Teresa's and it would stay Teresa's.

Teresa turned off the light and looked into the fire. She snuggled under the down quilt and drifted off to sleep, happy that finally she could feel some control over her own life.

16

Early the next morning, Teresa opened the front door of the house to usher Joe and Anthony into the foyer. The smell of spaghetti sauce permeated the house. "Come into the kitchen, I have coffee for you, bagels for toasting, some sausages, cream cheese, and beach plum jelly," chimed Teresa. She stirred her sauce in the large crock-pot, adding garlic, garlic powder, pepper, basil, oregano, and a touch of romano grated cheese. Then she added Youngstown's own DiRusso's mild Italian Sausage with a little of the olive oil in which it was fried. "Sit down and help yourself while I start these meatballs; and then we'll get down to business."

The men went about helping themselves to the coffee, orange juice, and bagels. Anthony opted for the cream cheese, while Joe took some wild beach plum jam and sausages. The strong 8 o'clock A&P coffee that was imported from Ohio was greatly appreciated for its flavor and was a family favorite.

Meanwhile, Teresa was mixing the hamburger, eggs, garlic salt, garlic powder, parsley, paprika, bread crumbs, and romano cheese into her famous meatballs. Frying them in olive oil and giving a couple each to Anthony and Joe, just as her mother did each Sunday to the men in the family. Teresa was trying, once again, to recreate the good old days. The men were smiling as they continued to chow down on the mini-feast. For a brief moment, Teresa felt as though time had never elapsed and that Robert would be walking through the door any minute.

After depositing the rest of the meatballs in the crock-pot and stirring the sauce once more, Teresa replaced the lid and walked over to the kitchen table with her coffee and faced the men. "I've made some decisions, and I hope that the two of you will support me. If you do support me, these decisions will also affect your lives."

"Well, Sis," exclaimed Anthony, "I think we are both all ears by now. God knows that we all have had a lot of surprises over the last month!" Joe replied that he hoped Teresa had thought things through. He restated his opinion that this was a difficult time in her life and that she should not jump into things or make hasty decisions.

Teresa began with her priorities. "First, we must straighten out any legal entanglements that could affect Sarah. The adoption must be clearly recognized. Later in life, she can deal with her biological mother. She may choose to have a relationship with Kelly Mahoney when she becomes an adult. We must get a team of attorneys to work on the issue. They can submit their reports to you, Joe. Kelly Mahoney may have been allotted a raw deal, but she is not going to pass it on to Sarah."

Joe indicated that he knew some top attorneys in Boston to work on the case and review the documents.

Teresa said that she wanted Joe to personally negotiate with Kara's attorney, John Swartz, the trade of the properties in York and Bethany for all stock held in the Viscomi Construction Company. If the stock were worth more, Teresa was willing to add cash to make up the difference. This way, John's daughters would not have to endure contact with Teresa.

Teresa told Joe that she only wanted the items in the York home that were antiques from the Blake and Viscomi families. Also, she would take personal items that were hers, the children's, or given to her by John. Her only request was that her one third of each house be divided equally among Kara, Shannon, and Sarah.

Teresa also offered to renounce the income given to her in the Trust that John had set up. Each daughter would then have thirty-three and one third percent of the estate, with Kara controlling her own share and that of Sarah's. Teresa believed that this arrangement would be satisfactory because Kara genuinely cared for Sarah. Sarah would never need to depend upon her inheritance from John like his two other daughters. Sarah would also have her share of the Viscomi fortune.

Teresa continued to explain her thoughts and goals to Anthony and Joe. "If this negotiation is successful, I will become the majority shareholder of the Viscomi Construction Company. My shares, combined with Anthony's, will give us enough clout to turn the company in the direction that Anthony envisions."

Anthony sat in utter amazement at his sister; his dreams almost within his grasp. Only Joe seemed to realize the danger in Teresa's proposal. "Ter, do you realize how dangerous this could be?"

"Stop it now, Joe," yelled Teresa.

"What do you mean, 'dangerous?' " asked Anthony.

"Oh, Joe is such a worrywart. It's nothing at all, Anthony, nothing," replied Teresa.

But Teresa could not silence Joe. "Someone killed two men that you loved, possibly your father, too! The motives for these murders had to be the wealth and power in directing Viscomi Construction. This move to control the company places you in danger by inciting the murderer or murderers. They could try to do something to you."

"Well," Teresa went on, "It must be done in order for Viscomi Construction to progress. I want to move regional operations to Washington, D.C., away from York. I believe that this is the time to make the change. The transition in the company's leadership will be cemented. Loyalties will have to shift to Anthony and me. I will move to Alexandria, Virginia and try to manage part of the business while Anthony carries on in Youngstown. What I can't do, we will ask Frank to pitch in and do. Anthony will call the shots since he has the most experience."

Anthony was very thoughtful about the plans. "You've thought it all out, Sis; it is the perfect time because we are trying to get those government contracts. I really like it, Sis. But you have to understand that we are going to ruffle a lot of feathers, especially our brother's."

Joe was very worried about the whole situation. He believed that the killers were committed to doing anything for money or control of the company. If that were true, Teresa was putting herself right in the path of danger. "Ter, we need to talk in private, please!"

"Not today, Joe, I have too much to do. Please start the negotiations right away. From now on please use my name as Teresa Blake Mahoney, not Teresa Viscomi Mahoney. I need to honor my boys by using their name, too. If I didn't have Sarah, I would drop the name Mahoney altogether."

"Sis, I'm surprised by your behavior. I knew you were shocked about Sarah, but he was your husband!" declared Anthony.

"Don't be too surprised, Anthony. After all, he was Irish!" Teresa smirked as she realized that she could not confide in Anthony about all of the family's secrets; but she could not believe Anthony was one of the murderers.

"Let's be serious for one more moment. We must keep all of these business plans confidential. We have to keep this among the three of us until the negotiations with John's daughters are completed. I don't want my stepdaughters ruining Papa's company or the birthright of Robert, Anthony, and Sarah. Joe, we need to hold all of this close to our chests until we are ready to move. Then we will need to make a formal announcement, with all the players gathered together."

Joe agreed and added, "Ter, we need to also look at the risks involved and provide some safeguards. Promise me that you will let me protect you. Promise me, for the sake of the boys and Sarah."

"Okay, Joe, okay," sighed Teresa.

Teresa stirred the sauce one more time. "I'm off to the beach with Betty today. We will be here at the Hyannisport Association Beach. We are going over details for the Fourth of July family picnic. This is the third week of June you know." Teresa continued to rattle on. "What's the use of owning two homes on the Cape if you don't go to the beach and enjoy the ocean? Maggie and Riggs are meeting with contractors and upholsterers. We hope that two of the bathrooms on the first floor of Sand Castle will be ready to use at the time of the picnic. If not, we will be looking for another suitable location. The small lawn here just simply will not do." Teresa then exited the room giving one more command to Joe and Anthony. "You two, come back here at 6:00 P.M. for pasta and salad."

As she opened the door to let Joe and Anthony out, Betty drove up in her little Jetta. She jumped from the car, gave both her husband and Joe pecks on the cheek, and grabbed Teresa. Betty swung Teresa around gaily back into the house. "Let's relax today, kid. We need to remember what it's like to enjoy summer, the way we used to do years ago." Teresa responded, "I'll do my best. With you around, it'll be difficult to be blue! Just let me run upstairs and put my suit on."

Anthony and Joe were still hanging around the front, talking, as Betty and Teresa came out the front door, arm-in-arm. The two women were carrying water bottles, beach chairs, sunscreen, and towels. They walked and then skipped down the hill toward Squaw Island, giggling like schoolgirls, laughing in the morning sun. The sun was gleaming over Nantucket Sound and the water was glistening. The gray cedar-shingled homes stood weathered against the brisk breeze coming offshore. Flags were flying and flapping in the wind. Whitecaps swirled on the water and seagulls called to one another. It was a beautiful morning in Hyannisport.

Meanwhile, Riggs had selected a temporary home for Claudia De-Roches upon the return from her honeymoon. He arranged for a rental of the mansion at the corner of Craigville Beach Road and Main Street in Centerville. Teresa told him that the rental should be charged to the company. Claudia and Carlo could lease it until October 31. The house was on the market, but the lease took precedence.

The house was impressive with its beautiful red brick and stately columns. The tall green hedges provided needed privacy from the street side of the house. Both the porch and the columns were picture perfect for formal and informal entertaining. The only thing that it did not have was a private beach. But Madame Claudia would not care about that since she did not like the filth of the ocean. This home would be more befitting her style. This home contained much more marble than was originally in Sand Castle. Riggs could imagine Claudia in this house because it had the air of an Italian villa.

Maggie, looking over Teresa's instructions, confirmed the details of Sand Castle's renovation with the decorators and upholsterers. The library was completed and the furniture for the formal parlor and dining room was about to be reupholstered. The family room, the solarium, and library were to be decorated in pine, wicker, and a nautical theme. The family room would be awash in blue and cranberry. Teresa had selected a blue checked sofa. *Yes*, Maggie thought, *the house is coming together.* But Maggie realized that there was no way that the bathrooms would be completed for the Fourth of July. Mrs. B's second plan would have to go into effect. The picnic would have to be held at Claudia's rental property in Centerville.

Maggie made the call to Teresa's cellular phone on the beach. Teresa told Maggie to inform Riggs that Sand Castle could not be ready for the party. After the call, Teresa grabbed Betty's hand, and pulled her to her feet and exclaimed, "Let's go, you old horse, lets jump in!" And in they jumped, splashing and playing, having a good time, and just forgetting everything else…for a while.

The group reconvened at Teresa's house at 6:00 P.M. This time, Maggie joined the crew for dinner. Joe poured the wine, while Anthony set the table. Betty stirred the pasta in the bubbling water, while Teresa scooped sauce into the spaghetti bowl. Then she scooped the meatballs and sausage into a serving bowl. She put additional sauce into another serving bowl. Teresa then asked Maggie to get the romano cheese from the refrigerator as she was retrieving the Italian salad dressing. Teresa stood back from the group just for a second, gazing at them. How much like the past this was. Friends and family gathered together, with true happiness in sharing a meal. But this meal was different. There was some tension here. The master plan loomed behind the scene; but Teresa decided to set aside the plan for the time, and just enjoy the company and the food.

The twinkle in Joe's eye, Maggie's laughter, and Betty's gaiety gave the gathering a lightheartedness. "Mangia, mangia!" gestured Teresa, "I've made plenty, just like the old times.

I invited Riggs, but you know him, he'd rather die than mix with those that write his paycheck," giggled Teresa.

Maggie defended Riggs. "Now, now. He is a born and bred, proper butler. He would never compromise the family; he just couldn't let his guard down."

"Not you, though, old Maggie, girl," Joe yelled, as he swung his arm around her shoulder and planted a brotherly kiss on her cheek.

Everyone joined the merriment, except Anthony. He seemed rather somber. Anthony just couldn't seem to enter into the revelry. "Come on, An," said Joe. "Cheer up, just for the evening, if nothing else."

"No, Joe," replied Anthony. "Claudia and Carlo are due home. If these negotiations are not successful, where are we with the company? I feel Papa's legacy slipping through my hands. I must eventually deal with Testa and Foccata, if things don't go our way."

Teresa had to intervene. "Enough, Anthony, let's discuss this thoroughly tomorrow, in private; and then make our plans. Let's eat and enjoy the dinner. We have lots of decisions to make. I have to decide a lot of things about Sand Castle. Fourth of July is coming and we must confirm the details of our celebration."

Teresa continued to expound upon the fine points that needed to be handled. "Are we going to Nantucket to get the kids? Or, should Tom and Naomi bring them over to us and stay for the celebration? There is so much to think about—all of those business decisions for Anthony, Frank, Claudia, and me. I haven't even mentioned the other minor details, like what to do with my stepdaughters." Teresa took one breath before she added, "Joe, get those details worked out with John's daughters and then, life will go on. So, mangia!"

17

As the last week of June began, Teresa selected the final touches for Sand Castle. Riggs called back the staff, who worked furiously polishing silver, putting it in place, and hanging paintings of seascapes and clipper ships. The exterior was beginning to look different as the old cedar shingles were being peeled away to make way for the new yellow shakes that would make the place look like a castle, rising out of the sand. Change was in the wind in the home.

Teresa walked around the interior of the house with a clipboard, selecting places for furniture, lamps, paintings, chandeliers. She was having the time of her life. The restoration was helping her to focus, since negotiations were dragging with her stepdaughter, Kara. She and Riggs were walking around the first floor when she heard a loud shriek coming from the direction of the double front doors. There stood Claudia, decked in her finest suit.

"What has happened to my home? Oh, my God, Dio mio! Holy Mother of God! This is outrageous!" cried Claudia.

Teresa walked toward her father's widow. "I'm confident this is a shock, Claudia. We did originally try to contact you and could not find your whereabouts since you did not leave forwarding information. As you can see, I've decided to keep the house and restore it."

"But where are my things, my furniture?" Claudia asked.

Teresa replied that they had been stored and saved for her when she found a new place to live. "I asked Riggs to find a home for the company to lease for you. That will enable you to be comfortable until you find something you want to purchase for yourself. Riggs found a lovely home for you in Centerville, where we plan to have our Fourth of July celebration, since we won't be finished here for quite a while. We didn't think you'd be home until mid-July."

"I am going to check with my lawyer. How dare you, Teresa. How dare you! I came home a few days early to prepare this place for Carlo, to make it more his place, and there is nothing recognizable.

I'm speechless and outraged. You will pay for this. I will see to it!" Claudia shrieked all the way back out of the front door.

Teresa instructed Riggs to get a driver to take Claudia and her luggage over to the leased home, and to offer any assistance that would be needed. The gardener agreed to take Claudia to Centerville and Riggs helped her into the car. He told her that one of the maids would be over shortly to find out what she would need.

Teresa chuckled to herself. She did understand Claudia's disappointment in losing Sand Castle. But Sand Castle had passed hands and was being restored to its former glory. The secrets that were hidden in the past would eventually be unearthed with the restoration. Teresa was determined to know the truth about Robert, Papa, and John.

Evening was drawing close and Frank was coming to pick her up and take her to dinner. Sarah, Frank's wife, had left for a few days of shopping in New York City; and Frank wanted some quality brother-sister time. He had offered to take her to the Roadhouse Cafe in Hyannis. Teresa told Riggs that she was calling it a day and drove the Jeep back into Hyannisport for a quick shower and change of clothes.

Frank arrived at 7:00 P.M. sharp, just as he promised. He jumped from his little green Mazda Miata and ran to Teresa's front door. Maggie answered and ushered him in. Frank was not one of Maggie's favorites, so there was little joking between them.

"Mrs. B will be right down."

"Thank you, Maggie," quipped Frank.

Teresa came downstairs in an elegant black pantsuit, smiling at her brother. She gave him a peck on the cheek. "Well, it's a real feat to get you away from Anthony and Joe. I'm starting to get jealous because I'm not invited to get togethers. How come, Sis?"

"Frankie, you're always invited, I didn't know that you and Sarah wanted to be part of the gang. I have always had the feeling that Sarah didn't really enjoy it. Come on Frankie, we were just being sensitive to your feelings and to Sarah's. Tell us what you want, and we will do it. You just need to communicate it."

As they walked out the front door, Frank felt the breeze that had begun to blow from offshore. "Should I put the top up?" he asked.

"No, Frankie, let's live a little. We'll enjoy the evening, so what if the tourists see me with wind blown hair. I'm from Ohio anyway!" Teresa teased.

The Roadhouse Cafe was quiet and elegant. It had just the kind of ambiance that Teresa needed for the evening. She needed to see Frankie in a different light. He and Sarah led lives that were unlike the lives of the other family members. They wanted to be accepted by Claudia and to be part of the real power in the company. Frankie was the fun loving brother, the trickster, the one who drove Papa nuts.

Mama had a soft spot for him, but she tried to keep him in line. His wild streak had made Claudia gravitate toward him. Who knows what made Carlo like him, if indeed Carlo was enamored of him. Perhaps Carlo was just using him, just like he used everyone.

Dinner was delightful. The seafood, as usual, was broiled to perfection. There was little talk of anything serious. Teresa tried to just enjoy the time with her brother. She wanted to share what positive time there was—life and circumstances were so uncertain.

As Frankie drove Teresa back to Hyannisport, he noticed that a small black Saturn was following him, at a distance. The car was maintaining a discreet distance and Frank tried very hard to lose it by driving down a side road. The car always followed behind them. Frank said nothing to Teresa, but decided to call Joe after he dropped Teresa off at the house. He walked her to the door and made sure she locked it. He then drove around the block, towards Squaw Island, where he saw the car parked on Atlantic Avenue, a side street. He drove around the block and sat near the Kennedy Compound on Irving Street and called the police. Then he called Joe.

Joe and the Hyannis police arrived at about the same time. The police talked with the men in the car and asked them to move on. The police then told Joe and Frank that the men were either private detectives or security guards.

Joe and Frank discussed Teresa's safety. They discussed the possibilities for the evening with the police. Joe arranged to hire off-duty policemen. Several were called and took positions at the front and rear doors of Teresa's home. Joe told Frank that he would notify Teresa about the necessity of the police and they would look at hiring a more permanent security detail.

Joe rang the doorbell. Maggie answered the door and was somewhat surprised to see Joe. Teresa came down the stairs. Joe greeted her with a peck on the cheek. "Ter, you and Frank were followed. He dropped you off and then called the police and me. I have arranged for an off-duty police detail to protect you for the evening. Tomorrow we will need to look at other arrangements. I'm going to sleep in your guest room. Do you have an extra toothbrush and towels? Hey, Maggie, now's your chance for that affair with me. I'm sleeping over."

Teresa took the news calmly as she listened to Joe's simply phrased description of their situation. She asked Maggie to bring something warm to drink into the living room and then asked Joe to light a fire as the night had turned cool. Maggie took her time and returned with hot chocolate and Boston cream pie. She set the tray on the coffee table and stayed in the background, listening to the conversation.

Teresa tried to be calm and rational. "I really don't think we were in much danger tonight, after all. I didn't even know anyone was close to us. No one knows about any of the negotiations with Kara or any of the future plans with the company. There shouldn't be any imminent danger. I really think this is too much ado about nothing." Teresa minimized.

Joe responded in a calm way. "I agree with you. However, we need to be on guard. We know that John was murdered. We believe that Robert and your father could have been murdered also. Those supposed murders might have been tied to John's murder. If that is true, then it is all tied to the company. You will now be a major player in the company—perhaps the real power. Changing the direction of the company will cause much anger and unhappiness for those who have been directing it. We have to be careful. We have to keep our cards close to our chest."

At the end of the conversation, Maggie began to straighten the room, fluffing the cushions and pillows on the sofa. She then ushered Joe to his room. Joe looked around the guest room and sunk under the covers in the four-poster bed. He drifted off to sleep, knowing that in the days ahead, Teresa would need his best and he would have to be alert to protect her.

Teresa went to her room and sat in the chair by the fireplace, thinking of the future and her plans. There were many things that would need to be accomplished this summer to get life moving for her and the children. She needed to protect the children and their investment in the future, their inheritance in the company, and the future of the company.

Teresa wanted to discuss her plans with Anthony to move the company to the next level with major government contracts for public housing. She wanted to know about Robert and Papa. She had to find out if John really did conspire with others to kill them and take over their assets. Teresa knew that if she discovered that John was part of a conspiracy, she would be terribly hurt. However, she would not rest until all the truth was uncovered. She believed that her family would not be safe until the truth was known and the responsible people were neutralized. She had to learn who killed Robert and why. Then, she had to avenge Papa.

18

The sun was peeking through the ruffled curtains and Joe awoke to see the leaves lightly blowing against the window. He stretched out in the bed and yawned, rubbing his eyes. The smell of coffee and bacon frying in a pan was wafting up to the second floor. He rubbed the hairs on his chest and then his arms, trying to focus on where he was. Suddenly, his cellular phone rang and he jumped to answer it. "Hello, oh... good morning Mr. Swartz. Yes, I can meet with you later in the day to wind up the negotiations. Good, I'm glad we have reached agreement. Yes, we can meet you at Anthony's home at 11:00 AM. See you then."

Joe jumped from the bed realizing where he was now. He pulled on his shorts and ran to the bathroom to wash his face, brush his teeth, and comb his hair. He came downstairs to see Teresa and Maggie in the kitchen. Teresa was pouring orange juice for the three of them. "Sit right down here, my big protector guy." She poured him some coffee and passed him the half-n-half. Maggie turned and dished the scrambled eggs onto each plate with the home fries and bacon.

Joe smiled a big smile and heartily exclaimed, "A man could get real used to this treatment." Maggie told him to stick around awhile and she would see that he would enjoy life. Teresa interjected that they should stop the flirting since it was making her jealous. Maggie exclaimed loudly in her fake Irish brogue, "While thank the Lord God Almighty, finally!"

Maggie's exclamation silenced any further banter. Both Teresa and Joe retreated back into their own private quietness; neither could express their feelings. Teresa could not admit to any feelings at this time. It just was too soon. Her husband was less than two months in his grave. She was overwhelmed with the suggestion that her second husband had her first husband and her father murdered. Much too much had happened; there was no time for love and entanglements, even with such a decent man like Joe.

"Ter, John Swartz called about thirty minutes ago and wants us to meet him at Anthony's to seal the deal. Kara will be there so we can wrap up the deal right away. She wants to get on with it and get back to York. I guess he asked Anthony to be a witness." Teresa looked intently at Joe as he continued. "We'll go and I'll look over the papers. If they are in order, we'll move ahead."

Teresa got up and walked around the table, knelt down, slipped her arm through Joe's, and gave him a soft kiss on the cheek. "We need to get moving on this so I can make some critical decisions about where we will live and school arrangements for Sarah and the boys."

Maggie began to clear the table before going over to Sand Castle to work with Riggs. Teresa told Joe that she would be ready to go to Anthony's as soon as she made a call to Nantucket to talk to the Blakes and the kids.

Teresa went upstairs to freshen up and make the call. After she left, Joe walked over and put his arms around Maggie as she faced the sink. "Hang in there sweetie, we have some rough times ahead of us. We need to take care of her, even if she doesn't want us to do it. I am scared Maggie; we need to be cautious. We need to keep a close eye on her and the kids. The changes she will be making with the company and Sand Castle are going to incite some people. If what we discovered about Robert and Mr. Viscomi is true, then, Teresa could be in danger herself."

Maggie held Joe's arms around her, her back to his chest. "Joe, we'll protect her. Robert would have wanted me to stay with her until I die. I will, for him, for her, and for the kids. And Joe, just for your information, you may not be Irish, but for you, too."

Teresa came running down the stairs, much more lighthearted than usual in the recent months. "I just talked to Grandpa Tom and arranged for him to bring the kids back on the third of July for our picnic on the Fourth. He and Grandma Naomi will bring the kids straight to the private docks at Sand Castle. I'll arrange to spend the day at the beach there, after working on arranging things at the house. We'll drive back here and the Blakes will spend the night."

Maggie took note to arrange the guest room for Robert's parents and jotted a few ideas down about things she could do to make the older couple more comfortable. Joe and Teresa left for Anthony's house on Long Beach Road; and the police went back to the station. Maggie jumped into one of the Jeep Wranglers to go over to Sand Castle to plan the layout for the informal gardens with Riggs and the landscapers. All of those formal gardens that Madame had designed were to be dug out. They were to be replaced with lovely informal flowers, shrubs, and sweeping green lawns, right down to where the beach grass and beach began.

Driving to Anthony's house, Joe and Teresa passed Craigville Beach. The beach was coming alive with joggers and cars that pulled into the parking lots. Traffic seemed particularly heavy this morning.

They drove straight into Long Beach Road and parked at Anthony's and Betty's home. They could hear the surf and the neighbor's kids wiz by with toys, blankets, and beach chairs. Joe noticed a black Saturn sedan parked along the side of the house; but John Swartz's Lincoln Town Car wasn't there yet.

Teresa and Joe entered the house, and were greeted by an obviously angry Betty. They asked her if there was a problem. She shrugged her shoulders and offered a short explanation, "I have always disliked some people that the family has employed, and I'm not about to change now." Betty showed Joe and Teresa into the vast living room with its huge picture window through which Nantucket Sound could be seen. Seated in the deep-cushioned seats were Anthony, Mario Testa Sr., and his two associates, Freddie Paolone and Bobby Faccia.

19

Anthony, Mario Testa, Freddie Paolone, and Bobby Faccia stood as Teresa entered the room. She was momentarily made mute by the surprise of seeing the men with Anthony. Joe was less surprised since he had observed the black Saturn sedan parked outside of the house. No wonder Betty was less than happy with her houseguests.

"Well, gentlemen, what are we doing here? Mario, who's running the company in York while all of you are here? I'm somewhat surprised to see all of you here. I thought Frank was dealing with you until things are more organized in York?" Teresa's questions were unexpected. Mario seemed a little tongue tied, as did Anthony. Mario had been Angelo Viscomi's right hand man in Youngstown until the company's expansion to the East. Tony Foccata stayed in Youngstown and Mario Testa helped John Mahoney in York, Pennsylvania.

"Mrs. Mahoney, I just thought that Mr. Viscomi needed to be aware of the company's developments in York. Frank has been a little scattered since the wedding, Mr. Mahoney's death, and Sarah's shopping trip to New York. Frank hasn't even been on the construction site of his new house, or visited your place in Wyndom Hills. I've been somewhat concerned," countered Mario Testa, in a quiet voice.

Before Teresa or Anthony could get a word into the conversation, Joe asked if they had traveled all the way from York in the little Saturn that was outside.

"No, I flew into Providence and caught a connection into Hyannis. The guys picked me up at the airport and brought me here to Anthony's house. Guess we will be staying at Mrs. DeRoches new house since Sand Castle is in the middle of restoration," replied Testa matter of factly.

With that, Paolone and Faccia immediately made excuses to leave. "We have to stretch our limbs and get a little rest," they said apologetically. Mario Testa agreed and made some polite excuses that he would return to talk with Anthony later in the day. Mario didn't want to interrupt a family discussion. He and the two men decided to go into Centerville, take a shower, and then look for an Italian restaurant.

"So Anthony, what was that all about? Why is Mario here? I really don't trust the man; and why is he here with two of his employees?" asked Teresa.

"Teresa, he told the truth, he was just here to talk about the company and his many concerns about Frank being in charge since John's death," replied Anthony.

Joe interjected that Teresa and Frank were followed the night before, and the police were called to guard the house for the night. "I think the two guys in that black Saturn were Paolone and Faccia. Why would they be following Teresa, Anthony?" asked Joe.

Anthony paused, poured himself a glass of iced tea, and told Joe and Teresa that he thought Joe was making a mountain out a molehill. "Maybe the guys were just looking around Hyannis and followed you because they wanted to see the area, your house, and the Kennedy Compound. For God's sake, everyone who comes here wants to drive around the compound to see everything that can be seen. Come on guys, let's be calm," pleaded Anthony.

Teresa wanted to agree with Anthony's reasoning, but Joe just didn't buy it. Joe's mind was working overtime, a mile a minute. He wanted to believe in Anthony. Anthony was his best friend, but it just all didn't jive. It just didn't all click, and Teresa had to be careful. He didn't want to think Anthony was part of the vast conspiracy of murders. Where did Anthony fit into this and why didn't Vincent Palmieri get back to him. Another trip to Boston might be needed since the first one didn't produce any results. Palmieri had to know more than he was saying.

"Well, Anthony, negotiations are finished with Kara and the Mahoneys about the estate. Kara is coming here soon to sign the papers with John Swartz. After that, you and I need to talk about the company, its future, and how it will affect each of us." Teresa was determined to take control of her life, her financial interests, and the future of her children. She was certainly on a mission and was not to be dissuaded.

Betty interrupted the talk and showed Attorney Swartz, Kara Mahoney, and Mario Testa Jr. into the room. They momentarily looked at the beautiful beach scene through the wide picture window. Mario Junior was quiet while Kara explained that she needed moral support in getting through this settlement.

"I told Kara that I did not think that this deal was in her best interest or that of her sister, Shannon. Of course, she now realizes that Sarah's adoption is legal. Her father was certainly thorough in his dealings. Sarah's future is assured since she will get her part of the property with her sisters, but she also benefits because she will inherit more from you. Kara wants to be as amicable as possible, since she wants to maintain a relationship with Sarah. She also wants the houses in York and Bethany to be their homes, without your influence or interference. Kara agrees to your terms. The shares of Viscomi Construction are to be traded for the two homes plus a settlement of two million dollars. She also agrees that your personal belongings and furniture are to be removed from the homes. One additional stipulation that Kara talked about this morning is that she wants a written promise that Sarah will be equal to your sons in all inheritance rights," offered Swartz.

Before Joe could respond, Teresa took over. "I agree to the terms. Of course, Sarah will have equal inheritance rights. She is my daughter." exclaimed Teresa. "I have always treated her equally; however, her rights will not be protected as they are in her father's will. If she receives her inheritance when she is a minor, Viscomi retainers or Viscomi family members will supervise it. This will protect her interests from all others. Mr. Cutruzzula has already prepared an interim will that names guardians and executors."

Joe then interjected that all were in agreement and they could proceed with signing the papers. After all the signing was completed, Teresa told Kara that the children would be returning to the Cape with Tom Blake on July third, in time for the annual Viscomi July Fourth picnic. She extended an invitation to Kara and to Shannon. Teresa had rightly decided that it was better to keep the Mahoney girls close for personal observation. She didn't want them to work against her, without knowing what was going on in their world.

"At the same time, I'll send Riggs and Maggie to York and Bethany. There are several pieces of furniture in York that are Blake and Viscomi heirlooms. They will be removed to storage as will a few pieces in Bethany. The rest, as agreed, is yours." Teresa instructed.

Swartz, Kara, and Mario Jr. left the house for the airport. Anthony, Joe, and Teresa settled down to discuss the future of Viscomi Construction. They agreed to call a meeting within three days to inform the family of the transfer of John Mahoney's share in the company. At the same meeting, the announcement of a new direction for Viscomi Construction would be made. The change of managerial authority that they had just decided upon would be explained to all concerned.

Joe realized that the announcement of these new decisions would probably compromise Teresa's safety. She could become a target for the group that killed John, Robert, and Mr. Viscomi. She needed to be protected, guarded. Her very life could be at stake, unless Anthony was the mastermind and power behind the deaths.

Betty knocked at the door of the room and told the three that Frank was pulling up to the house with his swimming trunks, towels, and two kids in tow. The kids were rambunctious and running around. Their mother's influence was not present when their devilish father was in charge. Angelo II and Katie Marie were boisterous kids under eight-years-old. They were the wild children of the family, spoiled by their father who tried to make up for the mother's frequent absences, which were becoming even more frequent as time passed.

Teresa, Anthony, and Joe quickly broke into a casual conversation about the weather, as Frank came into the room. Without discussion, they realized that they could not tell Frank about their decisions and the resulting changes until they were announced to the entire family and managers.

Frank seemed oblivious to the whole thing and kissed Teresa on the cheek, inquiring about her nerves. "Is everything okay today, Teresa? I guess I overreacted last night with the car thing. Mario Testa stopped over last night and told me that it was his associates who were looking around the area. When they saw me get in my car, they followed me to your house. I overreacted because of John's murder. I want you to be safe and I am worried since nothing has been solved and there are few leads."

"Well, brother, I am fine today and decided to drop over to discuss the Fourth with Anthony and Betts. Will you be there?" Frank told her that he didn't know Sarah's plans but hoped to persuade her to attend. "Well, when is Sarah coming back from her shopping trip in New York?" questioned Teresa.

"One evening, I'm going to meet her for a dinner and show. We'll return the night of July second, so we should be available to attend the picnic, wherever it will be. I'm leaving tomorrow and hope that you will put the staff on notice, in case there is an emergency with the kids. Okay, Sis?"

"I think Betty and I can lend a hand, if there is an emergency. We have some freedom since the boys and little Sarah are spending time on Nantucket with the Blakes. You and Sarah need some private time together, too," Teresa said supportively.

With that, Frank herded the kids out to the beach and asked his siblings to join in. Betty offered Teresa and Joe a choice from an array of swimsuits that they kept for guests at the house. Joe begged off, but Teresa decided to enjoy the sun. She wanted to spend one more carefree day at the beach before any company politics interfered with family harmony and personal safety.

Joe saw himself off and decided to look up Vincent Palmieri one more time. He needed to learn the history of Palmieri's investigation for Angelo Viscomi and he thought Palmieri knew more than he was willing to share.

20

Joe rose from bed in the morning of July second at his home on Craigville Beach Road. He jogged down the stairs and drank some orange juice, poured a cup of coffee from the pot that was programmed the night before to brew, and toasted his usual bagel. He wondered what he'd look like if Maggie made breakfast for him everyday, as she did when he stayed over at Teresa's home the week before.

Joe mentally prepared himself for the day. Anthony had called a meeting at the Hyannis Ramada Hotel and invited all the principal players of Viscomi Construction to discuss the management situation since the death of John Mahoney. What the group of players didn't know was that there were new changes in the ownership of John Mahoney's stock. The decisions that Teresa made after acquiring majority ownership would be more startling than the murder itself.

Frank and his wife, Sarah, had returned the evening before from New York City. He seemed rested after his two-day hiatus. Carlo would be at the meeting with Claudia. He had returned to the Cape three days before. Claudia had indicated that Carlo was looking for property in the Hamptons on Long Island since they were removed from Sand Castle.

Carlo, also, had traveled to York to inspect the construction progress of Frank's and Sarah's home. He had talked about looking for an additional home in York to be closer to the York regional office. If he were going to be a leader in the company, a home in York would be needed. Claudia was not happy with the idea. Her loss of Sand Castle really cut her ties to the Cape. She really didn't want another home there. Carlo had persuaded her to allow him to shop for a home in the Hamptons. Claudia had shared Carlo's thoughts about the Hamptons with Frank and Sarah, who looked at some homes in East Hampton after Frank joined Sarah for his two-day holiday.

Joe would be attending the meeting because Teresa and Anthony were going to announce his employment with Viscomi Construction. He would be legal counsel for the company. Mario Testa Sr., Tony Foccata, and several other associates would be there also to listen to the new strategic plan. Their role would be to support the plan and put it into action. They just had no idea what was coming their way.

Behind the scene, Frank and Carlo were both jockeying for power within the York headquarters. They realized that they needed each other to keep the balance of power. Claudia's vote, combined with Frank's vote, would allow them to determine the direction of the company as long as Kara Mahoney administered John Mahoney's shares. They were hoping that Kara's dislike of Teresa would keep her from forging a pact with Anthony and Teresa. Claudia and Carlo had to keep Teresa from exercising any power to change the company's management.

Joe knew he needed to arrange for security for Teresa after this meeting occurred. Any forces within the family or company that did not like the coming changes could endanger the lives of both Teresa and Anthony. He knew that someone would make a move against Teresa and Anthony after today's announcements. It was a matter of time before something happened. This meeting could be the catalyst for setting events into motion that would shed light on the murders of Robert, John, and possibly, old Angelo Viscomi.

Joe arrived and seated himself near where Teresa would be seated. The long conference table was set in preparation with coffee mugs, pens, tablets, and pitchers of ice water. The participants were beginning to arrive. Frank arrived first with Sarah. He seemed a little edgy. Soon, Anthony came into the room. Betty had decided to stay at her home and prepare for tomorrow's Fourth of July celebration at Claudia's rented home in Centerville. Claudia floated into the room with Carlo in tow. She swished past others and poured her coffee. Carlo made small pleasantries with Anthony and Frank.

Teresa was the last to enter the room. She seemed a little nervous and twirled her gold wedding band around her finger. Claudia noticed the ring and commented, "You've changed rings, Teresa. Isn't that your wedding band from Robert?" Teresa nodded her affirmation.

"I've been spending a lot of time rethinking the past and recent events. So much has happened over the last few weeks, I've needed to gather my thoughts," offered Teresa without further explanation. Teresa then stepped to the door and invited Tina, Robert's former secretary, into the room. "I've asked Tina to become my secretary, and she is going to take the minutes of this meeting," instructed Teresa. Claudia refused to go on with the meeting without Kara Mahoney, insisting that those shares controlled by the Mahoney family would be key in any vote.

Joe stepped in at that moment to announce the transfer of shares. "I'm happy to announce that through negotiation over John Mahoney's estate, Teresa Blake Mahoney has acquired those shares from the three daughters of the late Mr. Mahoney."

Claudia shrieked, and Frank turned pale. His face could not hide the rage. "How could all of this go on, Teresa and Anthony, without you mentioning any of it to me? I am your brother! Doesn't family mean anything to you?"

Carlo remained quiet, holding his wife's hand, squeezing it to help her gain control over her emotions. She was clearly emotionally distraught, and the anger was building.

Teresa decided that this was the time to take control of the meeting. "I know that this is a shock to all of you. However, I wanted Papa's legacy and the company to remain within family hands. John, as my husband, guided the company in York as he wanted to do. I'm confident that he had everyone's best interest at heart. But John is gone and I wanted to take control of those shares in order to have a voice in the direction of Viscomi Construction."

Claudia voiced her objection and then exclaimed that she could not believe that John's daughters didn't have the foresight to protect their interests in the company. Carlo remained poised and was intent on listening to Teresa.

"Therefore," Teresa continued, "I am announcing the reorganization of Viscomi Construction. Anthony and I have decided that I will become President and CEO of Viscomi Construction. Anthony will be Vice President and General Manager of the entire company. He will maintain his office in Youngstown, but he will travel back and forth to metropolitan Washington D.C., where we will be moving our eastern headquarters from York, Pennsylvania."

Frank exploded with rage. "How could you? How dare you! We are building a home in York, as will be Carlo and Claudia. So many plans are in motion, including moves of summer homes to the Hamptons. It's bad enough that you've required them to leave Sand Castle, now you are trying to devastate the rest of us in some kind of revenge. Teresa, you've gone mad because of John's murder, and you are spreading the misery around."

Teresa remained calm and in charge. "Regardless of your thoughts, Frankie, these things have been thoroughly considered. Anthony and I want to pursue federal government contracts, which necessitate a move to Washington. I have decided to look for a townhouse in Old Town Alexandria so that I can personally supervise changes in the company. Carlo and Frank will work with me to effect the change. But understand, the change will come; and for your financial interest, you will need to support the move. Tomorrow, I'll be greeting the kids upon their return at Sand Castle before the holiday celebration. Let's allow all of this to sink in and put a face on for all the kids."

With that, Frank fled the room in a rage, calling for Sarah to follow. Carlo made excuses and ushered Claudia out to his car. Anthony, Joe, and Teresa were left alone. Joe told Anthony and Teresa that he was going to arrange for security protection for Teresa. Teresa protested, but Anthony agreed. The case was closed. Joe and Anthony were set on protecting her.

Teresa reasoned, "You two are such cappadosts, you know, hard-heads, I don't have the strength to argue."

21

The morning of the Fourth of July was a typical, misty, foggy day at the Cape. A cold front had moved in and the sky was gray and ominous. Teresa awoke and looked out of her bedroom window, down towards Squaw Island. She dressed in jeans and a hooded sweatshirt with sneakers. She bounced down the stairs with the happy anticipation that she would soon be seeing the children later in the day. Teresa and Betty had planned to spend some time at the beach at Sand Castle this morning, before the family gathering. She didn't think Betty was going to be very positive about sitting at the beach in this weather.

Teresa loved the sea and the beach in every kind of weather. She longed to pull up a beach chair and read a good mystery, while sipping coffee. Perhaps the surf would be rough and she could watch the waves. The little cove that was the private beach at Sand Castle would allow her protection from giant waves but permit her to see the dramatic roll of the sea further out into Nantucket Sound. Teresa was glad that she would soon have a view of the Sound from her windows. Beyond the sweeping green lawn, the beach grass, and the sand, her eyes would feast upon the Sound. Sand Castle was stately and grand, not just a simple home on the beach.

While making the coffee, Teresa wondered how Maggie would feel when she woke up and found her making breakfast. She pulled the toaster out of the cupboard and retrieved the bagels, butter, and plum jelly. Maggie came into the room in a rush, "What are you doing missy? This is my job! Trying to save money by not paying me an adequate income?"

"Oh, Maggie," exclaimed Teresa, "I was just trying to help since you'll be helping with the Fourth's picnic." The telephone rang. Betty was calling with news for the day. Frank and Sarah had left for New York and house hunting in the Hamptons, leaving the kids with the nanny. They were accompanied by Carlo, who was on the same mission. Apparently, that group decided that they needed to be away from the family for the summer in a new location. Claudia was left behind at the house in Centerville because she wanted to relax and unpack the new treasures that she had purchased on her honeymoon.

The house on the corner of Main Street and Craigville Beach Road was the place selected for the annual picnic. Claudia had told Frank and Sarah that she would bring their children over to the house to be with their cousins, Robert, Anthony, Sarah, and Joey. Claudia had also told Betty that despite the lack of harmony in the family, the children deserved to have fun at the picnic. She even offered to take them across the street to the Four Seas Ice Cream store for a special treat after the dinner.

Betty told Teresa that she would meet her later at Sand Castle, knowing Tom Blake would be docking there at the private docks. They would bring the children directly over to the picnic and join Anthony, Joe, Mario Testa, and the Mahoney sisters. Teresa was off to Sand Castle to look at the restoration progress and then head to the beach for some serious reading.

It was obvious to anyone who passed by the estate that Sand Castle was under complete renovation. Teresa drove her Jeep up to the beautiful black, iron gates with a brass design. You could see the gigantic home, stripped of its cedar shingles. Large equipment, from the landscaping company, sat in front of the house. Trees surrounded the grounds that looked like a clearing in the woods. Here, one felt secluded. The magnificence of the house, even with the disarray, was apparent to anyone driving down the lane.

The gates opened and Teresa drove down the driveway and stopped at the front door. Riggs, spry as ever, met her at the front door and ushered her down through the center hall into the completed kitchen. Cherry cabinets, with stainless steel commercial appliances, added to a warmth and hominess that Teresa was trying to achieve. She wanted the feel of a home, not just a grand estate. She wanted the kids to have breakfast and snacks in the kitchen, not to be always waited on by the many staff members. Riggs poured another cup of coffee for her and added cream. The staff, the construction crew, and the landscapers had been given the day off. The place had the feel of being deserted.

Teresa and Riggs toured the house. They started with the completed, mahogany-paneled library. The formal living room and dining room had Queen Anne furniture. The wainscoting in the dining room was restored in cherry stain. The large great room/family room was being painted. It had large overstuffed chairs and a pillowed sofa. Wicker and pine were the accents in the informal living space. Teresa had looked through the old contents of the house and selected a nautical theme to enhance the entire decor.

In the master bedroom, Teresa sat down in a chair and selected fabrics for the walls, bedspread, and sheets. Riggs told her that he would get started on July fifth. Teresa asked him to locate a beach chair for her to sit on at the beach. She took her coffee, the chair, and a book down to the sand. She pulled the hood over her head to block some of the wind. This would be a pleasant day at the beach. The sun was peeking through the dark gray clouds that were being blown out to sea by the wind.

Teresa wanted to be engrossed in her murder mystery, but her mind refused to let her focus. She propped the book open against her stomach and thought about all that had transpired in the last few months. Her life had taken a big twist after Claudia's remarriage, John's death, and the negotiations with John's girls. Her mind was racing with thoughts of Vincent Palmieri's report, which suggested that Robert was murdered. She gazed out to Nantucket Sound, as though in a trance. She had the presence of mind to put a bookmark in her book. Teresa did not like to lose her place, even when reading a book. Similarly, she did not want to lose her place in the family, the company, and her ownership of Sand Castle. She was determined to remain organized and clear minded, thus protecting her position and power.

Teresa leaned over to place her book on a beach towel and reach for her coffee. At that moment, a shot rang out and seemed to buzz past her ear. She gasped and heard herself scream. Joe came running out of Sand Castle, down the crushed shell path leading to the sandy opening through the beach grass on each side. Out of breath from trying to get to her, he pushed her to the ground and threw his body on top of her. They remained that way for minutes, without moving.

Anthony, Mario Testa, and Freddie Paolone ran down the path. "Ter, Joe! Are you all right? Quick, get back to the house! Mario, Freddie, look around the grounds," screamed Anthony.

Joe gasped, "Someone took a shot at Teresa. Call the police!"

Joe and Anthony each grasped an arm and lifted Teresa to her feet and swept her into the house. She was pale but unharmed. "Are you okay?" panted Anthony, "We'd just arrived and were walking around the grounds when we heard the gun shot and your scream. We saw Joe running down to the beach and dive on you." Joe, again, insisted that the police needed to be called.

Anthony's mind was running a mile a minute. He was already in high gear, planning to protect his sister. He suggested that Freddie Paolone and Bobby Faccia should be asked to be Teresa's bodyguards. Joe quickly disagreed. They should arrange for professionals to guard Teresa.

Maggie, who had arrived in the middle of the chaos, came into the room and hugged Teresa. "What can I get for you to calm you down? Riggs has called the police and Dr. Rhodes."

The police arrived shortly thereafter. Barnstable County had the best and brightest local police on the Cape. The State Police came with the local cops. Sand Castle was surrounded with blaring sirens and blinking lights. Many state troopers began to search the woods around the grounds. The bullet shell casings were found in the woods near the clearing next to the driveway.

Sergeant Thompson, of the Massachusetts State Police, asked questions of Joe, Teresa, Maggie, Anthony, and the others. Joe was clearly concerned and was very worried about providing security for Teresa and the kids, upon their return.

Everything seemed to be mass confusion when Betty arrived on the scene. "Anthony, where have you been? I was waiting for you to come and pick me up? What in the world is going on here?" she questioned.

Anthony roughly put his arm around Betty and drew her into a corner, all the while explaining the incidents. He began to pace back and forth, anger building in him at each turn. Betty tried to calm him but he roughly pushed her aside. "Leave me alone. Everything, everything is coming apart. This has to stop and now!"

Teresa rose and went over to the corner of the family room. She placed her right hand on the mantle as she sipped the cup of coffee that Maggie had brought to her. "Anthony, what are you talking about? What is your take on all of this? Do you know something?"

"No," Anthony gruffly responded. "Because of all the company politics and maneuvers, I am concerned for your safety."

Sergeant Thompson was intent on getting all the specifics and Joe was becoming more impatient. "Officer, obviously this whole incident was carrid out by a professional. He would have killed Mrs. Mahoney had she not at the same moment bent over to pick up her cup of coffee. She needs protection right now." Joe continued to violently ramble.

"Can we have police protection until we can arrange for a private company to protect her?" pleaded Anthony.

"I'll do better than that," answered Sergeant Thompson. "I'll arrange for the Palmieri firm in Boston to come right away for the protection. Peter Palmieri Security is exceptional, professional, and can be trusted."

Joe's mind overflowed with all the possibilities of danger if the selected company could not be trusted. "Is Peter Palmieri related to Vincent Palmieri, the private investigator?" asked Joe.

"Why yes, they're brothers," Sergeant Thompson intoned. "Those guys are the best and most trusted in their fields. You couldn't put yourselves in better hands."

Joe didn't know whom to trust, but he couldn't allow Anthony to ask Faccia and Paolone to be around Teresa. No, he reasoned to himself, *Palmieri would be the better choice.* "Okay, Sergeant, get it set up."

Anthony, now in tears, was holding Betty. Teresa went over to him and told him to get his act together. She instructed him that he was needed and could not fall apart. The whole family would look to him and he needed to be the rock, the solid rock. After all, he was now the patriarch of the family.

Sergeant Thompson excused himself to make the security arrangements. Upon his return, he informed Joe that Peter Palmieri, himself, was coming with several security guards. He would personally survey Sand Castle and the house in Hyannisport and plan the measures for Teresa's protection and that of her children.

The men were huddled in a circle as Teresa, Betty, and Maggie went to the kitchen, where they sat on bar stools. Riggs stood by the door, as though he could bar any menacing force that would come from the grounds. Teresa seemed deep in thought; Betty sat in silence; and Maggie fussed, while making tea and rattling around the kitchen.

Suddenly, through the door came Bobby Faccia, Freddy Paolone, and Tony Foccata. Tony had been her father's close companion, a friend to lean upon. Freddy seemed to be his assistant. Are you okay, Teresa?" Tony bellowed out.

"I'm fine, Tony. When did you get here?" asked Teresa.

"I arrived a while back; and Freddie and I have been out roaming the grounds, looking for the shooter. The cops didn't like us mobsters out there so they sent us in," responded Tony.

Teresa chuckled. She decided to gather her emotions and take charge of the situation. She asked Riggs to usher all the men into the library for a short discussion. Betty and Maggie followed her. Then Joe, Anthony, Mario, Bobby, Freddie, and Sergeant Thompson came swiftly into the room.

"Listen and understand," Teresa began, "I am not going to allow this incident to intimidate me or affect my children. They are due to arrive here any minute now aboard the boat with Tom and Naomi." Anthony and Joe tried to interrupt her, without success. "I will allow the Palmieri Security Company to protect us, but they may not be overly intrusive. I will reimburse the Barnstable Police and Sergeant Thompson for today's protection. The Fourth is going to be celebrated in true Italian American style. Thank you for your care and concern. I will lean upon all of you until this thing is resolved."

Joe was wary of Testa, but could not believe that Anthony was behind any of this. Anthony and Testa seemed to always be together, huddled in some corner, discussing business. Testa had been John Mahoney's right hand in York, while the trusted Faccia served Angelo in Youngstown and later at the Cape.

The men started to disperse, Faccia telling Testa that Teresa was certainly a chip off the old block—the boss, Angelo Viscomi. Five state troopers had already arrived along with ten more officers of the

Barnstable Police Department. Every effort would be made to protect the family. Meanwhile, Anthony was talking on the phone with Peter Palmieri, who promised to be at Anthony's house by 9:00 A.M. on the fifth.

Suddenly, there was a shriek by little Sarah Mahoney. "Mommy, Mommy, where are you? We're home! We're home!" She scampered down the center hall and Teresa ran through the library's double doors and scooped her up into her arms. Robert and Anthony Blake followed and put their arms around Teresa.

"We've had so much fun, Mom," yelled Anthony.

Robert Jr. informed his mother that Grandma and Grandpa Blake were the best. Tom and Naomi arrived behind the group. The anxiousness showed on Tom's face, as Naomi wrung her hands, "Why all the security, Teresa, is something wrong?"

22

Traffic at the corner of Centerville's Main Street and Craigville Beach Road was extremely heavy. Lines of cars were headed to the beach. People streamed into the Four Seas Ice Cream Parlor. The Craigville Motel was overrun with tourists. The grounds of the large brick mansion were encased with shrubs, tall bushes, trees, and a mound of landscaped earth. Barnstable police were stationed around the perimeter. In addition, Testa, Paolone, and Foccata were strolling the grounds with men in their employ. The air of the past, which encapsulated the power and sins of Angelo Viscomi was evident. The dreaded past, far removed from his children, had now settled in their laps. The goal to move to a completely legal business may not have been totally accomplished.

Claudia looked out the window of the large elegant living room, as she pulled back the drapery. She peered at Maggie, who was giving orders to the caterers. Large picnic tables were set up with one great tent that provided shade. Traditional food would be served at the lunch—burgers, cheeseburgers, hot dogs, potato salad, and baked beans. The children would be delighted.

Claudia wished that she were back at Sand Castle. Although the elegance of this home rivaled Sand Castle, there was much more noise and much less privacy. The grounds were considerably smaller. But Claudia decided to make the best of the situation today. Despite the entire situation, she enjoyed the children who had been so loved by Angelo. He wanted to spoil them at every turn, as a grandfather should. Although she would never replace the beloved Catherine in Angelo's eyes, she wanted to have a relationship with the grandchildren. Claudia knew that Angelo's children, especially Teresa, would never allow her to have a grandmotherly relationship with them; but she could try to be a favorite aunt-like personality. Today, after all the eating, she would take them all across the street for the special ice cream cones that only Four Seas could serve.

Teresa's Jeep pulled into the drive, followed closely behind by Betty and Anthony's large Trail Blazer. The kids piled out of the vehicles and raced to Maggie, squeezing and hugging her. Maggie had relieved Riggs of the supervision for this picnic since he would be organizing the recently selected materials for the completion of the renovation of Sand Castle. Teresa skipped happily over to Maggie with young Anthony, her quiet child. She wanted to escape and shelter the kids from the terror that had occurred at Sand Castle only this morning.

Anthony and Betty were so glad to have their son, Joey, home again. Joey wanted to join in with the kids, but he was mindful that he had been gone from his parents for almost three weeks, so he stayed by their side.

Claudia stepped out of the front door in capri slacks, blouse, and sunglasses. She had never dressed so casually with the family. In the past, her formal attire had been an attempt to play the power game with Angelo's children. That game was not needed any longer. Teresa now had control of the Viscomi Construction Company. She now owned Sand Castle and Claudia was married to the love of her life, Carlo, the dashing Italian creature. Claudia realized that with Angelo's bequests, she was set for life; and although she had lost Sand Castle, she could relax and find another home that would bring her that feeling of luxury and safety.

Teresa went up to Claudia and extended her hand as a gesture for a truce, at least for the day. Teresa wanted to provide the children with a fun, festive Fourth of July.

Frank's children entered the grounds with their nanny. They had walked up the street to the house from their home. Young Angelo and Katie were very happy to be with their cousins. They yearned for companionship of family. Frank and Sarah seemed to be everywhere but with their children. Claudia went over to the children and embraced them. She brought them over to the other kids who quickly engaged them in conversation, before they all ran off to play. Teresa was touched by Claudia's care of Frank's children.

Maggie ran after the children and corralled them to the picnic tables, where they were served food. As soon as the children were settled, the adults lined up to sample the foods on the makeshift buffet. Tom and Naomi had arrived with Riggs, who was in casual attire. He and Maggie were asked to participate in the festivities. Other family retainers, including Tony Foccata, Mario Testa, and Mario Jr. with Kara Mahoney, began to stroll the grounds.

Teresa greeted Kara in a gentle manner, hoping that there would be no display of raw emotion. Kara was more reserved than usual. She inquired about Teresa. "Are you and the children okay? I am concerned for Sarah's safety. The person who killed my father must have been the one who took the shot at you today. How will you protect my sister?"

Teresa told Kara that they would talk a little later after lunch, when Claudia took the kids for ice cream. Claudia, overhearing the conversation, became very aggressive in questioning Anthony about the morning's events. She reacted in an almost hysterical way. Anthony and Mario ushered her back into the house to calm her down.

"Teresa is insisting that this not touch the children. Calm down now," commanded Anthony.

Claudia dissolved in tears. "What is to become of this family? Are John's murderers out to kill us all?" Anthony went to the bar and brought a stiff shot of whiskey over to Claudia. After Claudia calmed down, Anthony rejoined the group outside.

Joe had just arrived because he had stayed at Sand Castle to give information to the police. He was drawn into a huddled conversation with Tom and Naomi at one of the picnic tables. Teresa walked over to them and sat down with her lunch. Tom extended his arm around Teresa and drew her to him. "Teresa, you are my daughter just as much as if you were blood of my blood. You were the love of Robert's life and I will cherish you and the kids forever. That includes young Sarah, too."

Teresa leaned her head on Tom's shoulder. Her silent tears fell softly onto Tom's shirt. Naomi rose and came to the other side of her and hugged her gently. Teresa was with family who loved her very much. *Yes,* Teresa thought, *this love is comforting.*

After everyone had eaten, the men gathered into groups to select teams for bocce. Joe nagged Tom to participate. Claudia started to round up the children. Maggie would go with her and the kids across the street to buy ice cream cones. Maggie was concerned about the traffic and made the kids hold hands with her and Claudia. They all skipped happily across the street to stand in the long line that weaved its way down the slight hill past the parking lot.

After the kids made their way across the street for their treat, Teresa asked Joe and Anthony to join her inside for a brief discussion. Seated in the dark paneled library, on the large red sofa, Teresa sipped a glass of red wine.

"I've been thinking," she began. "Joe, you have to work with us full-time and you must take charge of the investigation and protection of the family. Is there a way to turn your current clients over to another firm?"

Joe looked deeply into her eyes. "I've already made those arrangements, Ter, right after John's murder."

"Joe, I need you, we need you at the company, and we will negotiate whatever you need." Joe smiled and responded that it would be very costly indeed, but that his heart would be in working with his second family.

Teresa continued: "Anthony, we need to take charge of the company and hold it firmly in our grasp. I had thought that I would be the one who would move the operations from York, but now I know that I do not have the talent and knowledge that you possess to do that. To do the job, you must be the one to move. Can you leave Papa's house in Youngstown and start anew in Virginia?"

"Teresa, of course. We need to make this move and make it successfully. It needs the family's personal touch. Frank is not in favor of the move and we cannot trust him or Carlo with such an important role. It is not a sacrifice for me and Betty, although I'm not sure how Joey will take a move. Betty has wanted to move out of the house for a long time, but I have been reluctant to sell it. Our family's heritage is wrapped in it as much as it is in Sand Castle. You realize, of course, that you will need to move your family back to Ohio in order to hold the reins tightly at the corporate office. That means you will need to be personally present. Can you do that? You were planning a move to Boston to be near the Blakes, weren't you?"

Teresa nodded at Anthony's wisdom. "Yes, Anthony, I've come to the same conclusion. Moving back to Youngstown will be different for us. The children only remember visits to see Papa. Perhaps you can arrange for us to use the house?"

"Sis, better than that. We will transfer ownership of Paone to you lock, stock, and barrel, including the furniture. Then you will own both family manses. Betty will look forward to a fresh start, using what she wants from our first house that is in storage. She really hates living at Paone, so a change will do us all good." Anthony seemed very enthusiastic about the proposed change in plans. He felt energized and wanted to make a difference with the company.

At that moment, Kara opened the door and peered into the room. "Teresa, I want to talk. What are you going to do to protect my sister?" Joe moved to the door and told her to follow him outside to the veranda where they could talk. He informed her that he was in charge of the security and that she should contact him in the future about these matters. He tried to soothe her fears, while impressing upon her the need to lay off of Teresa.

At the same time, Teresa decided that she would need to inform Tom and Naomi about the change of plans. Perhaps they would consider an extended visit to Youngstown at the beginning of the move, in order to reassure the kids. There was plenty enough room at Papa's house, Paone, which was named after Monte Paone in Italy. The house was even larger than Sand Castle and was pretty much the same as it was when Catherine and Angelo first moved in. Claudia had been allowed only a few changes, and Betty had taken no interest in changing the house at all. The eight bedrooms and twelve baths of the home would allow Tom and Naomi Blake some privacy while being there to support the children.

Teresa pondered at moving home to Youngstown. Life was strange. Here she was, Teresa, the daughter of the family, now in charge of the company and soon to be owner of two great houses. But how would she handle Frank and Carlo? How would she keep them in line? Who was the family member that planned chaos and murder? Which retainers were the traitors? She had to be careful, at least for the children's sake.

23

The fifth of July was distinctly different than the Fourth. The sun rose in the cloudless sky and there was a gentle breeze. Teresa and Maggie planned to take the kids to the Christian Association Beach at Craigville. There would be people at the private beach and an assault upon Teresa there would be less likely. Betty decided to bring Joey and Frank's children over to meet them. Maggie was preparing the children to leave, when Kara Mahoney arrived with her sister, Shannon.

Teresa ushered them into the living room of her Hyannisport cottage. They sat in the wing chairs opposite the sofa. Teresa poured coffee for them and asked Maggie to bring some of her freshly baked blueberry muffins. The girls politely accepted the offer. They were obviously restraining their hostility for Teresa.

"We've taken possession of the houses in York and Bethany. We thank you for all of the furniture that you left there. You left almost everything. Why?" quipped Kara.

"I took only a few sentimental things that John and I had acquired. I did take the Viscomi and Blake antique pieces that will eventually be important to the children when they have homes of their own. The rest I knew could be used by both of you. If you don't want them, you can replace them at your leisure," answered Teresa.

"Let's get down to business," continued Teresa. I agree that it is in Sarah's best interest to continue seeing you both. You are her sisters. I would have agreed to that before the revelations of her biological parents came to light. However, I will not allow your visits to be unsupervised because I do not want her to have access to your mother. The adoption was completely legal. I can thank your father for his usual thoroughness."

Shannon blurted that Teresa could not control Sarah for ever and that she will eventually know their mother. Kara quickly interjected, "Stop it Shannon. Teresa obviously holds the cards at this time. We'll have to abide by her wishes now."

Teresa quickly brought the discussion to a close and ushered the girls to the door where Mario Testa Jr met them. "I'll invite you to every holiday celebration, including family picnics. You can start with Sarah, and we will work to build the future. Right now, I'm taking charge of my child and her life, and we will work slowly together. I'll try to remain positive with both of you, but don't challenge me because you will lose."

Teresa closed the door and called Maggie to get the kids moving. As she changed into her swimming gear, she thought over the relationship with Mario Jr. and Kara. She hoped that it was a good one and not some dark partnership based on duplicity against her and Viscomi Construction. Could this relationship be entangled in all of the mess that threatens to bring them all down?

Teresa's thoughts drifted to the July Fourth celebration. Claudia had been almost polite and sociable. With all of her schemes and greediness, she did seem to like the children, especially Frank's children, who were not given much attention. It was good to have Tom and Naomi with them. They really were as much family as the rest of her siblings. Tom and Naomi symbolized all that was good, decent, and warm.

Then there was Frank and Sarah; what was going on with those two, who were off and house shopping in the Hamptons with Carlo, of all people? Why had he left his beloved wife of a few months just to go house hunting? He just got home from the honeymoon and he was off roaming again. Supposedly Carlo and Frank were going to York afterwards to look in on the office and the construction of Frank's new home. There is so much going on, it is difficult to discern what is happening.

A thought of Anthony also came to Teresa's mind. Why was he always in deep conversation with Mario Testa? Teresa trusted Anthony and Joe; but Joe seemed wary of all the cast of characters. She knew that he was troubled about Anthony's closeness to Testa. It sure was evident to both Joe and Teresa that an element of the initial illegal aspects of Viscomi Construction still existed. This element of the past must have brought about the demise of Angelo, John, and Robert. She reminded herself, *I must be quick, decisive, wise, and committed to making all of the operations legal.* This was essential to her safety and the safety of her children.

Teresa remained deep in thought as she, Maggie, and the kids took off toward Craigville Beach. Her Jeep was being followed by a two-man detail of the Barnstable County Police.

After securing a parking place, the kids jumped from the Jeep, eagerly anticipating fun at the beach. Teresa and her gang walked across the hot sand and were met by Betty and the other three cousins. Teresa took the hands of little Sarah and Katie and ran down into the water, diving under to quickly adjust to the temperature.

24

Joe drove up to Anthony's house on Long Beach Road. He had been asked by Anthony to come by for lunch and a quick meeting to discuss Teresa's safety and security measures. Anthony had also asked Peter Palmieri to join them.

Joe was ushered down the hall to the large family room overlooking the large expanse of the beach and Nantucket Sound. Rising from his chair to greet Joe was Peter Palmieri and his brother Vincent. Joe was truly perplexed to meet Vincent at this time. "I asked Peter to give me a lift down to the Cape since I heard he was coming to meet you and Mr. Viscomi," explained Vincent. "Peter informed me about the attempt on Mrs. Mahoney's life and the ensuing security measures. I think that it is wise to continue protection for Mrs. Mahoney."

Anthony interrupted the conversation by bringing in some fried clams and sandwiches that had just been delivered. He placed the tray on the bar and invited his three quests to partake as he mixed their drinks. Anthony handed Joe a strong rum and Coke. "I did think that Vinnie should be here as these incidents might fall into his continuing investigation," added Anthony.

"What continued investigation?" asked Joe.

"Mr. Viscomi hired me a year ago to continue his father's initial investigation request!" exclaimed Vinnie Palmieri. "Mr. Angelo Viscomi had hinted to Anthony about an ongoing investigation just before he died. The company's direction under John Mahoney and the impending nuptials of the merry widow with Carlo DeRoches seemed to trigger his need to know more."

"Vinnie and I will work to piece together the information while protecting the family. I don't think everyone is in danger, but because Mrs. Mahoney is key to control of the company and other assets, her safety is a priority. Her existence is a threat to someone," declared Peter.

Anthony seated each of his guests in comfortable chairs. Outside, the rolling surf sparkled under the clear blue skies. It was a picture perfect Cape Cod day that hid a dark and ominous terror. "Well, Vin, tell us what you've got," coaxed Anthony. "We need to understand who and what we are up against."

Joe had tried to take all of this in and spoke plainly. "Anthony," he began, "you are like a brother to me. You, Robert, and Teresa meant everything to me in my childhood. I have tried hard to trust you, but I've been concerned about your association with Testa. I am so relieved that everything is out in the open now and we can begin to work together to resolve these issues."

Vincent again interrupted and said that there was much to discuss. "Until John Mahoney's funeral, we had little information to go on, except that which was previously given to Mr. Angelo Viscomi. However, with the revelation about little Sarah Mahoney's parentage, we started to look in on some medical issues. It seems that Dr. Rhodes delivered Sarah in Youngstown. We learned this through a little investigatory discussion with Molly Mahoney, John's mother. She wasn't too happy to see the disarray in her grandchildren's lives and is not at all more favorable to the first Mrs. John Mahoney than she is to Teresa Blake Mahoney." Joe and Anthony thought that this piece of information was interesting, but other than revealing the deception to Teresa, what did it matter?

"Dr. Rhodes was present at Robert Blake's death in the Cape Cod Hospital after his arrival by ambulance. The good doctor was also present at Angelo Viscomi's bedside, being called there by Mrs. Viscomi. Since we believe that Mr. Viscomi was in the process of changing his will, we think that there is a connection between the doctor and Mr. Viscomi's death. Mr. Viscomi's death, Robert Blake's death, and little Sarah's birth all concerned John Mahoney. The previous two deaths benefited Mr. John Mahoney and his position with Viscomi Construction. We need to closely question Dr. Rhodes to find out the nature of his relationship with John Mahoney."

Anthony was becoming impatient. He exclaimed, "Let's get going on this!"

Vincent tried to calm him down. "We need to keep him away from Mrs. Mahoney and the children. Another physician should be called if there is a need by the family," suggested Vincent. Anthony nodded his head in agreement.

"There is a clear indication that Dr. Rhodes was not in this, without John Mahoney. However, does he know anything about what has recently occurred? Obviously, John was murdered, so someone else is now calling the shots. We need to know if that someone was partnered with John from the beginning or did he just take over after he decided to have John knocked off? Whoever it is, there is a concern about Teresa and the company," argued Vincent.

After a long and intense discussion, Joe sat back and looked at the surf while sipping his rum and Coke. Anthony escorted the Palmieri brothers out to their car. This was certainly a complex situation, and nothing was clear-cut; but Joe was relieved about Anthony's involvement in the mysteries.

25

After seeing the Palmieri brothers off, Anthony went back inside the house. He walked down his hallway and out the door to the deck overlooking the beach. He decided to grab an hour to take a dip into the Sound. The water was as still as a pool, the offshore breeze was very gentle. The water glistened as he swam through it. After a few minutes, he left the water and walked up to the beach chair. He stooped to brush a piece of seaweed from his ankle, then he sank into the chair and gazed out over Nantucket Sound, taking a drink of his scotch. Anthony decided that he must be the rock that Teresa demanded he should be. It was time to clear this mess up and move forward.

Joe, at the end of Long Beach Road, took a left turn to the north instead of heading home toward West Hyannisport. He drove into Centerville and decided to stop at the Four Seas for an ice cream cone. He felt lucky since there wasn't a long line of people like there was on the Fourth of July.

After getting a dark chocolate cone, he walked out through the doors onto Main Street. He stood looking across the street at Claudia's elegant mansion. The sun was streaming through the trees onto the grounds. Joe debated with himself about making a surprise visit just to see how Claudia was coping as a player in all the recent events. Joe went to cross the street but thought better of it and turned around to walk to the Centerville General Store. He decided that he'd go in after he finished his cone. He sat on one of the two political-labeled benches outside the store. He couldn't bring himself to sit on the Republican bench, so he sat beside a woman tourist on the Democrat's bench. She made polite conversation with Joe, and he asked her if she were from the Midwest because she was acting so friendly. New Englanders just didn't act in such a way.

After finishing his cone, Joe entered the store. Looking over the merchandise, Joe picked out a friendship card for Teresa and a small miniature of the Cape Cod Light. He stepped from the store in deep thought. He walked back toward Four Seas and was whirling around the corner when he stopped, turned about face, and crossed the street over to Claudia's mansion. He walked over to the drive and up to the main entrance. There were two vehicles in the semicircular drive. Claudia had visitors.

Joe knocked on the door and a new face opened it. "Hello, I'm Joe Cutruzzula. Is Mrs. Viscomi, I mean Mrs. DeRoches, in?"

The young woman nodded affirmatively. "Please step inside and I will inform her that you are asking to see her," informed the maid. "My name is Antoinette. I am Mrs. DeRoches's new housekeeper."

Joe smiled and wished her success. "Pleased to meet you and good luck in your new position." Joe knew that she would need it; only Riggs survived Claudia, and that was due to his long tenure in service with the Viscomi family.

Claudia came through the double doors of the parlor. "Well, Joseph, please come in. I was just serving lunch to a few friends. We would be delighted to have you join us."

Joe smiled and nodded to Claudia. "Of course, Claudia, but I will only take a little iced tea. I just had lunch with Anthony."

Claudia asked Antoinette to bring a pitcher of iced tea into the parlor. Inside the parlor, Joe was surprised to see Mario Testa Sr., Mario Jr., Kara Mahoney, and Shannon Mahoney. "Well, hello, Joe," bellowed Mario Sr. "Glad to see you here today."

Joe tried to cover his perplexing facial expression. "Good to see you all. Did you have a good Fourth?" The group seemed to respond together. There seemed to be a comfortableness within this group. Joe felt a little wary being in the midst of this crowd, but he had to observe them to understand any part that they could be playing in the current difficulties. Here were the Testa men, who were John Mahoney's associates. Here also were the Mahoney sisters, John's daughters and Teresa's difficult stepchildren. And then there was Claudia. She was back in true form today, semiformal, ever the mistress of the house and major player in the family and the company.

Everyone continued to informally chat when Antoinette announced the arrival of Tony Foccata, Freddy Paolone, and Bobby Faccia. Claudia, in her best hostess way, ushered them into the room. They looked around and shook hands with all, including Joe. Claudia made sure that everyone was seated comfortably after each person had selected food from the buffet.

"I have asked all the family's associates here for a post Fourth of July celebration. We seem to be in a slight turmoil with all of the changes in the company and John's death. I've asked John Swartz to see me tomorrow to discuss ways to stop Teresa from making these changes in the company. I can't believe John would want these changes. Teresa is just not thinking clearly," began Claudia.

Joe interjected, "Claudia, Teresa is the legal CEO and majority owner of Viscomi Construction. Neither you nor any of these family retainers will be able to legally make her change the company's direction. If the attempt that was made on her life didn't change her direction, how do you think anything else will?"

"Joseph, I am glad that you are here, even if it is only by chance. I want to enlist the help of my late husband's associates to jump ship if Ms. Teresa doesn't change. There is more than one way to make this okay. I cannot allow, I will not allow, her to run the company into the ground. I am confident that we can get Frank Viscomi to agree to pressure his sister. His future is at stake also," asserted Claudia.

Mario Sr. stood up and spoke. "Mrs. DeRoches, I have been very concerned about the business since Mr. Mahoney's death. I want to hear more of your plan. York has been a very good location for the business, and we have been very successful there. I'm not confident about your solution, but I am willing to listen."

Tony Foccata looked troubled. "I was Signore Angelo's right hand man in Youngstown. I hate to go against the family now. I'll listen to what you have to say, but I won't allow anything to happen to the family."

Joe excused himself as Claudia began to pontificate about the wrongs being done to her and the company. He walked out the door and across the street to his car in the parking lot of the Four Seas. This could beget a great turn of events. Anyone in that room could be Teresa's enemy. It seemed that Testa was willing to go against the family. Obviously Kara Mahoney would sway Junior's opinion. Junior could work on his dad. Foccata was willing to listen but seemed reluctant to cross Teresa and Anthony. Frank Viscomi, although not present, certainly seemed to be in Claudia's pocket.

Joe was trying to line the characters up. There was Claudia who is married to Carlo. John's right hand man was Testa whose son is dating John's daughter. Testa is unusually close to Anthony. Then there is Foccata, Angelo's right hand man in Youngstown. Foccata's associate is Freddy Paolone. Tony Foccata, while willing to listen, was certainly reluctant to cross the legitimate owners of the business. Frank Viscomi, Teresa's brother, was John's associate in York; and he worked closely with Testa. Joe had to figure all of this out, and he had to play it close to his chest in order to protect Teresa.

26

The weekend after the Fourth of July promised to be fair, at least weather wise. Joe, as prearranged with Teresa, was on his way to Hyannisport to pick up Robert and Anthony Blake, along with their grandfather, Tom. They were going to take a trip to visit the museum at the John F. Kennedy Library in Dorchester. He hoped to have a few day trips with the boys and, perhaps, even Teresa, before the summer was over. Joe had decided to kill two birds with one stone by meeting Peter Palmieri in the North End for dinner while Tom Blake took the boys to Old North Church and then out for some sandwiches.

As he came down Scudder Lane to Irving Avenue, déjà vu seemed to hit him. There at the corner of Scudder and Irving was a Barnstable policeman directing all traffic to the left. Joe remembered days in the 1970s when police manned the street corner to keep traffic from stopping at the Kennedy Compound. This was especially true when Jacqueline Kennedy Onassis was staying at her house behind the tall stockade fence. But this time the policeman was there to direct traffic away from Teresa's home. The police recognized Joe and signaled him on to go up the hill to Teresa's Cape Cod cottage. The boys, seeing Joe, ran to the Saab, followed by Tom Blake. "Are we all going to fit in this thing, Joe?" asked Tom. "No, Tom, Teresa is having one of the Jeeps sent over for us to use."

There were two Palmieri security men in front of the house. Other guards were casually strolling around the house. Joe put his arms around the boys and walked with Tom into the house. Inside, Teresa greeted Joe with a quick peck on the cheek. "Thanks, Joe," she said.

"Tom and the boys are looking forward to this outing. I hope that you will be comfortable with the Jeep."

She led Joe and Tom into the dining room, where they sat in the Windsor chairs. Naomi poured some coffee and juice for everyone, as Maggie brought in more of the famous blueberry muffins. Naomi smiled at the men and told them that they were to be carefree for the day. "Teresa and I will be going over to Sand Castle to look over the progress of the renovations and I get to help her select the final touches. After that, we're going to have a few hours on the beach, before going for lunch at Wimpy's in Osterville. Little Sarah will be getting a good dose of women bonding. Just us girls." Naomi, in a matronly manner, was overjoyed to be with Teresa and renew their relationship.

Maggie entered the dining room and addressed Joe. "The Jeep has arrived and you overgrown boys better get out of here and on the road. Be careful and take care of the boys, I want to see them safe and sound after dinner." Teresa then reminded the men of the plan to go out on Tom's boat that evening to watch the fireworks that had been canceled in Hyannis because of the overcast on the Fourth of July.

Joe sat behind the wheel with Tom in the passenger seat. The boys were merry and somewhat loud and boisterous. The boys and Tom began to play a license plate game, looking for different states to pass the time. Joe enjoyed the drive north to Dorchester. Over the canal and up Route 3, past Miles Standish Forest, Joe thought of taking the kids to Plimouth Plantation sometime in the near future. He hoped Teresa would go, too. It would be pretty difficult to go with several security men in tow. Hopefully, this would all be over in the future. Perhaps he would suggest a trip over to Mystic Seaport in Mystic, Connecticut. Tom and Naomi would probably enjoy that so much more, Tom being a sailor at heart. Nearing Dorchester, Joe turned from the highway and drove into the parking lot of the impressive Kennedy Library.

Tom took a photograph of the kids and Joe in front of John Kennedy's sailboat. They all went inside and sat to view the short film detailing President Kennedy's life. The boys took all the information in, since they lived on the same street as the Kennedy Compound. The walk through the museum was especially interesting. Young Anthony was particularly moved by the film on the assassination and the funeral. Robert could not have been more impressed by the short clip on former President Clinton, describing his short visit as a Boy Scout to the White House Rose Garden where he met President Kennedy.

Robert and Anthony both had not thought much about the large fence on their street with the large homes behind it. They decided that the next time they were walking down to the boat docks to sail with Joe, Uncle Anthony, or their Grandpa Tom, that they would peek inside the gate to see if anyone was there.

After a full day, the men headed for the North End of Boston. The short trip into Boston was uneventful. Joe drove up to a very nice Italian restaurant, Felicia's. He entered the building and climbed the stairs to the restaurant. He looked at all the celebrities' photographs that Felicia hung on the wall along the stairway. Joe hoped Palmieri was already there so that they could order dinner and discuss the future security arrangements for Teresa at Sand Castle and at Paone in Youngstown. Joe also wanted to have a good veal parmesan dinner and a cup of cappuccino, with cannoli for dessert.

Joe was informed that Peter Palmieri was not yet at the restaurant. A waiter guided him to his table. While sitting in a corner away from the crowd, Joe perused the room. He nearly gasped out loud as his gaze centered on a couple that he knew. Frank Viscomi and John Mahoney's ex-wife, Kelly, were sequestered in an opposite corner having an intense and heated discussion. Joe tried to keep his head down behind the giant menu, while observing the interesting interaction. He certainly wished he could hear the dialogue that seemed so intense.

Carlo was supposed to be with Frank and Sarah while they were in the Hamptons, searching for a summer home. After the home search, all of them were supposed to go to Pennsylvania to check on the regional corporate office in York. What was going on here? There was Frank sitting and sharing an intimate moment with Kelly Mahoney, the ex-wife of his sister's dead husband. Obviously, something was up because they were not where they were supposed to be. Instead they were in an out-of-the-way restaurant in Boston's North End.

Peter arrived and came over to the table where he sat down in front of Joe, blocking Joe's view of the room. Just as Joe motioned to Peter about the couple in the corner, Kelly rose from her chair, shouted something that was indistinguishable, and left the restaurant. Frank called for the check and left quickly, without noticing Joe's presence.

Joe and Peter were amazed at the revelation of events. "I think that we need to take this to my brother. There is something more to this," offered Peter.

"I just can't understand what Frank is thinking. This woman has hurt Teresa very much and has intruded in her life. What could Frank possibly gain from an association with her, or vice versa?" Joe thought out loud.

Later that evening, Joe and Tom arrived at Teresa's Hyannisport cottage. Naomi already had a jacket ready for Tom to put on. They began to walk down the slight hill on Irving Street to the Hyannisport Dock Association, where Tom's boat was docked. Teresa took Joe's arm as she walked behind her in-laws with the boys, Robert and Anthony. Little Sarah and Maggie brought up the rear with two Palmieri security men. The kids were especially excited to see the fireworks from a spot near Kalmus Beach.

As they crossed Scudder Lane, Robert and Anthony ran to the open gate at the Kennedy Compound and peered in. Teresa gasped, "Boys, what's got into you? Stop now!" The boys reluctantly backed away from the gate before they got to see anyone inside.

"Aw, Mom, how are we ever going to meet the neighbors?" asked Anthony.

"Well, send them an invitation to come over for brunch sometime," offered Teresa, smiling.

The whole group moved down to the docks, followed by two security men. Teresa's brother, Anthony, and his wife, Betty, were waiting there for them with Joey. "Aunt Betty, where are Katie and little Angelo?" asked Robert.

"Well, Robert, it seems that Uncle Frank just got home and he wants to take Katie and little Angelo to the airport to welcome Aunt Sarah and Carlo home," Betty explained. Joe knew that he and Vincent Palmieri needed to make a surprise visit to see Frank in the very near future.

27

Joe loved to jog along Craigville Beach Road. It made him feel the freshness of summer, the season that he really enjoyed. The South had little appeal to him, although it certainly would be tempting to go down to Florida during the winter. While jogging today, he noticed again that there was not a cloud in the sky. He also noticed cars pulling into the parking lot and tourists exiting their rented cottages to set up umbrellas on the beach. Kids were running about with giant beach balls, while lifeguards were announcing over the public address system that flotation devices were not allowed at Craigville Beach. The flags flew briskly in the breeze from the Christian Association Beach. The door to the large bathhouse was filled with lifeguards, who were preparing to do their exercises on the beach.

Joe continued to run past the Barnacle, where the management was preparing morning coffee and already taking a few orders for burgers and fries from beachgoers. His destination was Anthony's home on Long Beach Road, where he could sink into a wicker chair on the porch and sip juice and coffee while overlooking the water.

Traffic was picking up and Joe decided to concentrate on his running since he didn't want to be an accident victim lying on the road. Suddenly, a car screeched from behind and Joe swiftly jumped over a stonewall that encompassed a cottage colony across from the beach. He narrowly dodged being hit by the little sports car. Joe quickly turned to see if he could recognize the car, but he only saw the black trunk of the convertible as it sped away. He stopped, stooped over to touch his knees, and took a breath. This little incident was no accident, and Joe knew it. He chuckled out loud, "Where are the cops when you really need them?"

The attendant of the private parking lot adjacent to the cottages across from the beach ran over and offered to call the police. Joe told him that it wasn't necessary and that he would be more careful in the future. "Look sir," screeched the attendant, "that was a close call and that guy needs to be put away for awhile, so that he doesn't kill someone!"

Joe took a deep breath and wiped his forehead with the back of his hand and proceeded to walk to Anthony's home. As he reached the end of the beach, he changed his mind and decided to walk up Craigville Beach Road around the bend toward Centerville, instead of straight to Anthony's house on Long Beach Road. As he walked up the street, he crossed over to a beautiful newly-restored but moderate-size home covered by cedar shingles.

He walked up to the door and knocked. Frank's wife, Sarah Viscomi, answered the door in a becoming sundress. Her blonde hair was tied back in a ponytail. She did not smile when she greeted him. Her mood was that of aggravation. Her face was covered with freckles, like most blondes who have fair skin and spend extensive time in the sun. "Come in, Joe. Frank is in the kitchen having some breakfast. Go in and help yourself," she said.

With that, she called to the nanny to take the kids over to Anthony's and Betty's for a short swim. She grabbed a windbreaker, slipped it on, went out the door, and up the street to Centerville.

Frank was in the kitchen, his head in his hands, and elbows on the counter. Joe walked over and said hello, then poured himself a cup of coffee. Methodically, he strolled across the room to the refrigerator and poured a little half-n-half into the coffee. This was all done in silence—Joe looking at Frank, but Frank not acknowledging Joe.

"So, Frank, do you know what is going on here?" Joe inquired. "Your sister is in great danger. Someone tried to kill her when you were off house hunting in the rich glamour land of the Hamptons."

Frank stared at Joe, his eyes almost piercing right through him, as though he were drugged, dazed.

"Frank, wake up for God's sake! Your sister has been attacked; someone just tried to run me over while jogging here; and you're up in Boston, hanging with Kelly Mahoney. And what's up with that? What the hell is wrong here, Frank? Where are you? What are you doing? What are you feeling?" Joe's voice was at a fevered pitch. "Frank, what's going on with you? Claudia is trying to stop Anthony and Teresa from moving the company ahead. You are sitting here moping, with your head in your hand; and your wife just walked out the door like she didn't give a crap about any of it!"

Frank dissolved into tears. He began weeping, wildly moving his hands and throwing his juice glass against the wall, shattering it into pieces. "Oh, God! How did things get so out of hand?" His weeping seemed uncontrollable. Screaming, crying, holding his head, he seemed to have lost all sense of hope.

Joe grabbed Frank around the arms and hugged him, with Frank's back pressed against Joe's chest. Joe's chin dug into Frank's shoulder. "Frankie, it's all right. I'll help. You just need to get a grip and take hold." Joe squeezed Frank close to him, holding him as only a brother could. "Frankie, whatever it is, I'll help. I won't judge, I'll just help and do whatever I can. Come on, Frank, tell me," pleaded Joe.

Frank took a deep breath and Joe released him. They sat on the stools at the breakfast bar. Joe poured some black coffee for Frank. "Joey, I'm in trouble and I don't know what I'm going to do. I don't know how to get out of it, and I don't know how to fix it."

Joe sat in silence as Frank continued. "I've been seeing Kelly for a few months, and I tried to break it off. She says that she is pregnant and I thought she was taking precautions. Sarah doesn't know about any of it, but I'm sure she'll leave me if she finds out. I tried to break it off over a month ago, but Kelly threatened to tell Sarah and, of course, Ter. Ter is having it so bad and she doesn't need to know about Kelly and me, especially since she found out about little Sarah being Kelly's child with John."

Joe sat silently, just listening to Frank. "Sarah and I have been having problems and she is not responsive to my attempts to get closer. I almost feel that there could be someone else. Anyway, Kelly was around and Claudia seemed to fix us up together one evening, and now here is where we are."

"Well, Frank, what do you want?" asked Joe.

"I want my family and Sarah, my life in York or wherever, and a reasonable place in the company," quipped Frank.

"Well, Frankie, I could become your attorney, or set you up with one. Then, you could make a reasonable offer to Kelly for support of the child and for a settlement for her personally," recommended Joe.

"That would be fine and good, Joe. However, that's not what Kelly wants. She wants me to go along with Claudia's schemes for the company. Claudia has promised to take care of Kelly with a settlement and John Swartz is ready to set the papers up for Claudia to bestow a settlement on Kelly. Kelly will go away and disappear. Give the baby up, and live in luxury on her own little fortune. Otherwise, if I don't agree, Kelly and Claudia are going to tell both my wife and Teresa. I've really no choice."

Joe hugged Frank. "Stall, Frank, take your time. We will figure this one out. I am going to talk with Vinnie Palmieri, there's got to be more to all of this than is evident at this time. Okay, Frank?"

"All right, Joe. I'll try, for the family." Frank cried.

28

Teresa took a sip of her coffee as she looked out over Nantucket Sound and the private beach at the end of Craigville. Anthony's and Betty's home was comfortable and casual, the perfect beach home. Teresa mentally compared the family homes. The cottage in Hyannisport was lovely, a little haven of colonial charm. It was filled with antiques, Windsor chairs, and memories of life with her first husband, Robert. Sand Castle was a grand estate on the beach. Many of its rooms would be restored to formal New England charm. It would be appointed with Queen Anne, cherry dining room furniture and the formal parlor would be decorated with Chippendale sofas and Queen Anne wing chairs. The mahogany-paneled library was comfortable, but very New England. Teresa could envision evenings by the fireplace with the flames reflecting off the paneled walls; deep comfortable furniture; and a good book to read, with the sound of gentle music in the background.

Life at Sand Castle would be good, but Anthony's and Betty's home was the beach house that Teresa and her husband, Robert, had dreamed about. Robert and she had wanted a little cottage in the little village of Sconset on the island of Nantucket. The house in Bethany that she shared with John, her second husband, now owned by the girls, was a true beach house. It was modern and, therefore, not the kind of home Teresa ever liked or wanted. She was glad to be rid of it and the memories that went with it. Sand Castle was more of a home, even with its sweeping lawns running down to the beach grass and beach. It was a haven. Teresa had also come to the decision that she would keep the Hyannisport cottage for herself and the boys to use in the off-season, when opening Sand Castle would not be practical. She would also allow guests to utilize it.

Teresa slowly became aware of the bustle going on about her. Betty was running around playing hostess. Anthony, Joe, and Teresa were waiting for Frank and Claudia to come for a discussion about the move of the regional offices from York to the Washington, D.C. metro area. Not long ago, she would have been assisting Betty in her role as

John would have been the person participating in the meeting. Now, she, Teresa, was the major player and the largest shareholder of the company, with thirty percent. Twenty-four percent was her outright share and six percent was purchased from John's daughters, including little Sarah's share. Each of her siblings and Claudia had twenty-four percent. Her late father, Angelo Viscomi, allowed each an equal share, in his will, with John being a pivotal vote, to ensure family harmony.

Teresa took a bite of a blueberry muffin and sipped her coffee. Joe and Anthony talked about the previous day's events. Joe was almost killed, or was he being warned? Frank was desperate to cover up his sins. Joe had not yet told Teresa and Anthony about the pressure Frank had to endure.

Anthony was becoming intolerant of the tardiness that Frank and Claudia repeatedly demonstrated. "We will start this meeting in a few moments without those two. We have the majority between us; and we will just make the decisions, if they don't have the courtesy to show."

Immediately after Anthony's declaration, Claudia, with John Swartz at her heel, swooped into the room. This was the Claudia that everyone knew. She was regal in her formal attire; yet, rather trendy, with extravagant taste; and she talked to the family in a haughty condescending manner.

"Good morning," Claudia purred. "Mr. Swartz offered to come in my behalf, but I wanted to deliver the news myself," she continued. "Mr. Swartz has filed suit in Youngstown to stop the move you are planning for the regional office. We have been granted a stay and you will need to stop immediately."

Anthony stepped forward and accepted the papers that Swartz handed to him. He handed the papers to Joe. Swartz delivered the reason to them in a low monotone voice. "Joe, you will see that Claudia Viscomi DeRoches is objecting to the purchase of the late Mr. John Mahoney's shares by his second wife, Teresa Mahoney. She and Mr. Mahoney's first wife, Kelly Mahoney, mother of the minor, Shannon Mahoney, have filed a complaint about the inappropriate sale of those shares."

"But John's will left the control of those shares to Kara, and she legally agreed to a settlement, including the York and Bethany properties, not to mention a sizable amount of cash," Teresa declared in an authorative manner.

"Well, Mrs. Mahoney, Mr. Mahoney's first wife is Shannon's legal guardian; and she believes that she should be involved in any transactions that involve Shannon's welfare. Mrs. Kelly Mahoney's permission should have been sought before an agreement was made with Kara," Swartz reasoned.

Anthony began to shout, but Teresa intervened. "Stop this nonsense now! We finally have Frank's support and we will make the move anyway," reasoned Teresa.

"Why, Teresa, how do they say it here in America? I know. Counting your eggs before they are hatched? Frank is certainly not going to vote with you. He worked with John and Carlo. He wants what is best for the company. Therefore, he will solidly support our side. Without your pivotal percentage, you are dead in the water."

Claudia turned and walked out the door, leaving the trio in a trance. Anthony followed her to the door and watched Claudia and Swartz get into her limousine and drive off.

"Well, this is certainly a turn of events," declared Teresa. "I'm going to walk down the street and talk to Frank right now. I'm not going to let that strega control our lives anymore."

Joe tried to calm Teresa, but she wouldn't be calmed. She wanted to rant, she wanted to scream to let out her frustration. She slipped on her sandals and hurried out the door to the drive, bypassed the security men, and walked down Long Beach Road, turned left, and walked briskly up the road away from the beach toward Frank's house. She was going to give it to him good. It would be a knock down, drag out fight, just like when they were kids and their mother, Catherine, would have to chase them with a wooden spoon, swatting at them as she got close. A security guard ran after her while a second jumped in his vehicle to follow.

Teresa marched up to the door with the security guard running right after her. Joe ran down the street after both of them, huffing as he came up to the porch right behind the two. The nanny came to the door and told Teresa that Mr. Frank was out sailing and that Miss Sarah had left without telling anyone where she was going. The nanny was just preparing to take the kids to meet Teresa's children at the Association Beach. Teresa demanded to come in and leave a note for Frank. She scribbled hastily, "I need to talk to you immediately."

Teresa turned, walked past Joe and the security guard, opened her car door, and told the driver to drive up to Our Lady of Victory Church in Centerville. The other guard hopped into the rear of the car and they sped away. At the traffic light, Teresa looked over and saw Dr. Rhodes go into Claudia's house. John Swartz's car was still in the drive.

The car turned right, drove down the street, and turned left into the church driveway. Teresa directed the driver to drive to the front of the church. She stepped out of the car and walked up the few steps into the church. She blessed herself, walked to a front pew, genuflected, and knelt on the kneeler. She tried to pray, to calm herself, but she could not come up with words. She sat on the pew and looked at the crucifix. She pleaded with God to help her to understand what was happening. She prayed for the safety of her children, herself, and the rest of the family. That was all she could manage. Her thoughts were running over her in waves. She couldn't think or regain calmness.

Teresa rose from her knees, genuflected, and left the church. Joe was waiting for her at the entrance with the security guard. She walked up to Joe, squeezed his hand and leaned over to kiss him on the cheek. "I'll be all right. I'm going to stay here in the churchyard for about thirty minutes, then you can take me up to the Light, please," Teresa pleaded.

Joe put his arm around her and squeezed her to him. "I'll drive home, shower, shave, and meet you in Hyannisport. We'll drive up to the Light and then have a relaxing dinner," suggested Joe.

"That would be great. Maggie will take the kids for the evening. Thanks, Joe," Teresa said softly, "I need a trip to the Lighthouse."

Joe got in his car and watched as Teresa walked over to the rosary garden that was planted in front of the church. She began her prayers, words that were memorized but never failed when her own would not come. The two guards stood under the trees, watching as Teresa moved from bush to bush, each signifying a prayer.

29

Joe arrived at Teresa's cottage in Hyannisport and noticed Anthony's car parked outside. Maggie opened the door and led him into the living room. There sat Teresa, Anthony, and Vincent Palmieri. "What's going on?" Joe asked. "I thought we were taking a short jaunt up the Cape to Truro. Did something come up?"

Vincent Palmieri said that he had called Anthony and asked to have a short meeting. "Too much is going on in your family and I have decided to use some of my men to follow members of the family. There is a lot of coming and going in the DeRoches house and in the Frank Viscomi house. Claudia and Carlo are moving constantly, and they are rarely together. When we locate Kelly Mahoney, we will tail her also. We must see what's up her sleeve. Also, Frank and his wife, Sarah, are going their separate, but very interesting, ways. I'm very concerned that they may be part of the equation of evil that is happening to the Viscomi family.

Teresa interrupted, insisting that Frank must be in trouble to completely side with Claudia and Carlo. Joe told the group that there were some circumstances that could not be discussed with the children in the house. However, there were some very complicated issues of which he made Palmieri aware.

Teresa told the group that Betty had picked the children up when Anthony came over with Palmieri. "They are staying the night at Anthony's because Joe and I will be getting back late from Truro. I'll pick them up after my morning meeting at Sand Castle with Riggs."

"Good, let me tell you and Anthony what I know," started Joe. "I stopped to see Frank and Sarah yesterday. Sarah walked out and went up the street, but Frank was in the kitchen. I've never seen Frank so low." Teresa interrupted to say that she would try to help Frank.

Joe continued. "You might not want to help Frank when you hear this." Teresa protested but Joe asked her to remain silent so that he could spit this out. "Claudia is blackmailing Frank. He has been having a relationship with Kelly Mahoney, who has aligned herself with Claudia. The terms of the alliance require Claudia to give Kelly a settlement for helping to break Teresa's control over Viscomi Construction. Frank is desperate, and he does not want Sarah to know because they are not really getting along."

Teresa sat dumbfounded. "Surely he could buck Claudia in some way; we could help him." Joe told them that the situation was far more complicated than that. "Kelly is pregnant with Frank's child."

Anthony groaned; Teresa wept. Vincent Palmieri continued to explain his plan. "I will have Frank, Sarah, Carlo, and Claudia followed. When we locate Kelly Mahoney, we will tail her also."

Palmieri's face turned somber. "I have to say that this investigation is getting more difficult everyday, but we are making some headway. I've been reviewing legal medical paperwork. I did not realize that Dr. Rhodes had signed Robert Blake's death certificate, as well as Angelo Viscomi's. There were no autopsies or other medical investigations. In addition, Dr. Rhodes actually delivered Sarah Mahoney, as arranged by your late husband, John Mahoney. Dr. Rhodes also took charge of the DNA test for Sarah's paternity. You must all know that I am very suspicious of all of it."

Teresa said that she didn't know about the rest of the family but Dr. Rhodes had been a longtime family retainer and it didn't seem that strange to her, except for the delivery of little Sarah. "Now that sets my mind to thinking. That is very unusual."

"Well," continued Vincent, "I want to start with redoing the DNA tests for Sarah's parentage by a new independent source. If that brings up new information, then I have a feeling we are on the right track."

Teresa and Anthony sat as though in a trance. They nodded their heads and agreed to Palmieri's plan. Joe told them that he would be Vincent's contact. At this time, they need a clear mind to take control. Neither Anthony nor Teresa could really assimilate the information about Frank. It was the worst of betrayals. What would become of the family and of Viscomi Construction?

Palmieri told the group that he needed to be on his way in order to put some people in place to carry out the enlarged investigation. Joe saw him to the door and shook his hand. "Good work, Vinnie. I have a feeling that this will just be the first of many surprises."

Joe entered the living room and poured a rum and Coke for both Anthony and Teresa. They sipped the drinks in silence. "Listen guys," started Joe. "We need to get on with this. I know this is disturbing news, but we will make the best of this and probably help Frank also."

Teresa smiled and Anthony stared into space. Joe continued, "Anthony, let's go with the original plans. You keep the boys and little Sarah tonight. Teresa and I will be going down Cape for the evening and will be back rather late. We will regroup in the late morning hours with a meeting right here when Teresa comes back from her meeting with Riggs. Okay?"

Teresa began to protest, but Anthony told her that they should follow Joe's lead. "Take my sister up to her special place and look out over the sea. Take some coffee in a thermos and relax. I agree completely with you, Joe."

Teresa nodded her head and, with a smile, rose to her feet. "Just let me run upstairs to get a windbreaker in case there is a chill. I'll be right down."

Joe held the door for Teresa as she got into the little red Saab. Joe put the top down. "Let's enjoy the drive and the wind blowing through our hair," insisted Joe. He drove through Hyannisport past the Kennedy Compound and the Hyannisport Dock Association. The site, brought into focus by looking out over the sea in Hyannisport, was one of his favorite views. He got over to Sea Street, passing the Kennedy Memorial and the Sea Street Docks. The traffic was pretty congested on Route 28, so he decided to access the Mid-Cape Highway on Route 132, past the Cape Cod Mall.

Teresa leaned her head back on the headrest and she sat in silence, as they drove up the highway toward Truro. She sighed and put her hand upon Joe's as he shifted into fifth gear. He looked over and smiled at her, staying silent and enjoying the moment.

Joe knew that Teresa needed his company but not his voice. He savored the moment when their hands touched and drove on in silence. The trip seemed to calm both of their spirits. Teresa did not notice the security guards in the car that followed them. Entering Eastham, Joe pulled into the National Seashore for a quick stop. He then drove down to the Coast Guard Station to look out over the water and then over to Nauset Light. Both looked out to the sea and said not a word.

Teresa was silent and appreciated Joe's understanding of her need. God, how could things get so messed up in the family? Teresa agonized about Frank, his relationship with that Mahoney woman, and his need to side with Claudia. And then there was Claudia. Teresa wondered if her late father had really loved Claudia, or if he had only a physical need for her. Could it have been loneliness since he had been married to her mother for so many years?

Teresa sighed as Joe pointed to the Cape Cod Light sign on the highway. They drove to the parking lot and exited the car. There were a few tourists, but since the sky was starting to darken, most were at various restaurants getting dinner. Joe and Teresa walked hand in hand to the cliff and looked out to the sea. The little overlook was empty of people so Joe and Teresa sat on the built-in bench. They both gazed out to sea, without speaking. Joe poured some coffee from the thermos for each of them. Teresa nodded her head in thanks.

They sat there for an hour until Teresa broke the silence. "Gosh, Joe, I'm famished. Let's get something to eat."

"Where would you like to go?" asked Joe. Teresa told him it was up to him.

"Well, babe, I'm taking you into Provincetown for some fried clams, French fries, and beer," Joe suggested.

"I do not like Provincetown in the summer, when tourists are around. But maybe, just maybe, it'll get my mind off the family," Teresa said.

In the Saab, they returned to Route 6 and headed toward Provincetown. The guards were right behind them in their car. The streets in the little town were packed with walking tourists. The cars came to a standstill several times. Joe headed over to the Pilgrim's Monument to park the car. He put up the convertible top. Then he and Teresa walked over to Commercial Street to get some food. The guards tried to be as inconspicuous as possible.

Teresa held Joe's hand and he felt very protective. The crowds were unbelievable. Over by the town wharf, Joe ordered some fried clams, fries, and coleslaw. Teresa got two beers at the same time. They found an outdoor picnic table and decided to dig in.

They did some people watching, as they finished their feast. The guards, at an adjacent table, were also eating their meal. Joe suddenly gasped, held Teresa's head and pulled it to his, as if in a passionate kiss. "Stay like this," he whispered, "until they pass."

Teresa whispered back, "Who, where?"

"Wait one more minute," answered Joe. "Okay, there." Joe pointed.

"Oh, my God!" gasped Teresa. "It's Carlo and my sister-in-law, Sarah, walking hand-in-hand."

Joe pulled Teresa from the table, and walked a respectable distance behind Carlo DeRoches and Sarah Viscomi. Carlo's handsome tan was spectacular against his white shirt and shorts. Sarah's hair was pulled back in a ponytail and she wore that sexy sundress with sandals. They seemed very comfortable, without the fear of being discovered.

Teresa and Joe kept the crowd between them and the couple. The guards were also more alert, spying other family members. The group followed Carlo and Sarah to a quaint Bed and Breakfast off Commercial Street. They entered the building, hand-in-hand.

"How convenient Provincetown is for them, since they know how much we all avoid it in summer. Such freedom, without being discovered; and Frank is worried about what Sarah will think of him," declared Teresa.

"Well, after I tell Frank, he'll change his stance with Claudia. And what of Claudia? She can't know of this!" exclaimed Joe.

"Joe, you have to promise me, we can't tell Frank, not now, maybe not ever. However, we've got to tell Vinnie Palmieri right away," demanded Teresa.

30

Teresa sat in the paneled library at Sand Castle. Riggs had prepared a fire for her. The glow of the flames reflected on the mahogany-paneled walls. It took the chill from the morning air. Riggs had prepared a tea, which she poured from an elaborate silver teapot that had been her mother's. Teresa had decided to take another look at the swatches for the master bedroom.

In previous years, when decorating the master bedroom at her homes, she had thought of the men with whom she shared those rooms. In Hyannisport, the four-poster bed with the flowered walls was very New England and, therefore, very Robert. Perhaps that is why John hated that house. In York and Bethany, she had thought of John; and in Bethany, the bedroom was very modern. Now Teresa planned the room for herself. Her father's four-poster flat, canopied bed was the center of the decorated room. The dark, cherry, Queen Anne furniture was somewhat masculine, but still very traditional New England.

Teresa thought about her mother and father, and then Claudia. Catherine, her mother, had decorated the home in a very American way, with traditional period pieces. These were the touches that Teresa had decided to bring back to the beloved family home. But with all the Americana, Catherine never lost her Italian heritage, both in family tradition and in food that the family ate. Then there was Claudia, who had redecorated this house in a very Mediterranean decor, which Teresa didn't think befitting the house or Cape Cod. And with all of this, Claudia had discarded her Italian ways and traditions.

Teresa fought hard to concentrate on the task before her. She sat back and looked at the restored library. She wished that she could hole up in this room, read a good book, and never leave. The situation with Claudia, Carlo and Sarah, along with Frank and Kelly Mahoney was very difficult to fathom. How could things have gotten so messed up?

Back to the swatches, she picked some very nice flowered wallpaper, beautiful but plain white bedding with lots of pillows. Then she selected a deep cushion, six-pillowed sofa and two matching club chairs for the sitting room of the master suite. The furniture was to be covered in a white linen slipcover, very beach-like. There would be lots of pillows to enable her to be comfortable while lounging there. A small television and stereo would be placed in the room, along with some bookshelves. Cherry accent tables would be placed next to the sofa and chair. This would be her solitary sanctuary.

"There," Teresa said aloud to herself. "Finally done." She took a sip of her tea and walked to the rear of the house to look at the recently completed family room in nautical prints and blue and white checked patterns. From there, she went out to the solarium, where the beautifully restored wicker sofa and furniture were being put into place. Blue flowered cushions were placed on the wicker pieces. A soft blue tablecloth covered a wicker table, which had matching chairs. Dining in the solarium would be very comfortable.

Teresa went back to the library where Riggs joined her. "Miss Teresa, the rooms are taking less time to complete than the grounds. I believe that I will be able to have the entire house completed for Labor Day weekend, just in time for the annual picnic."

"That's great, Riggs. I will not be moving in until that weekend, when everything is completed. You and Maggie can start planning for the annual picnic for that Sunday. We'll have a traditional lunch with lobster, clams, chicken, potatoes, and roasted corn. Please have hamburgers and hotdogs on hand, too. For the dinner, we'll do the traditional Italian dinner like my mother used to prepare. I'll make the sauce myself that weekend. Wedding soup, pasta, meatballs, and DiRusso sausage from Youngstown will be the first two courses. I want you to send to the North End for desserts, cannoli, and other pastries."

"Will that be all, Miss Teresa?" asked Riggs.

"Not really, Riggs. I think you should know that I will not be living at Sand Castle full time. We will close the house for the winter after Thanksgiving. I will host a family Thanksgiving here with a large guest list. The staff should be told about this immediately. Please make arrangements to offer the staff an invitation to move with us to Paone in Youngstown. It'll be like old times going between Sand Castle and Paone. I hope you will consider staying with me. Those staff members who want to remain could be placed with Mrs. DeRoches. However, you better tell them to make up their minds before she selects new people."

"Miss Teresa, I'll look forward to moving back to Paone, but I'm sure it will need a lot of work," answered Riggs. "Well, as you know, Mrs. DeRoches did not redecorate Paone. Betty and Anthony really didn't change it much either. I'll be going back to take the children for the Feast of the Assumption celebration in Lowellville this August. If you remember, it is a big Italian celebration with food, games, fireworks, and lots of fun. Papa took us every year, and I want the children to experience the same. The kids and I will try to get somewhat settled in the house. I will have to register them in a school. If you give Maggie a list of things you want to be looked after, she will take care of it while you finish the restoration here. As time goes on, we will tackle needed changes at Paone. We'll come back to the Cape after deciding what needs to be accomplished before the move. I'm so looking forward to seeing this house completed."

Teresa then shook Riggs's hand, thanked him for all his hard work on Sand Castle, and left the house. The security guards followed her. She headed toward Centerville. As she turned right onto Craigville Beach Road, she decided to drop in on Claudia. As she walked up to the door, it opened. The maid was showing Mario Testa to the door. He greeted Teresa, then went out to his car and drove down toward the beach. Teresa stepped into the grand foyer and looked around. She heard some loud discussion but could not understand what was being said. A door to the parlor opened and her sister-in-law, Sarah, walked out. She looked at Teresa, said a hasty goodbye, and was out the door.

Carlo followed her out the door, but stopped when he saw Teresa. "Hi, Teresa. Come in," he said with a wide smile. "Claudia is not home right now. She left mumbling something about going to John Swartz's office and then for a bit of lunch with Bobby Faccia in Hyannis."

"Oh," said Teresa, "What was Sarah doing here?"

Carlo was perplexed that she should ask a question like that. "Sarah just stopped in to see my wife; but, as I told you, Claudia isn't available."

Teresa ended the conversation by inviting the DeRoches to a big family dinner at Wimpy's in Osterville. She was going to invite the entire family to discuss the Feast of the Assumption Festival and her attendance. "We'll be there. Seven, correct?" asked Carlo.

"Yes, and we'll try to get the entire family there," replied Teresa.

Teresa exited the driveway and stopped briefly at the home of Frank and Sarah. "Frank's sailing again, Teresa," Sarah informed Teresa. "I suppose we'll come and bring the kids, right?" asked Sarah.

"Yes, let's make it a big family occasion," said Teresa.

Teresa then drove down the street and turned right onto Long Beach Road. She entered Anthony's and Betty's house. Anthony was grilling cheeseburgers and offered Teresa one with a beer. Teresa accepted as she walked toward a bathroom to change into her one-piece bathing suit. Walking back onto the deck, she joined Anthony, Betty, and Joe, who had just arrived. They watched the kids playing in the gentle surf as they ate and discussed the previous evening's discovery. Betty was silent throughout the whole discussion. Teresa said that she wanted the entire family to dine together at Wimpy's, and she invited Joe to come along.

After lunch, the group discussed all of the recent events and then reasoned that little would happen until the court made a decision on Claudia's complaint. In the meantime, Teresa was probably safe. All business initiatives came to a standstill, as a consequence of Claudia's lawsuit. Both Teresa and Anthony talked about the need to show no negative emotion in the presence of Claudia, Carlo, or Frank.

When Teresa arrived home with the excited children, she met Tom Blake in her living room. She bent to give him a kiss on the cheek. He turned and smiled at her. He looked a great deal like Robert, except he was much more mature. Robert would be forever young in her memory. How could she tell this man, this second father, that her second husband, John, had murdered his son, Robert? She decided that if she could not prove it and find the murderers, then she would never burden him or Naomi with the truth.

Tom greeted Teresa, "Hey, hon. You've been gone a long time. Naomi went into town to the Main Street Puritan Store to do some shopping. She'll be back soon."

"All right, Tom, but I hope you'll join the family for a dinner at Wimpy's. Going to have the whole crowd together," Teresa announced. "I'm going up to jump in the shower, after I get the kids moving with their clean-up."

After she had showered, Teresa came downstairs to find Naomi fixing little Sarah's hair, just like any grandmother would do. To Naomi, Sarah was her grandchild because she was Teresa's child, no matter who the father was.

Maggie was given the evening off and she decided to catch a movie with Riggs. *Boy,* thought Teresa, *what a pair!* As the phone rang, Teresa moved swiftly to answer it. "Yes, Vinnie, we'll meet at Sand Castle tomorrow to discuss the results of the test. I'll invite Anthony and Joe to come along. Shall we say 10:00 A.M. sharp? I'll have a few refreshments for you."

Teresa and the kids went out the door with Tom and Naomi. There was a small caravan of vehicles that went down Scudder Lane and turned left onto Craigville Beach Road. They stopped and pulled into Joe's drive. Joe came out of his small, Dutch colonial house and jumped into the car with Naomi and Tom. He kissed Naomi and shook Tom's hand. Tom then warmly embraced him. "Let's all try to have a peaceful and relaxing dinner." Then they drove to the Osterville restaurant.

The family entered Wimpy's and were shown to a large set-up of tables in the rear dining room. The kids were very well behaved. Teresa told everyone that she would pick up the tab since the dinner was her idea. Everyone was there but Claudia and Carlo. "Let's wait a few minutes to order in case Claudia and Carlo are on their way," suggested Teresa.

After about ten minutes, Anthony grew impatient and called the waitress over. Drinks were already at the table. Anthony ordered some appetizers and each person ordered an entree. Conversation remained light; and although subdued, both Frank and Sarah tried to be sociable.

Just as three waitresses were bringing the entrees, Carlo arrived with a blurry-eyed Claudia. His white shirt complemented his dark wavy hair and deep tan. He was barely five years older than Teresa, and he looked almost like a Greek God. Teresa wondered how Claudia, or for that matter, her sister-in-law, Sarah, could ever withstand his charm.

Claudia looked very distressed. She had obviously been crying. She seemed to have aged. Although significantly younger than Papa, she was about three years older than Carlo. Carlo looked and acted as though nothing was wrong. He apologized for being late and asked the waitress to bring some menus. He instructed all to continue eating, while he ordered for himself and Claudia, who was unusually quiet; but she still maintained the haughtiness and aloofness that so characterized her demeanor.

Teresa, too, was very quiet, yet observant. Teresa thought, *it really is too bad that we don't see the side of Claudia that she showed with the children on the Fourth of July.* The men talked a lot; the women ate quietly and attended to the children.

As the group was finishing the meal, the waitress brought over the dinners for Carlo and Claudia. Carlo seemed famished and scarfed down the food. Claudia just picked at hers with a fork, moving it around but taking only a few bites. Her eyes were fixed upon her plate as Carlo talked with the men. Sarah looked at Carlo with a pleasant smile. Teresa hoped Frank would not see through that.

Teresa interrupted the conversation. "I'm glad you all came tonight. I want to announce the reinstitution of an old family tradition tonight."

"What's that?" Frank asked.

"I am going to take the kids and as many of you who would like to go back to Youngstown and Lowellville for the Festival, food, and fireworks. We'll be leaving on August twelfth and returning on August seventeenth. That way, we will be able to settle into Paone, register the children for Catholic school, and attend the Festival. Just like the old days. I hope some of you will go."

Sarah, Frank's wife, said that she would attend and bring the kids. Tom and Naomi said that they would sit this trip out. Carlo said that he wanted to go and it would allow him to visit the Viscomi Corporate Headquarters to discuss some accounting procedures. Claudia said that she would stay home in Centerville. Though not stated, she did not want to return to the old homestead that so reeked of her late husband, Angelo, and his first wife, Catherine, and their long life together.

Joe and Anthony, both, wanted to go to protect Teresa from the reoccurrence of the violence that had come close to Teresa. They were not confident that the violence had stopped. In reality, everything depended on Claudia's court case. Violence could be renewed if Teresa, and not Claudia, won the case.

As the group began to dwindle, Teresa wished Carlo a peaceful night. All were making their way home. Robert and Anthony Blake, along with their sister, little Sarah Mahoney, went back to Hyannisport with Tom and Naomi. Joe and Teresa were alone once again. She leaned over and whispered in his ear. "Joe, please get the court to reevaluate its schedule. Perhaps it would be better if you got the case moved to the days when we are home." Teresa smiled at Joe and gave him a soft kiss on his cheek. "Let's get going," she urged.

31

Days seemed to come and go quickly on the Cape. July was rapidly coming to an end. Joe was heartened by his time with Teresa. They seemed to be growing closer. Joe knew he had always been attracted to her, but she had been Robert's girl; and later, Robert's wife. After she became Robert's widow, there was interminable grief, both for her and for Joe, himself. Just when enough time had passed to respectably approach Teresa, she pulled away and married John. It was a terrific blow for Joe, so he threw himself into his work and had several shallow relationships, but nothing that would stand the test of time. He loved Teresa and Teresa only.

Joe worked and built a practice in Boston, and then he bought his second home on Craigville Beach Road, in West Hyannisport. He loved the Cape and since Teresa and John didn't frequent the Cape, he could drown himself in activities there. But now, since John Mahoney's death, Teresa, her family, and his love for her again surrounded him. His law practice had suffered because of the time he was devoting to Teresa, Viscomi Construction, and the Viscomi family. Joe forwarded his caseload to other colleagues in Boston and all but closed his office. His income almost doubled from his work with Viscomi Construction, and he was close to Teresa. He worried about her and was protective of her. This widowhood was different; Teresa was not pulling away from him this time. All that had happened seemed to draw them closer together.

Joe had decided that his Cape home would be the place for future meetings that needed to be confidential. This morning he rose and went downstairs to make some coffee. The doorbell rang, and he went to the door in his boxers to let Maggie in. "Joseph, get dressed. I've come to set up the breakfast for your meeting. Get dressed, you exhibitionist!" cried Maggie.

"Oh, Maggie, you know you love it; you want me!" he responded as he bounded up the stairs to get dressed.

When Joe had come back down the stairs, Vinnie Palmieri was already settled in the living room, drinking coffee. Maggie was bustling around the makeshift buffet, which held juice, coffee, scrambled eggs, home fried potatoes, bacon, and homemade rolls. Maggie looked at Joe, pulled her sweater around her shoulders, and told him to blow out the flames under the serving trays when all were finished eating. Teresa and Anthony entered the door as Maggie exited.

"I see everything is in order," announced Teresa. "Let's dig in and get on with the business." All gathered around the buffet and filled their plates. As they began eating, Vinnie Palmieri told them that he had news. "I received the DNA results on little Sarah. John Mahoney is not her biological father."

Teresa sat as though in shock. "Oh, my God," she exclaimed. "How could this all be true? Thank God John had insisted on a legal adoption or we would be in more trouble right now. At least I have Sarah, legally, and forever."

Vinnie continued, "I think this brings into question Dr. Rhodes's veracity and other medical incidents surrounding him." Joe and Anthony began to talk about all the family that Dr. Rhodes had treated and that he was the one person who had been present when both Robert Blake and Angelo Viscomi were pronounced dead. He had talked with the family about how unnecessary an autopsy would have been in each of those deaths. Joe voiced the obvious, "What other lies is Dr. Rhodes covering up concerning Robert and Angelo?"

Palmieri struggled to gain control of the discussion. Everyone continued to chatter with the unbelievable news about Sarah's parentage. "I don't know how or who to look at next, except maybe Frank Viscomi. He is seeing Kelly on the side. Perhaps, Anthony, you could get a strand of his hair for another DNA test?"

"I will try," Anthony quickly responded.

Vincent Palmieri had not finished. "We know that Frank had been seeing Kelly Mahoney and that she said she is pregnant with his child. He could very well be little Sarah's biological father. We do know, however, that he is not seeing Kelly Mahoney anymore. We have been following him and he is spending a great deal of his time sailing alone. We also know that Mrs. Mahoney has been spending time with her daughters in Bethany, Delaware. When she is not with them, she has been lavishing away at the DeRoches house in Centerville. In addition, Sarah Viscomi, Frank's wife, continues to sneak little getaways with Carlo DeRoches."

"We've got to formulate a plan to extricate the company from Carlo and Claudia. We've got to come up with something!" exclaimed Joe. "Well, Joe, let's stick to one issue right now, Dr. Rhodes." Vinnie brought them back to the original subject. "We've got to look into other incidents that involve Dr. Rhodes. I brought some papers for Teresa's and Anthony's signature, and for your perusal, Joe."

Joe took the papers from Vincent's hand and looked them over. "I guess that this is the logical step to take next. I do believe that it needs to happen." Joe then looked straight at Anthony and then took Teresa's hands in his. "Vinnie has an order here for you to sign. It gives permission to exhume your father's body for an autopsy."

Tears ran down Teresa's face. She wiped her eyes and cheeks. "I understand. We need to know and the sooner the better. If Papa was murdered, then Robert probably was also. We've got to get to the bottom of it, including John's participation in the murders and the participation of any other family member who may have been involved."

Teresa took the order, signed it, and handed it to Anthony. He looked at her, smiled, and signed. "Sis, we'll get to the bottom of this and avenge both Robert and Papa."

"I'll be going to Youngstown immediately to get this accomplished," Vinnie informed the group. "I'll need you, Joe, to help us block any fight that Claudia or Frank might put up."

Joe responded in an affirmative manner. "I've retained the firm of Altvater, Patton, and Reindl in Youngstown. We need a battery of lawyers for the complex issues involving Viscomi Construction. John Swartz won't do anymore because he is representing Claudia De-Roches. His firm is out. Murray Patton, Patrick Altvater, and Louis Reindl run a tough law firm with plenty of associates to do the background work. I'll inform them right away about the exhumation. They'll be able to handle any protest."

Vincent Palmieri thanked them, took a cup of coffee in a travel mug, and headed out the door to the Hyannis airport, where he would take connecting flights to Pittsburgh and on to Youngstown.

Even though this was Joe's home, Teresa took over as hostess and poured Joe and Anthony additional cups of coffee. "We've got to tackle the situation with Frank. We need to extricate him from Claudia and Kelly Mahoney. If we can accomplish that, we will nix Claudia's move to control the company," Joe reasoned.

"I've been thinking about this," Teresa began. "I need to be pro active. I'm going to confront Sarah, on my turf, at Sand Castle. Joe, you and Anthony will be there, and I'll make sure that the meeting takes place when Frank is out sailing. I want to get Sarah alone. If we neutralize her, we can neutralize Frank and, maybe, even Carlo. I need to set the stage and do this in the family home, Sand Castle. It will have the aura of elegance, history, and family power. It's time to act like we control our destiny. It is time to take the wheel and do the directing."

"Okay," responded a convinced Anthony. "But, Joe, we need to call Peter Palmieri and beef up security. If we turn up the heat, someone is going to get desperate. That could mean harm to Teresa. If we dislodge Frank's support of Claudia, Teresa again becomes a target because she controls the largest share of the company. Our father's will allows for the siblings to control a deceased sibling's share until the children of the deceased sibling become adults. Frank's share, combined with one half of Teresa's share, if something happens to her, will enable Claudia to be in control. Of course, if Frank is still being blackmailed."

Teresa then decided that the group should break for the day and that she would contact Sarah to get her over to Sand Castle on some pretext. Then she would get Sarah under tow.

32

Teresa was busy in the breakfast room of Sand Castle, arranging flowers in a vase. Just yesterday, the plan had been formulated. Today was the day that she would meet with her sister-in-law, Sarah, to discuss Frank's support and Sarah's relationship with Carlo DeRoches. Joe and Anthony were sitting in the library awaiting the arrival of Sarah, who was invited on the pretext of planning the Labor Day grand opening of the house, including the traditional picnic, and the Italian dinner in the evening.

Teresa continued to move the flowers around in the vase until she achieved perfection. The flowers were bright and added a gaiety to the surroundings. Although the landscaping was incomplete, the view from this room was undisturbed by the work on the grounds. Looking out toward the beach, the blue of Nantucket Sound was gleaming. Teresa looked around her. The room had three walls of French doors that looked out over a terrace. At one end of the terrace was the beautiful, wicker-furnished solarium. How many family mornings she remembered in this room. Now, she had redecorated it in her favorite blue. Blue-flowered wallpaper accented the blue upholstery of the chairs. The round table allowed for good conversation. The sun streamed through the French doors to cast a bright glow over the room.

Teresa was pleased. Soon, the house would be finished and all remnants of Claudia's decorating would be history. How she loved this house. She was grateful to Papa for giving her the chance to live in it once again. It was too bad that she wouldn't be here year round. The only consolation was that she would be living at Paone, her childhood home. Neither Anthony nor his wife, Betty, seemed sad about leaving that home. Yet, here she was, loving the idea of living within the historical walls of the family.

Maggie and Riggs were the only staff in the house. Teresa did not want to be overheard. The kids were outside playing catch. Teresa saw her brother's children, Katie and Angelo, run up to little Sarah and young Anthony, hoping to participate in whatever game they were playing. Teresa took a deep breath because she knew that Riggs would soon announce the arrival of her sister-in-law.

"I'm delighted with the changes that you have made at Sand Castle," Sarah exclaimed as she burst through the door. Teresa was a little surprised that Sarah had circumvented Riggs in his duty to announce guests. "I never really liked Claudia's decor. Now you have restored it to a truly dignified and stately home."

Teresa thanked Sarah and instructed Riggs to have the refreshments brought in. Maggie filled the serving trays with scrambled eggs, bacon, and home fries. They would serve themselves after Maggie exited the room. "I can't wait to plan this picnic and celebration. This should be a truly happy time for you and your... Joe, Anthony, what are you doing here?" asked a surprised Sarah.

"We've dropped in for a conversation with you," explained Teresa's brother, Anthony. Joe remained silent. He just wanted to observe. After all, this was a family affair.

"That's kind of strange," observed Sarah. "Why would you men want to talk with me when you have so many things to do for Viscomi Construction?"

Anthony did not answer. He had decided that this was Teresa's show; he and Joe were just the witnesses. This way Sarah will understand the family power behind the conversation. "Please get your food and take a seat," suggested Anthony. Each of the four filled a plate and toasted a bagel. After that was accomplished, all were seated and coffee was served. Teresa began the conversation.

"The family is in trouble, Sarah. I asked you over here to discuss the issue and to gain your support," Teresa said. "I can't imagine what I can do for you, Teresa," expressed a baffled Sarah.

"For starters, you can stop your affair with Carlo DeRoches," insisted Teresa. Sarah froze. She looked at the men and back to Teresa. Her eyes welled up with tears. "This affair is complicating many issues," Teresa explained. "It has to stop right now. I insist on it."

"Okay, Teresa. How did you find out about this? And even more important, how do you think that this will affect Viscomi Construction?" Sarah asked.

"For starters, your distance from Carlo will enable Frank to disagree with Claudia," explained Teresa.

"I don't understand," cried Sarah. Joe and Anthony sat looking at Sarah without any sympathy, wondering what Teresa would say next. Sarah sobbed and tried to play the martyr.

"Calm down, Sarah. You need to get a grip." Teresa's voice was now more elevated. "I need to get a few points across to you. Number one, Frank has had a brief affair with Kelly Mahoney. Number two, she claims she is pregnant with his child. They could not have been seeing each other for more than a few weeks. Number three, Frank is being blackmailed by Claudia about this information. Frank felt that he would lose his family if he didn't side with Claudia."

"That bastard!" screamed Sarah. "Well, he damn well has lost his family. I'm going to get a divorce and take him for all he's worth!" exclaimed Sarah. Joe and Anthony kept eating, Joe with his eyes downcast into his plate. Anthony noted that Teresa's demeanor was changing into one of anger.

"That's just what I thought you would say, Sarah Viscomi. But you are not going to get away with that. Although Frank saw that woman for only a few weeks, she could take some of his money to support that child. For nearly a year, you have been seeing Carlo. You even spent the night with him before his wedding to Claudia." Sarah began to get up from the table. "Sit down," screamed Teresa. "You are not going to divorce Frank. You are going to tell him that you know he had a brief relationship with Kelly Mahoney. You will then tell him that you forgive him and want to move forward and make your marriage work. Then, after any confession that he makes, after he takes you in his arms, you will convince him to side with Anthony and me in the changes that we want to make in the company. Am I clear, do you understand?"

Sarah looked into Teresa's steely brown eyes and smirked. "And just what makes you think, Miss High and Mighty Viscomi wannabe C.E.O., that I'm going to do what you want? I'm out of here, and I'm getting my share of your bastard brother's money."

"Listen to me Sarah Viscomi, not only will I inform Claudia about your indiscretions with her newly wedded husband, but I will do everything in my power for you to lose your kids. Frank will get them; and you know him, he will never let you see them again. As much as you neglect those poor kids, you still won't want to give them up because they are yours." Teresa's furious gaze was fixed upon Sarah; her eyes did not leave Sarah's face, which was filled with rage. "I've retained a prestigious law firm, and they are already working on taking those kids from you, in case you don't listen to me. Then of course, you will have to deal with Claudia's ire because you betrayed her friendship when you slept with her husband."

"All right," whimpered a broken Sarah. "I'll do what you say, but how can I be assured that you will live up to your promises?" Sarah probed.

"Listen, Sarah Viscomi, you can't be sure I'll keep my word. You know me and have for years. Think about it. I'll give you one thing; I will not tell Frank of your indiscretion. You sway his vote, and I'll lay off. But you turn him around, and do it very soon."

"Okay," Sarah interjected, "I'll give in, you win. I'll try to work this out!"

"Oh, yeah," Teresa said matter of factly, "and you won't see Carlo anymore. You will go to a marriage counselor or all bets are off. Understand?"

"Yes, I understand," said Sarah. "I'll do what you say and try to talk Frank into siding with you and Anthony."

With that said, a teary-eyed Sarah rose and went out through the French doors to retrieve her children. She left hastily. Anthony smirked at his sister and Joe smiled with pride at Teresa's restored confidence.

"There is no point in having power unless you wield it. I have the power and I'm going to use it," quipped Teresa.

33

Teresa relaxed in the living room of her Hyannisport cottage. The fire was aglow in the fireplace, and she had just sunk into the chair, experiencing that homey feeling that one gets in loving one's surroundings. She looked at the kids. Robert Jr. was reading the latest Harry Potter book, while little Sarah and Anthony were playing a very long game of Monopoly.

One would hardly know that there were security guards posted outside the door. They were protecting Teresa here and were also stationed at Sand Castle to prevent any future trouble there. Since the last meeting with Joe and Anthony, after the confrontation with her sister-in-law, Sarah, Joe arranged protection for Anthony and his family. If and when Frank turned around and supported his sister, Teresa, and brother, Anthony, one of them would be in danger. Teresa, because of her gender, would be the most likely target. If Anthony or Teresa were not in the picture, Frank could be swayed to support Claudia with his share in the company, and with his one half control of Anthony's or Teresa's share. Joe could not take the chance. Anthony, Betty, and Joey had to be protected.

Teresa looked around the room that was filled with so many memories. It was truly special to be able to spend the summer in this house. Teresa had thought that she would never do that again. Summers in Bethany were very nice, but it just was not the Cape. This house, with its colonial décor, meant so much more to her than the house in Bethany. Staying in this house, while decorating Sand Castle, the Osterville mansion, would have given Teresa the time of her life, if it hadn't been for the murders. Teresa was having a lot of fun diving into the restoration and redecoration of Sand Castle. It provided a lot of diversion from the problems that had come her way. Teresa hoped that the problems, the secrets, and the security guards would not ruin the summer for the children. She would do her best to make sure that they enjoyed this summer. She had one other goal, to enable the boys to enjoy what would probably be the last summer in their father's house, the Hyannisport cottage.

As Teresa leaned on the arm of her chair and looked into the fire, she felt a caress on the back of her neck and a kiss on her cheek. She turned to see Frank smiling at her and the kids. "Hello, brother, what brings you here?"

"Hey, Ter, I came over to see you and talk. We really haven't been together since the night we had dinner at the Road House, when we thought we were being followed. How are you?"

"I'm all right, Frank. I'd like to get to the bottom of the mess this family is in so that I can feel safe again." Teresa sighed. "There is so much going on that my head is spinning."

"So, Ter, tell me about it. I'm here for you, but I've something to tell you first," said Frank.

"Let me go get some coffee first and scurry the kids up to bed. Maggie, please come and get the kids up to bed," Teresa said softly.

Teresa returned with coffee and some sweetbreads. She sank into the sofa, opposite Frank, and looked intently into his eyes. They both sipped their coffee and Frank smiled a more genuine smile than she had seen in a long while. "Ter, I've come to tell you that I'm going to support you and our big brother in moving the company's regional office to the Washington, D.C. metro area. I was wrong, but there were some extenuating circumstances that kind of forced me to throw my support to Claudia. Please don't ask me what they were, because they are somewhat embarrassing. Just know, I'm going to rectify the situation and move ahead with you and Anthony."

"Oh, Frankie, thanks so much. I know that you will never be sorry about this. We Viscomi kids need to pull together!" exclaimed a more lighthearted Teresa.

"Ter, I've been very unhappy for a long time. It has not been good between Sarah and me," explained Frank.

"I know, brother; it hasn't been difficult to see. My heart has been aching for you." Teresa said through some tears. "I would do anything to make it better for you, Frankie."

"Oh, Ter, I have been so introverted, thinking of myself. I am finally seeing some light at the end of the tunnel and here you are crying for my pain. You, who just lost a husband a few months ago; and then, you were almost killed in some weird kind of attempted mob hit. But still, you are here crying for me. I love you."

Teresa and Frank embraced. Teresa was very touched by Frank's expression of love. She hoped that he would really find happiness. She wasn't sure that his wife, Sarah, would be able to do it with him, but then stranger things were happening in this family all of the time.

"There are a few things that I need to tell you, Frank. You have not been privy to several dark secrets that possibly only the walls of Sand Castle have heard in entirety. I think you need to understand what's been going on. I am going to tell you that..."

At that moment, Claudia came bursting into the room in her usual haughty and condescending manner. "How dare you, Teresa Mahoney. How dare you! How could you do this without my knowledge? I stopped at Anthony's, but he went to Youngstown on short notice, probably to oversee this nasty mess. How can you bring all this disgrace upon me and the rest of your family. It's going to be in all the papers, and you will not be able to shake the dishonor that you have brought on us all!"

"Whoa, whoa, wait a minute Claudia," interrupted Frank. "What in God's name are you shouting about? The kids are upstairs, take it easy. Calm down. What is this all about?"

"Your sister knows what this is about." Claudia was shrieking out of control by this time. "She and your brother, Anthony, are having your father's body exhumed! What do you really expect to find, Teresa? What? You've always hated me for taking your mother's place. You hated me living in Sand Castle and making it my own by redecorating it. You've taken that home from me; you're about to ruin the company; and now you are trying to insinuate that something was wrong about your father's death. How dare you! How dare you!"

"Try to calm down, Claudia." Teresa tried to assuage Claudia's out-of-control tirade. "Some alarming facts have come to light."

Claudia stood staring icily at Teresa. "Teresa Viscomi Mahoney, there is nothing you can say to me that will change this, and there is nothing to discover. Your father was an old man, who died; that is all there is. I'll see that John Swartz prevents this; I will not permit this. Angelo and John Mahoney must be turning in their graves."

"Claudia, you can do nothing. We have the legal right to do this and we have the justification. All precautions have been taken, and our attorneys are prepared to argue and win. You can't prevent it; do what you may!" dared Teresa defiantly. "And, Claudia, John Mahoney may be turning in his grave, but that won't change a thing!"

There was no pretense here between these two women. They were enemies now, and there would be a war for control. Neither would back down. Claudia stormed out the door, leaving it open. Frank followed and closed the door. As he was about to ask Teresa what this was all about, Maggie came downstairs and told them that the loud argument had disturbed the children. "I'll go up and tuck them in right now," said Teresa. "Stay here Frank, we will talk after I hear their prayers and make sure they are calm. Maggie, please make a fresh pot of coffee because I think Frank and I will be staying up tonight for a long talk."

After tucking in the children, Teresa came down the stairs into the living room. Frank was adding a log to the fire. The coffee was in a silver pot on the butler's coffee table. Teresa sat back on the sofa, opposite Frank, and refilled their coffee cups. She added cream to hers and sugar to his. She looked into his eyes, took his hand, and began the explanation.

"It all began with the restoration of Sand Castle. I was thinking a great deal about Robert, while living here in this house. I took off my wedding band and replaced it with the wedding band that Robert gave me. I sent Maggie over to Sand Castle to place John's ring in the safe to keep for little Sarah, when she grows older. Maggie found some documents in the safe that held some dark secrets. These included a report by a private investigator, Vincent Palmieri, and an unsigned will. This will was dated the day Papa died." Teresa cried.

Frank listened intently as Teresa told him about the investigation, the possibility that Robert had been murdered, that John was involved, and that their father's life had been suspiciously blotted out. She also told him of the will that disinherited Claudia.

Frank never swayed from listening intently. Both he and Teresa wiped tears from their eyes, as she came to the end of her story. The only segment that she kept close to her heart and did not divulge to Frank was that his wife, Sarah, had been unfaithful with Carlo De-Roches. Teresa would not hurt Frank with the knowledge that his wife had betrayed him.

34

Anthony Viscomi stood in the rain under a large umbrella. The heat of the day was unbearable. It was Ohio and it was summer. Here he was outside a large mausoleum, in Calvary Cemetery in Youngstown. Around the corner was the grave of John Mahoney. Next to him was Father Francis Montillo, who was saying prayers for the dead. Angelo Viscomi was being reinterred. "Eternal Rest grant unto him, O Lord!" Anthony responded, "And let Perpetual Light shine upon him." Father Francis continued, "May his soul and all the souls of the faithful departed rest in peace." Both concluded, "Amen."

Father Francis put his arm around Anthony. Anthony was choked with emotion; here was his father being buried again. It was as though it was the first time and he had just died. Anthony stepped inside the mausoleum and placed a bouquet of flowers on the large, newly-sealed sarcophagus. The large printed letters indicated that this was the tomb of Angelo Viscomi. Next to him lay his first wife, Catherine Viscomi. Off to each side of the tomb were spaces for each of the children and their spouses. Neither Robert Blake nor John Mahoney was buried here. There was room here for several of the grandchildren. Anthony looked around and knelt, blessed himself, and said a prayer. He then left and turned to watch the men lock the gates.

Anthony returned to the rectory at Our Lady of Mount Carmel Church for a brief lunch with Father Francis. Then he headed directly for a flight to the Cape. Vincent Palmieri had already gone back to the Cape. He called ahead and asked his brother, Peter, to tighten security on Teresa and other members of the family. News of the findings of the autopsy would be scandalous. That fact, combined with an unexpected gathering of many family retainers at the DeRoches house, was a cause for alarm.

Anthony and Father Francis sat leisurely over bowls of pasta and meatballs. Little conversation permeated the dinner. Anthony was deep in thought; the confirmation of a suspicion did not make him feel better.

Meantime, at the Cape, Joe had arrived in Hyannisport. Maggie and the kids were at the Hyannisport Association Beach. Joe and Teresa walked hand-in-hand down the hill from her cottage, toward the private beach club and Squaw Island. Teresa just wanted to check on the children and Maggie, before she and Joe walked the private beaches of Squaw Island.

As they walked down the hill, Joe told Teresa about Youngstown. "The autopsy has been completed. Vincent Palmieri will be here tomorrow for a meeting with the entire family. He even requested that Claudia and Frank be present. I've taken the liberty to ask Riggs to set up the library at Sand Castle for the meeting. Claudia will be bringing John Swartz and Anthony will be bringing Patrick Altvater. The Barnstable Police will be sending a detective."

Teresa was speculative about this information. "I guess the autopsy revealed that my father was murdered?"

Joe responded in an even voice, "I don't know the specifics, but I do know that foul play is indicated. I'm so sorry, Ter." Teresa leaned her body closer to Joe's, as they walked. Her silent closeness was enough for Joe.

When Teresa saw the kids in the water, she waved at them. The lifeguards seemed to be paying close attention to them. Maggie was busy eating an apple, while watching the kids. Teresa stopped and kissed her on the cheek. "Joe and I will be going for a long walk along the beaches and coves, she said. "A guard is following us close behind. It will be a few hours before we return. Perhaps the six of us can have a small dinner together on the porch? You pick the menu, it doesn't matter."

Maggie patted Teresa's hand lovingly. She watched as Joe and Teresa disappeared around a bend into a small cove on Squaw Island. She smiled. It looked like her Teresa, despite the recent trials, might find real happiness with a good man. Maggie loved Robert, having been with the Blake's many years, but she disliked John Mahoney. He seemed like a sleaze and an opportunist, who was out to get whatever he could. Joe was a good man, a good person, a gentle and caring spirit. If Teresa couldn't be with Robert, Joe should be the guy. He should have been the guy even before Mahoney was in the picture.

Joe and Teresa walked silently hand-in-hand. Occasionally, one would stop and select a beautiful seashell on the ground. They carried their sandals in their free hands. Joe was the first to break the silence. "Vincent called Peter early this morning. His investigators have reported a gathering of the old family retainers at Claudia's house in Centerville—Tony Foccata, Mario Testa and his son, along with his girlfriend, Kara. Kelly Mahoney is there with Shannon, also. Bobby Faccia, Freddie Paolone are there, too. I don't want to be too alarmed, but I do believe that trouble is brewing."

"Joe, they will probably all come to Sand Castle tomorrow. All of them will expect to hear the results of the autopsy. It will be like at an old royal court, with people lining the foyer and sitting in chairs, waiting to be presented. Treachery will be present there tomorrow. We just don't know who the treacherous ones are. Tomorrow will be the beginning in learning the truth. I'll pick you up on the way to Sand Castle. We'll face this one together."

The remainder of their walk continued in understanding silence. At times they clasped each other's hand firmly to prevent the other from stumbling. The sun was starting to descend. Wearing sandals, they walked up the hill on the street away from the beach. Entering Teresa's cottage, they saw Maggie preparing to throw some steaks on the grill. Teresa went upstairs to freshen up, while Joe poured some wine for Teresa, Maggie, and himself.

After washing up for dinner, the children went out to the porch. Teresa followed them. The kids were oblivious to any trouble—laughing and screeching and talking about tomorrow's fun at the beach.

Teresa served the baked potatoes and Maggie brought the vegetables to the table. Joe served the steaks and the adults sat back to enjoy the lightheartedness of conversation with the young children. Teresa looked around and smiled. *At least the children are enjoying the summer and the boys are so at home here in this old Hyannisport cottage.*

35

Teresa and Joe turned the corner in front of Claudia's house and headed toward Osterville where Sand Castle was located. There were no cars in the driveway at Claudia's Centerville home. It seemed strangely peaceful. Beach traffic was already picking up. Many cars were headed in the opposite direction, toward Craigville Beach. Teresa had hoped to get an earlier start. She liked to go to morning Mass at Our Lady of Victory and then say the Rosary out in the garden Rosary. She felt such solace in prayer, especially after dealing with all the revelations about the murders. Her plan now was to go to lunch with Joe after the meeting at Sand Castle and then go to church.

On the way to Sand Castle, Teresa talked with Joe about the situation. "Joe, I had to tell Tom and Naomi about Papa's autopsy. They know that it could be linked to John's murder, but I want to protect them from knowledge about Robert's death. They should be spared the knowledge, if at all possible. Today is their last full day before going back to Nantucket. They are taking the kids up to Salem today for a day trip. They are taking Joey also, so the kids will be spared any knowledge of all this mess."

Joe responded in a soft gentle manner. "I understand, Teresa, but don't you think they have the right to know? I think they may hold it against you, if you don't divulge the information as you glean it. Think about this, Ter. Think long and hard about it. Would you want to know if it had been your son?"

Teresa steered the Jeep into the drive of Sand Castle. The house was being stripped of the cedar shingles, in preparation for new ones. The grounds were covered with heavy, earth-moving equipment. The rear grounds between the house and the ocean were complete, just leaving the street side in disarray. Teresa sighed as she noted that the drive was filled with automobiles. An assembly had gathered. They were here to learn the fate of their fallen leader.

Riggs met her at the front door and one of the gardeners took the Jeep to the garage. Joe and Teresa entered the house to see a large group of old family retainers and officers of Viscomi Construction. The men parted for Teresa, who entered the formal parlor to greet the guests. Mario Testa rose to his feet immediately, followed by Tony Foccata. Tony was the first to greet her and express his sorrow for the need to meet like this.

The restored room was simply elegant. She briefly glanced up at the portrait of Angelo and Catherine over the fireplace. It once again presided over the room. Claudia had removed it for obvious reasons. Teresa asked Riggs to bring some refreshments for the group. As she exited the room, Teresa nodded to Mario Jr., Bobby Faccia, and Freddy Paolone.

Teresa crossed the foyer and entered the paneled library. Riggs had already prepared a fire and brought the refreshments. Teresa sank into a sofa. Joe poured a cup of coffee for her and sat down beside her. She clasped his hand. She looked around the room and managed a brief smile. Across from Teresa and Joe sat Claudia, Carlo, and John Swartz. Claudia looked pale, but some of that was probably rage that she was feeling deep within. Additional chairs had been brought from the dining room for Betty and Anthony, Frank and Sarah, and Attorney Patrick Altvater. The room was filled with obvious dread and dead silence.

Vincent Palmieri entered the room with his brother, Peter. Sergeant Thompson of the Massachusetts State Police followed them into the room. As the group began to introduce themselves to the rest of the family, Father Francis Montillo slipped into the room. He had decided to take a short vacation to the Cape so that he could be of support to the children of Angelo Viscomi.

Sergeant Thompson began with a short statement that an autopsy had been conducted on the body of the late Angelo Viscomi. The findings had been sent to the Massachusetts State Police and the Barnstable Police. Claudia was the first person to respond. "This is all so ridiculous, there can't possibly be anything wrong in this. I was there the day he died. I was with him most of the day and several of the days before."

"Mrs. DeRoches," responded Sergeant Thompson, "I am sorry to inform you, but you are wrong. The autopsy indicated that Mr. Viscomi died from being injected with bovine insulin. He slipped into a coma and died. Insulin is difficult to detect in a body. However, with sophisticated tests, bovine insulin can be detected. This crime almost went undetected."

Teresa put her hand to her mouth to suppress a gasp. She grasped Joe's hand and looked into Anthony's eyes. Anthony remained silent. "How can this be?" asked Frank. "I was in the house with the rest of you. You were, too, Anthony. The only one not here was Teresa, who was on her way when he died."

Teresa reacted strongly, "Papa wasn't a diabetic. He never told me that he was; did anyone here know? What about you Claudia; you saw him everyday; you were his wife; didn't you take care of him?"

Claudia slowly and deliberately responded through choking tears. "Angelo never bothered me with such things. It would not have been something that we would have discussed. He tried to protect me from unpleasant details. I would have never thought to question him. I left that to his assistant, Tony Foccata, and Dr. Rhodes."

Sergeant Thompson responded: "There is going to be a complete investigation into Mr. Viscomi's death. It is now being reclassified as a homicide." The Massachusetts State Police will be working with the locals because of Mr. Viscomi's stature in the community."

Claudia was gasping and crying. She screeched so loudly that even the family retainers across the foyer in the parlor could hear her. "My God, this can't be, this can't be!" She stood up to run out of the room, but fainted. Carlo caught her before she hit the floor. He carried her out of the room. No one followed them. Riggs met them at the door and took them to the solarium in the rear of the house. The family retainers, in the formal parlor, stood at the open door to the foyer and realized that something was indeed wrong. The news was not good. Claudia's performance as the distraught widow rivaled any Italian woman who would throw herself into the coffin, crying, "take me, take me! Not him, not him!"

Sergeant Thompson continued, "We will be interviewing those of you who were here that day, plus all of the people who had close contact with Mr. Viscomi. We will start with Mrs. DeRoches and all in the house the day Mr. Viscomi died, then we will move out to other family members and business associates."

John Swartz immediately stood and told them that they would have to make an appointment to meet with his client, widow of the deceased, Claudia Viscomi DeRoches. He believed that she was not in any condition to be interviewed at this time. Teresa told Sergeant Thompson that he could use the family room for interviewing and perhaps the other detective could use the breakfast room. "Riggs," she assured him, "will be available to make you comfortable."

Sergeant Thompson indicated that they would start with non-family members first, in order to give some time for the family to regain composure. He was a little concerned about the fainting Mrs. DeRoches. Teresa told him not to be concerned. "Italians are very dramatic. You would never feel like you were in a stressful situation, funeral, or other difficult time, if someone wasn't moaning, crying, or fainting. Don't let that affect your feelings or impressions." Then she looked at Anthony and Frank and asked them to take the Sergeant to the breakfast room to prepare a list of people who were in the house the day Angelo Viscomi died.

Preparing the list, Anthony observed that most of the people in the house were here today. "Even Mr. DeRoches, the new husband of the widow?" asked the Sergeant.

"Well of course," answered Frank. "He was, and is, an officer in the company. He controls the financial offices."

Anthony added that it really wasn't unusual because Carlo traveled back and forth between Youngstown, the Cape, and his home in York. "Dr. Thomas Rhodes is the only person, who was here on the day my father died, but is not here today.

There was no way that the two investigators would be able to interview all of the people in one day. They decided to talk with the Testas, father and son; Tony Foccata; Freddy Paolone; and Bobby Faccia. After that, they would start the family interviews with Claudia and her husband, Carlo. Anthony and Frank decided to stick around for the interviews. Betty and Sarah had already begun to leave. Teresa managed to thank Father Francis for coming. She invited him to Hyannisport for dinner, along with her siblings and their spouses. Then grasping Joe's hand, she told him that he must come for dinner also, especially since the family was to be there.

When Teresa and Joe got up to leave, a composed Claudia entered the room with Carlo behind her. "Teresa, I don't understand all of this and I wish none of this had happened. I can't help believing that you are trying to pull something here. I'll get to the bottom of it," Claudia sneered at Teresa. "You know, Frank indicated to me that he was switching sides to support you and Anthony. You may be moving on now, but I'll stop you. You are not going to make a mess out of Viscomi Construction like you have with this house." With that quip, she abruptly turned and walked out, leaving Carlo to follow her out the door like a puppy.

Joe, Teresa, and Father Francis left the house, as the interviews were about to begin. Joe looked at the retainers in the parlor. *Were any of these men involved? Testa was John Mahoney's right hand man. Foccata was Angelo Viscomi's. Bobby Faccia was working with Testa and Testa's son, Mario Jr. Freddie Paolone was Foccata's protégée. How did they fit into this intrigue?* Joe only hoped that John Mahoney was not as involved as the current evidence suggested. He wanted Teresa to feel as though her life was not wasted with Mahoney and that she had not married and slept with the man who had killed Robert, the love of her life.

Joe and Teresa walked out the door, hand-in-hand. Father Francis entered the rear of the Jeep. Teresa indicated that they would stop for lunch at the Barnacle and then, after dropping Joe off, she would go to church for the Rosary in the garden. Father Francis told Teresa he would stick with Joe until dinner and would come to her Hyannisport cottage later with the rest of the family.

140

Teresa drove the Jeep down the driveway and out the large, cast-iron gates of Sand Castle. Teresa turned right and headed down the street toward Centerville and Craigville Beach. The security guards were in a car behind them. As they approached Centerville, Teresa stopped and told the car's occupants: "We're going to do it backwards. We're going to stop at Four Seas for ice cream cones, before we have lunch at the Barnacle. I think we deserve it."

Father Francis, who had been quiet all morning, responded, "I think you deserve it, too."

36

After most of the interviews were conducted, Sergeant Thompson and Vincent Palmieri headed toward Claudia Viscomi De-Roches's Centerville house. While driving there, they were putting the pieces together. No one could confirm that diabetes was in Angelo Viscomi's medical history. Dr. Rhodes needed to be located. All the company and family retainers were in the house on the day that Angelo died. They didn't question John Swartz about the changed, but unsigned, will. He would claim confidentiality of his client. He also continued to represent Claudia Viscomi DeRoches, so questioning him was just not possible. It was obvious that someone in that house killed Angelo and possibly murdered John Mahoney, too. But would they ever tie Robert Blake's death to the whole thing?

As Sergeant Thompson and Vincent Palmieri pulled into Claudia's drive, they noticed that John Swartz was already there. The presence of many others was made evident by several parked vehicles. The two were escorted to the door of the living room, where Claudia and Carlo, along with John Swartz, were having a drink of sherry. Claudia stood when Vincent and Sergeant Thompson entered the room. "Please sit down gentlemen. May I offer you a drink?"

"No thank you, Ma'am, I don't think we should while we are on duty," responded the Sergeant.

John Swartz then asked why Vincent Palmieri was there since this was official business. Thompson quickly responded, "I have invited Mr. Palmieri because he has pertinent evidence to the investigation. Mr. Palmieri had contracted with Mr. Angelo Viscomi to investigate certain family and company matters before his death. In addition, Mr. Anthony Viscomi continued the contract after Angelo's death."

Thompson continued. "Mrs. DeRoches, we would like to talk with you alone, but your attorney may stay, of course."

Swartz nodded for Carlo to leave the room. "Mrs. DeRoches, you stated before that you were not privy to any information that would indicate that your late husband, Angelo Viscomi, was a diabetic. Is that correct?" asked the Sergeant.

"Yes, that is correct," responded Claudia.

"Did you notice anything suspicious on the day of your late husband's death?" asked the Sergeant.

"No," responded Claudia.

Changing the subject slightly, the Sergeant asked different questions. "Who was alone with your late husband on the day of his death?"

"Well," responded Claudia, "many people were there—his sons, Anthony and Frank; along with company employees and associates." Sergeant Thompson asked for the names of the company's personnel. "Well, Tony Foccata for one, and then there was Freddy Paolone. They were his right hand men in Youngstown and here at the Cape. Mario Testa and Bobby Faccia were there. Mario is a longtime member of the company and a family friend."

The Sergeant then asked, "Did your current husband, Carlo De-Roches, or Freddy Paolone, or Dr. Rhodes attend your late husband alone?"

"Dr. Rhodes was with him shortly before I came in at the end. John Swartz tried to see him, but he was already in a coma," answered Claudia.

"One final question, Mrs. DeRoches," Sergeant Thompson said, saving the best for the last. "Were you aware that your late husband had planned to sign a new will on the day of his death, leaving everything to his children?"

Visibly surprised, Claudia almost choked. Bringing her handkerchief to her mouth, she reached for her drink of sherry. Breaking his silence, John Swartz interjected, "Mrs. DeRoches did not know about the will change. I think that Mario Testa and Tony Foccata may have been aware. Not even his children had been told."

"Attorney Swartz, were you there on the day of Angelo Viscomi's death to attain his signature on the new will?" inquired the Sergeant. Attorney Swartz responded with an affirmative answer.

"I thank both of you for your cooperation. I have a few questions for Mr. DeRoches. Could we use this room?" Claudia nodded. "Of course, I'll go get him. John, please stay here with Carlo, when he arrives."

Carlo entered the room and began shaking hands with the Sergeant and Palmieri. He poured himself another drink of sherry and refilled John Swartz's glass. A maid brought in iced tea for Palmieri and Thompson before they got started.

"Mr. DeRoches, what was your relationship with the late Angelo Viscomi?" Thompson began.

Carlo responded that he was an employee in the company, Vice President of Financial Operations.

"Did you have contact with Mario Testa, Tony Foccata, Freddy Paolone, Bobby Faccia, and John Mahoney?" Sergeant Thompson asked in a follow-up. Carlo said that he had the most contact with Mr. Viscomi, then Anthony Viscomi and John Mahoney, who were the heads of the regional offices in Youngstown, Ohio and York, Pennsylvania. "I did have some marginal contact with Mario Testa and Anthony Foccata because they were second in charge at those locations. I had minimal contact with the others," responded Carlo.

"Mr. DeRoches, were there any difficulties or disagreements between Mr. John Mahoney and the late Mr. Viscomi?" asked the investigator.

"None that I knew about," responded Carlo. "I believe that Mr. Mahoney was deeply in love with his wife, Teresa, Mr. Viscomi's daughter. There is no way he would have breached the family's solidarity."

"Did you have any contact with the late Robert Blake, Teresa Mahoney's first husband?" asked the Sergeant.

"Not a lot. I only came on the scene shortly before his death. What does that have to do with anything?" asked Carlo. Sergeant Thompson ignored the question.

"Did the late Mr. John Mahoney ever make remarks about the late Mr. Robert Blake?" asked the Sergeant.

"Well, he did remark that he was disgusted with Robert Blake's saintly memory that everyone seemed to cling to, especially Teresa Mahoney," recalled Carlo.

"Mr. DeRoches, were you aware that the late Mr. Viscomi planned to change his will and had arranged to sign it on the day of his death?" asked the Sergeant.

Carlo looked very surprised and uncomfortable with the question. "Well, no, not exactly. I believed something was up, but he never said anything directly to me."

"Just a few more questions, Mr. DeRoches. What is your current relationship with Sarah Viscomi?" Sergeant Thompson was now getting to the heart of it.

Carlo choked. "Well, this is a bit uncomfortable. We were having a brief relationship but have cut it off, with my marriage and all. I don't want to divulge any more because of obvious reasons. I hope we can keep this information under wraps."

The Sergeant ignored the plea. "So, Mr. DeRoches, your relationship has ended?"

"Yes, of course," responded Carlo.

"Okay, Mr. DeRoches," said the Sergeant, "just one more question. What is your relationship with Kelly Mahoney?"

Carlo turned visibly pale. "Well, I don't have one. She is John's ex-wife and Claudia's friend."

"So, Mr. DeRoches, you are telling us that you have no personal relationship with Mrs. Kelly Mahoney?" repeated Thompson.

"Right," answered Carlo.

"Then why, Mr. DeRoches, can I place you and Mrs. Kelly Mahoney at several locations away from the Cape, at hotels in York and Youngstown and at Mrs. Mahoney's private residence?" countered Thompson.

"I don't believe you," said Carlo. "The whole thing is absurd."

"Mr. DeRoches," asked Thompson, "would you consider having a DNA test to rule you out as the biological father of Sarah Mahoney?"

"How ridiculous is this?" asked Carlo, as he looked at Swartz. "Everyone knew John was the father. If he wasn't, look at Frank Viscomi. He has Kelly knocked up now."

Thompson interjected, "Frank Viscomi has agreed to a DNA test, which is being conducted as we speak. How about you?" Carlo responded that he would have to get back with him after in-depth discussion with his attorney, John Swartz.

"One last question, Mr. DeRoches. Since you are aware of Kelly Mahoney's current pregnancy, what participation have you had in coercing Frank Viscomi to support your wife in her bid to take over controlling interest in Viscomi Construction?"

John Swartz interjected, "This interview is at an end; I need to confer with my client. Thank you gentlemen."

With the conclusion of the interview, Palmieri and Thompson were escorted out of the house. As they entered the car, they discussed the interviews and the information gleaned from Carlo and Claudia. "There is more than one private agenda in that house," speculated Vincent Palmieri.

"Oh yeah," said Thompson. "I think Claudia Viscomi DeRoches has a few secrets, but I really think she is going to have a few surprises, too."

As Thompson pulled the car out of the drive, he turned left onto Craigville Beach Road, then right onto Main and into the Four Seas parking lot. "We're here. We might as well have one of the best ice cream cones in the world."

37

Vincent Palmieri and his brother, Peter, met at the hotel. They were to spend the evening with the Viscomi siblings and Joe Cutruzzula at Joe's house on Craigville Beach Road in West Hyannisport. They were running a little late. Vincent wanted to freshen up and change into casual clothes after his round of interviews with Sergeant Thompson.

The drive through town into West Hyannisport was somewhat slow because of the heavy flow of tourists who were out and about everywhere; and there were few parking places available on the street. Vincent was happy that Joe declined his offer to pick up food for the group on his way to the house. Joe indicated that he was having the food delivered. He hoped that they didn't mind the usual chowder, lobster, baked potatoes, and corn on the cob. Vincent indicated that was fine for his palate.

Vincent and Peter were the last to arrive. The others had already started to dig into the food. Joe reheated the Palmieri brothers' lobsters in his microwave. The Viscomi siblings were unusually quiet, none of the boisterous behavior associated with family gatherings. Joe observed the somber behavior. It was clear that Anthony, Teresa, and Frank were grieving all over again for their father.

After dinner, Joe served the coffee to the group gathered around in the living room. The evening was unusually warm, and there was no need for Joe to start a fire. They all sat quietly and studied Vincent's face. Joe settled in next to Teresa on the sofa. He took her hand in his. She looked at him and smiled; but her eyes were filled with tears.

Vincent began, "Well, folks, things may begin to happen now. I believe the extra force to protect Teresa and her children, along with Anthony and his family, is very necessary. The person we are dealing with will tip his or her hand soon because Frank has changed sides. The obvious action for them to take is an elimination of Teresa or Anthony, or both of them. We must be careful and take extra caution in everything."

Teresa shuttered. "Tell us what you have learned through Sergeant Thompson's interviews today." Vincent replied that the whole situation was quite complicated, especially in the relationships of Carlo and different women. Vincent had almost slipped, because he agreed that he would not piece Sarah Viscomi into the picture with Carlo unless it meant that she was a knowledgeable accomplice to one of the murders in the puzzle.

Vincent told the group that Carlo DeRoches was cheating on his wife only a few months after his wedding. "The most notable of his liaisons is Mrs. Kelly Mahoney."

Teresa gasped, as a startled Frank shrieked out. "What? What are you saying?"

"Yes, Mr. Viscomi," continued Vincent Palmieri, "I am sure that this is quite a shock; but, yes, Mr. DeRoches has been seeing Mrs. Mahoney for quite some time."

It took a few minutes for this one to sink into their minds. "In fact, I think that it is very possible that Mr. DeRoches is Sarah Mahoney's biological father. I believe that John Mahoney was tricked into believing that he was the biological father, thus his move to adopt the child. Frank has agreed to a DNA test just to rule him out. We are conducting the test, but just the fact that you are so agreeable, Frank, tells me that you are not the one. In fact, I doubt if you are the father in the current pregnancy. In fact, you were probably tricked the way John Mahoney was."

"Oh, my God!" Teresa exclaimed as she realized that so much depravity was intermingled in the investigation.

Vincent Palmieri continued, "I know that John Mahoney was not present at Sand Castle the day Angelo Viscomi died. He was in route with Teresa at the time. Dr. Rhodes has not been accounted for, but Sergeant Thompson and I have spoken to all of the remaining people in the house."

Vincent decided to be brutally truthful. "Anyone in that house could be the one who administered the bovine insulin. They all had access to Angelo Viscomi; although, as much as I hate to say it, Claudia DeRoches seems credible. I think she is telling the truth."

Joe then interjected that there had to be some clues.

"Well, both Testa and Foccata talked to the late Mr. Viscomi, individually, the day that he died," Vincent observed. "Testa was the right hand man of John Mahoney. We know that Mr. Mahoney was involved in Robert Blake's death because he had the Jeep towed and overhauled immediately. Mr. Mahoney had called Dr. Rhodes in on the case and Dr. Rhodes indicated that there was no need to conduct an autopsy, as he did with Angelo Viscomi's body. All evidence in regard to Mr. Blake's death was destroyed. There will be no way to implicate John Mahoney, except by theory."

"I believe that Mario Testa, John's right hand man would be the one to turn traitor. Tony Foccata was too close to Mr. Viscomi. He worked with him at the Cape and in Youngstown. Too much loyalty there for him to betray his chief," continued Palmieri.

"I can't believe it, no, I refuse to believe that Mario had anything to do with Papa's death. He's been a family friend for a long time," asserted Teresa.

Anthony then added, "Papa always quoted the famous saying, 'keep your friends close and your enemies closer.' I know that Mario is a friend. Tony worked closely with Papa because Papa wanted to watch him."

"But," Vincent interrupted, "Mario Jr. is closely aligned to Kelly Mahoney's daughter, Kara. That could mean some kind of alliance."

Teresa continued to speculate. "Anthony, you are correct. I won't believe negatively of Mario Testa. It would be natural, given the working relationships in York, that the two young people from Youngstown would gravitate to each other. I'm with the Foccata explanation."

"Either way," Palmieri deliberated, "things will soon shake down. We must be prepared and we must play it safe. Don't take any chances," commanded Vincent.

"Well, I'll soon be going to Youngstown with the kids for the Feast of the Assumption. We will enjoy that tradition and begin setting up Paone for us. I will also be registering the children at St. Edward's Catholic School. There is much to do. Peter, please get whatever security together that I will need there," requested Teresa. "We will be leaving in a few days."

Frank indicated that he and his wife, Sarah, were going with Teresa and taking their children, little Angelo and Katie. Carlo would be present also, as he had to conduct some business at the office. All would be flying aboard the corporate jet. "I am going, too," said Joe. "I need to take a look at this gatehouse that I'll be moving into until I find something more suitable."

"Unfortunately, I can't go. However, I do understand that Mario Testa, Tony Foccata, and Bobby Faccia are going. I feel that this is the time for extra security," Anthony speculated. "I am a bit uncomfortable that all of those people will be there."

As the group settled into a second cup of coffee, the telephone rang. Joe answered it and called Vincent to the phone. Vincent listened intently to the caller. His face turned ashen as he put the receiver back on the phone. "That was Sergeant Thompson calling. He wanted to inform me that there has been a terrible traffic accident on the Mid-Cape Highway in the Upper Cape. A semi hit a car in a head-on collision. Unfortunately, the driver of the automobile, Dr. Thomas Rhodes, died at the scene of the accident."

38

Teresa Mahoney had difficulty this morning in concentrating on praying the Rosary. Each morning, she went to pray in the garden Rosary at Our Lady of Victory in Centerville. This morning was no different, except she remembered Dr. Rhodes, who was killed the previous evening. The death could not have been an accident. That would be too coincidental. This one was convenient. There would be just as much difficulty in tying this one in to the other deaths. There were just too many loose ends, and no one was talking. It would seem that Viscomi Construction was not the completely legal organization that Teresa thought it to be. Was it connected in some way to organized crime? How could she find out if that were true; and did either of her brothers know?

Teresa thought over the previous night's meeting. After the telephone call from Sergeant Thompson, the meeting reconvened. Vincent Palmieri went over the pieces to see how they tied together; but much of the outcome would be supposition, without hardcore evidence. Some pieces of the puzzle fit together. The rest was conjecture.

Vincent was very blunt about the investigation. He informed them that it would be very unlikely that any new evidence would come to light, without Dr. Rhodes or any of the individuals involved coming forward. This news was particularly devastating to Teresa. Not only was her father's murder the issue, but the supposed murders of her two husbands. The thought of going through life without knowing the truth about Robert's death and John's alleged involvement could drive her crazy. She knew John had been murdered and she wanted his murderers caught. She also wanted to know if both Robert and her father were victims of a murderous plot to gain money and power. She wanted to know for certain.

After praying the Rosary in the garden of the church in Centerville, Teresa met with Riggs at Sand Castle to discuss and review the restoration and the estimated time of completion. She walked around the mansion and wondered what secrets the walls had heard and were keeping. *Who murdered Papa? Someone had been in this house*

149

and injected Papa with insulin—so much that he went into a coma and died. Surely Dr. Rhodes had been aware of that? Did John want me to give this house up so that we would be away from the things that occurred here? How long would he have been able to keep these revelations from me had he lived? How much did he know about the events and was he the one who orchestrated them? She realized that it was pretty futile to speculate. She had to move on carefully; her life and the lives of her children depended upon it. She would establish her power and her children's heritage and eventually make sure she pulled the strings.

Driving back toward Centerville, Teresa was accompanied by her usual security guard. She was growing used to having one close and she felt some relief and safety with him nearby. Driving to Joe's house, she turned in front of Claudia's house down Craigville Beach Road. She was meeting at Joe's house to review the previous day's developments and plan the next step.

Before she reached Joe's house, Teresa noticed that Carlo's car was at Frank's house. She pulled into the short driveway and jumped out of her Jeep. She did not bother to knock as she entered the house, the security guard only steps behind her. She found Sarah in the kitchen, crying. Carlo was holding her arm and twisting it roughly.

"Stop right now! Carlo! Right now!" commanded Teresa. Carlo looked over at her and sneered. "Right, Teresa Mahoney to the rescue. You are probably the one who caused all of this, right?" asked Carlo.

"Carlo, I think you need to understand that you are talking to your employer. You are dangerously close to losing more than your job," stated a seriously calm but determined Teresa. "I am confident that Claudia would be interested in this little interaction with Sarah. Should I give her a call?" Teresa asked as she took her cellular phone from her purse.

Carlo released Sarah's arm and started to walk toward the front door. "Listen Boss, you think you've got the upper hand here, but you need to know that you are in way over your head. Think about it," warned Carlo. Then he walked out the door.

"Are you okay, Sarah?" asked Teresa.

"Oh, I guess. He came over here so angry because I refused to see him. Then he demanded that I ask Frank or plead with Frank to realign his support with Claudia. He pleaded, he cajoled, but I stood my ground. Then he told me about Kelly Mahoney's pregnancy. I guess it slipped out that I was aware of it," reported Sarah.

"Well, what happened then?" asked Teresa. "He guessed that you were behind my knowing and said that he would not be seeing me again. I know he won't tell Frank about us because he'll lose Claudia. I am fearful of him though; I've never seen this side of him," said Sarah.

Sarah was shaking and crying. Teresa asked where the kids were. "Thank God, they are swimming at the beach," screeched Sarah.

Teresa tried to calm Sarah down. "Sarah, Carlo is out of here, at least for today. You must try to be more careful. I'll try to delicately suggest that we put a guard on your family also. I want to keep you as a sister-in-law." Sarah hugged Teresa, who embraced her firmly. Teresa rocked her gently and kissed her gently on the cheek. "It's going to be all right, trust me," Teresa assured Sarah.

Teresa and her guard got back in the Jeep and drove past the beach to Joe's house. Anthony's and Frank's cars were already there when she pulled into the drive. She would suggest that Joe try to convince Frank that it was a good idea to add a detail of guards for his family.

"Well, hello, men," Teresa called out as she walked through the front door. The men were enjoying a cup of coffee, while waiting for Teresa. Teresa sat on the sofa and poured herself a cup. "Let's talk about the move from York to Washington," she suggested. "No, Sis," answered Anthony. "We've got to talk about your move to Youngstown, at least for a year. Frank has agreed to go back and forth between Youngstown and Washington to be of assistance to both of us."

"I have aspirations to eventually run one of the regional offices," interjected Frank. "I do eventually envision Teresa finally moving to Boston or the Cape as she originally planned to do. She will eventually be able to carry on from here, long distance, just like Papa did," suggested Frank.

"Thanks so much guys, but I think I'll work out my role as time goes on. I am glad that we three are a team." Teresa added, "Joe, of course, you are with us."

"Of course," Joe responded.

"Okay, let's talk about next week and the Feast of the Assumption," suggested Teresa. Frank reaffirmed that he and Sarah were going, and that Carlo had already said he wanted to help recreate the tradition. We can't oppose Carlo in accompanying us without tipping our hand to Claudia. Claudia is fighting the trip though, saying that she will not go."

Neither Teresa nor Joe would be able to offer Frank a reason why Carlo shouldn't be there since he also wanted to go to the offices on business. It looked as though they would be stuck with Carlo this time. Teresa was determined to protect her sister-in-law, Sarah, by keeping Carlo at a distance.

"Betty and I are staying here, although she may be doing some house hunting in the Old Town section of Alexandria, Virginia. I do believe that Mario Testa Sr. and other company officers will be in Youngstown. They wanted to meet and talk about the move to Washington and the effect it will have on several of our employees," Anthony offered.

151

Joe decided that he would also go to Youngstown as so many of the people, whom he mistrusted, would be going. He wanted to be there to personally supervise Teresa's protection.

With that round of discussion, Teresa decided to go back to Hyannisport and treat herself to a full day with her kids at the beach. She drove to Scudder Lane and turned right at the Kennedy Compound. The policeman was still stationed at the corner there. He waved her to turn right when all others had to turn left. She drove up the hill on Irving Avenue and parked in front of her house. The guard drove her Jeep around to her garage.

As Teresa entered the front door of her cottage, Kara and Mario Jr. rose from the sofa in the living room. "Teresa, home finally? When do you spend time with little Sarah? She needs a mother. Perhaps she should come home to mine?"

39

Teresa took a deep breath. She wasn't ready for a confrontation with Kara or anyone.

Maggie took the kids to the beach. She said that they will be waiting for you to join them," said Kara. "You spend so little time with your kids lately, I wonder what my father would have said about his little daughter living here in this Hyannisport house. I bet he would be turning in his grave to know you and his daughter are living here as though he didn't even exist. Look at you, the perfect widow; but the widow of which husband? You're wearing the wedding ring from your first marriage. Now that is very interesting. Where is the ring my father gave you on your wedding day? Have you erased him completely from your life?"

Teresa looked very stern. "Mario, could you excuse us; please leave us. I want to speak with Kara alone. I'm sorry."

"I want Mario to stay," insisted Kara. "I need him with me right now."

Mario Jr. stood up and squeezed Kara's hand. "It's not appropriate for me to be part of this conversation, Kara. I'm going to step outside on the porch in the back. I'll wait for you," said an embarrassed Mario Jr. "I'm sorry, Mrs. Mahoney, I don't mean to intrude; I just want to support Kara."

"That's okay, Mario, just pour yourself some iced tea and stick around," Teresa reassured him.

Mario left the room. Teresa looked at Kara and just shook her head. She didn't really know what to do about Kara. Kara was her father's daughter. She was the apple of his eye, until Sarah was born and adopted. John had seemed to look at Sarah as a new hope. The other two daughters, Kara and Shannon, were left to fend for themselves. Teresa had tried to integrate the girls into the family; and for a while, it seemed to work. However, over the last year, especially toward the end of John's life, the girls seemed more estranged from Teresa. The reason had to be Kelly Mahoney. Teresa wondered what John would think if he had known little Sarah was not his biological daughter.

"Kara, try to calm down," pleaded Teresa. "I realize that you have had terrible losses in the recent past. You were so close to your father, and now he is gone. I guess that I have been so in tune with my own problems that I wasn't aware of what you are going through. I am so sorry, Kara. I want to help."

Kara refused to be comforted, especially by Teresa. "How dare you! You are incredible. You sit here, in the house you shared with your first husband. You are wearing the wedding band from that marriage, and you want to comfort me about my father's death. That's incredible," Kara shrieked. "How can you sympathize with me? You've tried to erase my father from your life. You've gone back in your mind to Robert, precious, saintly, incredibly handsome, and romantic Robert. Robert, the man who haunted my father's marriage bed." Kara seemed out of control and was building up to complete hysteria.

"Stop it right now!" commanded Teresa, as she slapped Kara across her face. Kara looked stunned. She started crying and shaking uncontrollably. Teresa hurried to the kitchen and poured some iced tea and brought it to Kara. She accepted it and tried to calm down.

"I'm so sorry, Teresa!" exclaimed Kara. "I don't hate you; if I did, I wouldn't have settled with you on the house and the company shares. I just hate to see you eliminate reminders of my father as though he never existed. He always thought that Robert was there in your marriage, interfering with his life and your commitment to him." Kara was sobbing again.

Teresa moved from her chair to the sofa and put her arm around Kara. Kara allowed Teresa to hug her and comfort her. She cried the tears that had been held back. Teresa sat in silence for a while until she thought Kara could focus on what she wanted to say.

"Kara, I am so sorry. You and Shannon have lost a dear father. I have not been the person to comfort you because of my own grief. Much has happened in recent months and some of the secrets of the past have been disclosed to me in documents that I never knew existed. It has made me re-evaluate everything—Robert's death, my re-marriage, and little Sarah's adoption, though I would do that again in a moment. Your father's murder was especially brutal, and I was quite shocked about it," affirmed Teresa.

Kara gave Teresa a puzzled look. "What are you saying, Teresa? I keep feeling like there is an incredible omission to this story and your feelings."

"Yes, Kara, there is," stated Teresa in a matter of fact tone. "The newly discovered documents clearly show that John was not the man I thought him to be," Teresa rationalized. "It has been very disturbing to me."

"Just what should be so devastating to you about my father?" asked Kara.

"I'm not at liberty to say right now. It's all wrapped up in Viscomi Construction." Teresa tried to steer Kara away from the possible link to Robert's death and her father's murder.

"I don't see how any company business, even with the millions of dollars that you have, could possibly be a reason for you to stop honoring my father's memory. For God's sake, you have his child!"

Teresa tried to respond in a soothing manner. "I think you need to understand that I just learned that my father had been murdered. It happened as John and I were on our way to the Cape to see him for the last time. You have to understand, I'm dealing with a lot."

"I guess that is a lot. I'm sure when you realized that little Sarah was my father's biological daughter, it was a slap in the face. He cheated on you with his first wife, my mother," sneered Kara.

Teresa tried to ignore the feelings that welled up in her breast when Kara made the remark. "Yes, Kara, that hurts. It hurts a great deal." Teresa sighed. "John must have cheated on me for him to think that Sarah was his daughter."

Kara caught the remark immediately. "What do you mean by that?" she asked. "Well," Teresa responded, "To tell you the truth, we've recently discovered that your father was not Sarah's biological father."

"How could that be?" asked an incredulous Kara. "I knew my mother was pregnant. She told me it was Dad's. What are you trying to pull here? Are you trying to get back at me because my mother pulled a dirty trick by trying to stop our settling of the estate?"

Teresa took a deep breath and proceeded. "No, although I understand how you could think that. You have tried somewhat to get along with me, but Shannon has always kept her distance. Your mother always seemed to act as though she and John would get back together. Nothing was further from his mind."

"Dad did accept Sarah as his own, as was indicated in the letter that was delivered to you after his death." Teresa looked at Kara with compassion and stroked her cheek. Tears were falling from Teresa's eyes. Kara did not pull away.

"That's what hurts. Because John thought that Sarah was his, he had to have had at least a brief encounter with your mother." Teresa cut Kara's next question off before she could get it out. "But," Teresa continued, as she squeezed Kara's hand, "Sarah is not John's biological daughter."

Kara almost crumbled, and she looked as though she would start another angry discourse. Teresa hurriedly continued her explanation. "Recently, we had Sarah's DNA checked. It was conclusive that Sarah is not John's daughter. In fact, we believe Dr. Rhodes changed the results. He also concealed the reason my father died."

Kara was left stunned. "Well, contact Dr. Rhodes. Get some answers," demanded Kara.

"I'm afraid that he was killed in a traffic collision last night near Orleans. Many answers to many questions died with him," Teresa articulated.

Kara sat with her head in her hand, elbow on the arm of the sofa. "I've got to contact my mother and ask her about all of this. If you are telling the truth, she tricked my father and she used me to hurt you at my own father's funeral. God, this is all a mess."

"Where is your mother right now?" asked Teresa. "She is in Bethany with Shannon, but she will be going to Youngstown to pack up her house at the same time you will be there in August," replied Kara.

"I think that you can fly with the kids and me to Youngstown and surprise her there. Keep Shannon out of this. She is too young to know," suggested Teresa. "You are probably right," agreed Kara. "But, my mother and I have a lot of things to iron out."

"I know, Kara," replied Teresa. "It will be very difficult."

Teresa got up and went to the back porch to join Mario Jr. It was obvious that he was very uncomfortable in these surroundings. He came into the living room and sank next to Kara, kissing her lightly on the cheek. "Take her out to dinner, Mario. She needs to relax. Help her to take her mind off all of the recent troubles," suggested Teresa.

The two young people stood up and Kara took Teresa's hand and softly thanked her. "Take care of yourself, Kara. Rough times are still ahead of us," Teresa remarked. Teresa followed them to the door and waited until they drove off in Mario Jr.'s car. Then Teresa sighed, wishing that she could have withheld the details from Kara. But Kara was an adult; and she had to face the cruel adult world, especially if many of her actions were based on incorrect premises.

Teresa decided to switch gears and concentrate on spending the remaining part of her day with the children and Maggie at the Hyannisport Association Private Beach. She changed into her suit and walked down the slight hill toward the beach to join Maggie and the children. The kids were splashing and rollicking in the surf. Teresa bent, kissed Maggie on her cheek, and then settled into her beach chair and looked out over the waves. *How beautiful the Cape is! The children are really enjoying this summer, seemingly oblivious to adult problems. That is a real blessing.*

40

Teresa was following her usual routine. The kids were at home with Maggie, while Teresa and her guard progressed through the morning. Teresa drove to Our Lady of Victory Church to pray in the garden Rosary, and then on to Sand Castle, which was nearly completed. A brief discussion with Riggs ensued during the daily inspection of the progress on Sand Castle's renovation. She later walked down to the beach. The grounds were guarded by the security force, and she felt safe. *How long will I be safe?* she wondered. *There are murderers out there. Even if John had been part of the plot, there are accomplices out there who took over after John's death.*

Teresa looked down at her wedding ring. She had made the conscious choice in replacing John's ring with Robert's. She wished she could do the same with her name, but it would be unfair to little Sarah since she knew John as her father.

After walking back to the house, she sat in the solarium and called for Riggs. Teresa was thoughtful about the coming move. "Riggs, please sit and join me in a cup of coffee," she requested. "Maggie is going to Youngstown with me to review what needs to be accomplished at Paone. I will not make too many changes there because I like the fact that it looks much as it did when I was a child, growing up there. It is remarkable that Claudia did little to the house when she lived there."

"Miss Teresa," Riggs began, "Madame, I mean Mrs. Viscomi, disliked that house. You see, this one is by the sea—bright and airy. Paone is a little stuffy, formal, and tied too much with the past. Mr. Viscomi would only allow major changes here at Sand Castle, but there, none!" Riggs said thoughtfully.

Teresa then inquired about the number of staff who would go to Youngstown. Riggs answered in a businesslike voice. "I've asked the gardener to stay here because he needs to keep up the grounds. The cook will stay here from May to October, when she will take the winter months off. One maid will go to Youngstown and the other is being retained by Mrs. DeRoches. So, we'll have to do some hiring in

157

Youngstown. Paone is much larger than Sand Castle. I am looking forward to spending my time with you, Miss Teresa. It will be like the old days."

"Thank you, Riggs," Teresa said appreciatively. "I am so grateful that you are staying with me; we will have some adventure at Paone, bringing its decor and entertaining up to the quality of the good old days. I have a feeling that we will be doing a great deal of entertaining because of Viscomi Construction and my position as Chairman and CEO."

Having completed the meeting with Riggs, Teresa sent her guard to retrieve the Jeep. They drove towards Centerville and turned onto Craigville Beach Road. She drove into Claudia's driveway and exited her vehicle. Entering the house, she found Claudia eating breakfast on a tray in the formal living room. A fire was blazing in the hearth to warm the house on a cool, overcast morning.

"Come in, Teresa," Claudia said while waving her in. "Are you really going to Youngstown in the last month of summer?"

"I guess so," acknowledged Teresa. "I want to recapture some of our heritage for the children. If it goes well, we will make it an annual tradition."

"Then, I want to ask a favor of you," countered Claudia. "I want to use the grounds of Sand Castle for a small gathering on the Feast of the Assumption. I want to do our own fireworks, like we did when your father was alive. Could you allow us to do that this one time?"

"Why of course Claudia, please be my guest. I'll inform Riggs before going to Youngstown today." Changing the subject, Teresa asked, "Is Carlo around today?"

"No, he has been in York and flew to Youngstown yesterday to prepare for the big meeting that you will conduct upon your arrival. Why couldn't he use the corporate jet?"

"The jet is being repaired and overhauled right now. I chartered a small jet for a direct flight from Hyannis to Youngstown. I hope that the corporate jet will be finished for our return. Of course, you will be attending the annual picnic, right?" asked Teresa.

"How could I miss it?" asked Claudia. "After all, I still want to maintain my presence in the family and with the officers of Viscomi Construction. I haven't given up my role as an owner."

Claudia was somewhat snide in her response, but Teresa ignored her demeanor and offered good wishes. "Well, I've got to go, hope you have a good party."

Teresa took in a deep breath as she exited Claudia's home. *This is a nice home*, she thought. *It doesn't have the privacy of Sand Castle, but it is every bit as elegant.*

Teresa drove past Frank's home, where she saw him putting suitcases in the car, getting ready to go to the airport. Then she drove past the beach, where the joggers were out. Due to the weather, the traffic was lighter than usual. The dreariness may have been a good thing, in that the children would be less inclined to balk at leaving for Youngstown.

Teresa pulled into Joe's driveway to pick him up. He was sitting on his front stairs waiting for her. He put his luggage in the rear and hopped into the back seat. "Good morning, you've had a full day already. Hope everything is okay." Joe flirted with her.

Teresa smiled as she backed out of the drive. "Well, we are leaving the Cape. Even though it is my choice and it is only for a few days, I get sad. I love it here."

The airport limo was waiting at Teresa's door as she pulled up. The guard took the Jeep to the garage and then came around to help the driver load the luggage. Teresa, Joe, Maggie, and the three children were on their way to the place they would be calling home during the school months. They would be meeting Frank, Sarah, their children, in addition to Kara Mahoney and Mario Testa Jr. at the airport.

"The gathering is already convening in Youngstown. Tony Foccata, Mario Testa, and Bobby Faccia are there for a meeting today. It seems that Carlo DeRoches has been there for a few days," Joe informed Teresa.

"This trip is part business, part relocation, and part family tradition. We will just have to come to grips with the situation and take as much control as possible," reiterated Teresa.

Settling in on the jet, Teresa sat with Sarah; and Maggie sat with the boys. Preferring to be on his own, Joe sat alone, reading a book. Sarah Viscomi sat with the nanny; and her husband, Frank, sat with little Angelo and Katie. After take-off, Disney's *Lady and the Tramp* played on the television for the children. The flight was smooth and only took about three hours and fifteen minutes.

A few cars were waiting at the airport for the travelers. Teresa, Maggie, and the children drove straight to Paone, while Joe took off for the company office. Frank and Sarah decided to stop at a nearby restaurant, the Airport Tavern, for some veal parmesan and spaghetti. Teresa had thoughtfully ordered a car for Kara to be taken to her mother's house on Fifth Avenue in Youngstown where she would be packing for a move to Teresa's former home in York. There, Kelly would live with her two daughters. Her daughter, Shannon, had stayed behind at the beach house in Bethany with several friends.

Teresa and the kids arrived at Paone and drove through the gates that were at the entrance between the large concrete walls. The estate was massive in Tudor grandeur. Passing the gatehouse, where Joe would settle in, they drove to the front entrance of the house. It was all but deserted. They exited the car and the children began to busily run around. A maid came to the door and helped them into the house with their luggage. This was a very different homecoming than what she received in May at Sand Castle, the day before Claudia's and Carlo's wedding.

Teresa turned some lights on and asked the maid to adjust the air conditioning. They were in the middle of a hot and humid Midwestern summer. Teresa directed Maggie to the rooms the children would be using. Teresa would use her childhood room rather than the master suite because her brother, Anthony, and his wife, Betty, still had their things in the room.

She strolled through the house, looking out the windows at the formal gardens. As she surveyed the house with the maid, she identified the rooms Frank, Sarah, their children, and nanny would be using. Then she told the maid to prepare the rooms in the gatehouse for Joe. Teresa felt that this would be more like camping out than settling into a plush grand house. Maggie showed the kids their rooms, after which she and Teresa rummaged through the kitchen.

Betty had called ahead and requested that the staff provide some iced tea and lunch, which would soon be delivered. "Maggie, there will be much for you to do in these few days. We need to get by until Riggs gets here. We will call some more staff this week. Betty has already called a few of them to get rooms ready for this visit. Tom and Naomi Blake are coming for the month of September to help the children with the transition. I may be taking a lot of time for the company's business." Maggie was ready to dig in and get all house issues resolved, so she could go back and attend the annual picnic at Sand Castle.

Across town, Joe entered the office of Viscomi Construction, newly located in downtown Youngstown. He reviewed his office, introduced himself to the secretary, and then looked around. He asked Mario Testa and Tony Foccata to join him. They talked about the changes in the company leadership and what it would mean for all the employees. Frank would be working closely with each of them. He was really into the change and would watch the details as needed. Joe noted that both Tony and Mario were uneasy about much of this. Joe was worried. *Could these men be trusted?*

On Fifth Avenue, Kara entered her mother's home. It was in disarray because of the packing. Boxes were everywhere. *They must be taking a break,* she thought, *no packers are in sight, and no Kelly.* Kara called out, "Mother, are you here?" No answer. She went up to the master bedroom and opened the door. "Oh, my God!" Kara exclaimed. There was Kelly, lying on the bed, while Carlo DeRoches stood next to the bed in a silk robe.

41

Kelly and Carlo were frozen in time. Kara was stunned. The things Teresa had told her came falling instantly into place. "I've got to get out of here," hollered Kara. She turned around, ran down the stairs and out the door, where the driver was unloading her luggage. She told him to put the luggage back into her car and drive her to Logan Avenue in Liberty Township, to the estate named Paone. The driver hurriedly replaced the luggage and began to leave as Kelly Mahoney, wrapped in a robe, called to Kara from the front door of the house. "Hurry, driver, get me out of here," bellowed Kara.

Kara's driver drove through the giant gates of Paone. Frank, Sarah, and the children had just arrived and were unloading their own luggage. The driver pulled up behind Frank's car and Kara jumped out of the car and dashed through the door, calling out to Teresa. She was practically hysterical. "Teresa, I need to stay here. Teresa, where are you? Tere...sa!"

Teresa bounded down the stairs as Frank and Sarah ran through the door to see what was the matter. Kara had dissolved into tears. Maggie sent the children out to explore the grounds. Frank's children, Katie and little Angelo, followed them. Teresa led Kara into the living room and Maggie brought her a glass of iced tea. Kara could hardly catch her breath. "I can't believe it. It is so awful. It is so disgusting. How could it be true?" cried Kara.

By this time Frank and Sarah came into the room and sat, hoping to be of some support. "Teresa, everything you told me must be true. Everything!" Teresa asked what could have happened in this short time. "I arrived at my mother's home and there they were in the master bedroom."

"Who was in the master bedroom?" asked Frank.

"My mother and Carlo, Carlo DeRoches. She was in the bed and he was standing next to her in a silk robe. It's true; it's all true, Teresa. Everything you told me," groaned Kara. Both Sarah and Frank turned pale, each hoping that the other would not notice their reaction.

"What is she talking about, Teresa!" exclaimed Sarah. Before Teresa could offer an explanation, Kara interjected, "My mother has been having a long-term affair with Carlo DeRoches and he is little Sarah's biological father! It is true, everything, everything that you said!"

Frank and Sarah began firing questions at Teresa and Kara all at once. Who was doing what? Who was the father? Why did John think he was the father and what about Claudia and her new marriage to Carlo? Did she know? Teresa told them all to hold on, that she would explain.

"It is quite possible that Kelly tricked John into thinking that he was Sarah's father. The results of a second DNA test clearly showed that John was not the father. Dr. Rhodes was part of a cover-up about little Sarah and about our father's death. That's about all I know."

Frank's mind was swirling. *Could Carlo be the father of the child Kelly was carrying? Perhaps I was tricked, just as John had been.*

Sarah's mind was working equally fast. *Carlo has used me to control Frank. All along, he really wanted Kelly, not me, not Claudia. He only wanted Claudia's assets. What a dilemma it all was, except Teresa had really bailed me out of it, and without Frank knowing. Life could go on without terrible complexities if Frank were not the father of Kelly's baby,* Sarah mused.

There was silence in the room. Each person was evaluating how he or she would be affected by this discovery. The central figures of Carlo and Kelly affected each person in the room and the tangled web was woven into everyone's lives. Teresa even felt a little sorry for Claudia, thinking that at least she did not know about Carlo's relationship with Kelly. Teresa understood what it was like to find out that the man you married was not the man you thought he was.

The ringing of the telephone interrupted Teresa's thoughts. Maggie had gone outside to give the family a little privacy and to supervise the children's activities. "Hello," said Teresa.

"Is Kara there?" asked Kelly.

"Yes," answered Teresa.

"Is she all right?" asked Kelly.

"I'll get her for you," acknowledged Teresa.

Kara went to the phone, as Frank and Sarah looked on. "Hello," answered Kara.

"Baby," cried Kelly, "I am so sorry that you found out this way. Can we talk? Come home, please," pleaded Kelly.

"I am staying here, Mother. I can not stay in that house with you after what I just discovered," Kara retorted.

"But baby, I'm your mother," Kelly continued to plead.

"I feel like an orphan," retorted Kara. "I'm staying here and that is final!"

Kelly then asked her to come over tomorrow on the Feast of the Assumption when Teresa and the family would be going to Mass and on to view the fireworks at the festival in Lowellville. Kara relented and told her mother that she would be there tomorrow.

Teresa then hugged Kara. "I'll show you to your room and you can get freshened up. In the meantime, I will prepare a special sauce for the spaghetti. We can all relax after a good dinner. Everything is better after having some pasta. Trust me." Kara was grateful to Teresa. Frank and Sarah resumed the unpacking, while Maggie supervised the kids. Teresa changed her clothes and got down to the business of making meatballs and browning DiRusso sausage for the sauce.

Time passed slowly. Frank and his wife, Sarah, seemed to be drawn closer together. Both realized that Carlo and Kelly had duped them. They knew that these ruthless people had almost destroyed their family. Carlo had even used Claudia to blackmail Frank. Frank did not understand how these revelations affected Sarah because he did not know of her relationship with Carlo. But Sarah, keeping silent, knew that Teresa had pulled her from drowning; and for that, she was grateful.

Maggie decided to prepare the children for dinner. Kara was sleeping, trying to erase the awful revelation about her mother, Carlo, and the trick they had perpetrated upon her father. Sarah decided to help Teresa in the giant kitchen by making the salad; and Frank offered to set the table. They would eat in the kitchen this evening to encourage some family intimacy rather than in the imposing grand dining room.

When Joe arrived, everyone sat down for dinner. Kara was very quiet and Joe was more than surprised to see her. The sauce was excellent and the spaghetti was cooked al dente, to perfection. When the dinner was ended, the kids were allowed to go outside to play. Maggie told the family that she would be the sole person to clean up. The family then moved into the living room for coffee and dessert.

"It was an interesting day at the office. Both Testa and Foccata were very wary of me. Then Carlo, who hadn't been there all day, burst into the meeting that I was having with them. He looked harried and a bit spooked," reported Joe.

"I'm sure he was a bit taken aback. After all, I walked in on his little dirty secret," offered Kara. "I walked in on him and my mother."

Joe was stunned. He sat quietly and took a sip of coffee. He knew that he needed to pass news of this incident to Vincent Palmieri as soon as possible. "Are you all right?" asked Joe.

"I am going to be fine," Kara responded. "I do need to know about my mother's involvement with Carlo; and I intend to ask her tomorrow, when all of you go to the various festivals."

Teresa tried to change the subject, but Kara would have none of it. "My little sister, Sarah, must never know about her parentage. We

163

must protect her. But with so many people knowing who her biological mother is, it's going to be very difficult," concluded Kara.

Teresa reassured Kara, "I am going to do all that I can. Our little Sarah should just know that she is adopted, nothing else. Nothing at least until she is an adult."

Frank and Sarah decided to take their children, Angelo and Katie, to the festival in Lowellville for some carnival rides. Joe talked Teresa into going and taking the kids. Maggie begged off and went about the house making notes about needed changes. Kara decided to turn in for the night. Her depression took over and she lay in a fetal position on her bed for the entire evening, eventually drifting off to a restful sleep.

Tomorrow would be the Feast of the Assumption. There would be a brief meeting of the company's officers at Paone and then the family would take off to eat, drink, and be merry at the festival. Teresa felt guilty for leaving Kara alone, but Joe reasoned with her. "She needs to be alone. She needs to put the pieces of the puzzle together. Let's give her time, her whole world is topsy turvy right now."

42

On the morning of the Feast of the Assumption, it was very misty at the Cape. Claudia was up at the break of dawn, hoping to recreate past times and festivities. Her celebration had little to do with the Assumption of the Body and Soul of the Blessed Virgin Mary into Heaven. Claudia saw this day as a celebration of her position and power. She had always entertained in grand style on this day. Claudia had worked with Riggs to have a fireworks show in Osterville, at Sand Castle. She planned an organized caravan of vehicles to go to Sand Castle after a very nice buffet dinner in her Centerville mansion. The grounds at Sand Castle were more appropriate for fireworks than those at her new residence; and she vowed that someday she would once again be its mistress.

Claudia was very disappointed with her day. Most of the important people, who had been invited to her dinner party, were in Youngstown for a company meeting. However, she had been successful in securing promises from Carlo, Kelly Mahoney, and Mario Testa Jr. to join her and the other guests for the fireworks, after the Youngstown meeting at Paone ended.

In Youngstown, Teresa woke and helped Maggie to prepare breakfast for everyone in the full house. The kids were excited about going to the festival. Teresa had arranged to go to Mass at the Italian Church in Campbell, Ohio, St. Lucy's Parish. This small community on the east side of Youngstown would be awash in festivities. After Mass, there would be a parade, like in the old country; and the statue of the Blessed Virgin would be carried around the block. Then Teresa would take the kids to Lowellville for that church's festival and fireworks. Lowellville was east of Campbell and populated with Italian immigrants, who celebrated the Assumption in grand fashion.

The security guards were already checking the credentials of people coming to the meeting at Paone. Mario Testa arrived with his wife

Maria, who was in town visiting her family. Tony Foccata arrived at the same time as Bobby Faccia. The guests gathered in the living room.

Kara finished her breakfast in the dining room. She moved through the foyer to go upstairs as Maggie ushered Carlo DeRoches through the door. He looked at her sheepishly and offered a hurried "good morning."

Teresa, standing nearby, observed how Kara lifted her head high and ignored his greeting. Kara went upstairs. Teresa moved forward and greeted Carlo, shaking hands. "We will be meeting in the living room. Please make yourself comfortable." Carlo joined the others and helped himself to the coffee and juice.

Kara was upstairs when the meeting convened. She was running yesterday's events through her mind and mentally preparing herself for a confrontation with her mother. She was determined to uncover the extent of Kelly's duplicity and Carlo's treachery to John Mahoney, the Viscomi family, and the company. After dressing, Kara called for the driver to take her to her mother's home for lunch. She walked softly down the front stairs so not to interrupt the meeting.

Teresa and Frank had opened the meeting by greeting each person in the room. Teresa talked about the new leadership created by the death of John Mahoney, and the changes that were being made. She talked about the goals and objectives to gain new business, especially with the federal government. Frank then took over and explained the objectives that they hoped to achieve by moving the regional office from York, Pennsylvania to the metro Washington, D.C. area.

All of the company officials were quiet, except Carlo. He asked many questions and informed the attendees that Claudia was opposed to the move and was trying to block it in the courts.

Frank interrupted Carlo to say that a majority of the owners now agreed on the move and that Claudia's legal maneuvers would not be a factor. Carlo tried to protest, but Teresa shut him down. "Carlo, I know this may be difficult for you, but this is going to happen. You cannot prevent this. In addition, I have asked Joe Cutruzzula to employ a financial firm to conduct an outside audit on the company's finances, especially the regional offices in York." Carlo turned pale. As Vice President of Finance for Viscomi Construction, he was the obvious target of the proposed audit. He sat quietly through the rest of the meeting, stewing over Teresa's blatant attack.

On Fifth Avenue, Kara entered the house where her mother had prepared chef salads for lunch. They ate in the formal dining room. Kara looked around the room. This was the house that she grew up in, with her father and mother, before their divorce. She felt secure here. It was a place that she often returned to when she needed comfort and solace. Both Kara and her mother ate silently.

"Kara," Kelly spoke breaking the silence. "You were quite shocked yesterday, weren't you?"

Kara looked at her mother quizzically. How could her mother ask such a question?

"Well, Mother, what would you have thought, if you had walked in on your mother in her bedroom, in an obvious intimate situation, with a newly married man? You are sleeping with a man who is married to someone you supposedly consider a friend? It is outrageous!" Kara responded.

Kelly sat silently, not knowing how to respond. Kara neither spoke nor looked at her mother. Both continued to eat in silence.

Across town on Logan Avenue, the meeting at Paone was concluding. Carlo got up, walked out of the room, and exited the house without saying anything. He got in his car and dashed down the drive and through the gates. Teresa and Frank watched as he sped down the street. "Well," said Teresa, "It certainly looks as though we've struck a nerve in Carlo. We need to keep an eye on him."

"I agree, Ter. I think Joe is one step ahead of us; he is calling Palmieri as we speak," answered Frank.

In Centerville, Claudia was becoming more depressed about the guest list. The lack of attendees certainly showed her diminished prominence in Viscomi Construction. In spite of her disappointment, a crew of caterers set up a fabulous array of foods on the grounds of Claudia's home at the corner of Craigville Beach Road and Main Street. The table was resplendent with silver, serving platters, and flatware. Claudia was going all out with elegance and show. Her guests, even if not the top echelon, would be served and entertained in style, the way Angelo had encouraged her in the past; the way she would continue in the future.

Meanwhile, in Osterville, at Sand Castle, Riggs supervised a crew that prepared the grounds down by the beach for the fireworks. Valets were hired to park the cars. Riggs, himself, would be there to direct the flow of foot traffic to the rear of the property.

Back in Youngstown, Kara helped her mother clear the table in the dining room and brought the dishes to the kitchen. Each had avoided the subject that was on their minds. Finally Kara couldn't take it anymore. "Mother, what are you doing with Carlo?"

Kelly stopped and looked into her daughter's eyes. "I'm in love with Carlo, Kara. I've been in love with him for years. Right after your father left me for Teresa, I fell for Carlo."

Kara was seething with disgust. "What lies! Dad left you before Robert Blake died. How could he have left you for Teresa when she was completely devoted to Robert Blake? And why are you with Carlo? He just married Claudia Viscomi."

Kelly reached out to stroke Kara's cheek to comfort her just as Carlo burst through the door. Kara glared at him with hatred. "What are you doing here, Carlo?" asked Kelly.

"I couldn't stand it anymore, I had to get up and leave that meeting. It ended as I left. Get ready, we'll be going back to the Cape tonight."

Kara couldn't stand it anymore and stormed out the back door. Kelly tried to follow, but was blocked by Carlo. "Stay with me, we've got to be together today."

"Carlo, I've got to follow Kara, I'll be back, I promise," answered Kelly.

Kara hurried down the street, trying to call her driver on her cellular phone. Kelly drove in her car and pulled up along side of Kara. "Kara, stop. Get in the car," called Kelly.

"No, why should I?" demanded Kara.

"Kara, we need to talk. Stop, get in."

Kara stopped as the car slowed. She walked toward the car and Kelly stopped. Kara entered the car and said that she could not go back to where Carlo was. Kelly responded, "I know. I'm going to pull around the corner and call Carlo to tell him I'll go back to the house in a little while. Then you and I will drive and talk."

Kara listened as her mother called Carlo and tried to soothe his ruffled feathers. Kelly then began to drive around town to the places that were special in their lives. She drove to the rose garden in the park, where they got out and talked. "I love Carlo. I am pregnant with his child," explained Kelly. "He is my life and he has promised that we will eventually be together when things work out financially for him."

"But, Mother, he is married to Claudia. Is he going to take her money? Is that how he will become financially secure?" asked Kara.

Kelly sat on a bench in the park as Kara settled in beside her. "Things are far more complicated than that. Carlo is involved in the company takeover, which has been temporarily stalled. The sale of your shares to Teresa has gummed up the works. After today, some things will be resolved and the future will be within our grasp."

"How so, Mother?" Kelly didn't respond. "No answer, Mother? What's going on here?"

Kelly responded quietly, "I don't know everything, but I just cannot share what I know now."

Kara felt that she was wasting her time. Hours went by and there were no answers. There was no honesty here. Kara asked one more question. "Mother, who is Sarah's father? I know that Dad thought he was, but I also know for a fact that he was not the biological father."

Kelly was flabbergasted by Kara's declaration. She took a deep breath and sighed. "Let's go back to the car and take a short drive. Let's go to Calvary Cemetery." Kara followed her mother to the car.

In Centerville, Claudia was happy to see that her stepson, Anthony, and his wife, Betty, had come to her dinner. They had even brought their son, Joey, who was a bit bored since his cousins were away in Youngstown. Claudia put on a public face and played the perfect hostess for the crowd. The only other notable guest was Freddy Paolone. Anthony and Betty took a seat and pretty much stayed to themselves. They did not feel like socializing, but decided that their attendance showed that they were not afraid of Claudia. They sat back in the sun and enjoyed the dinner.

At Paone, Teresa and the family, including Joe and Maggie, were driving off to St. Lucy's for Mass and the Procession. Father Francis Montillo had been asked to fill in for the church's pastor who was recuperating from a stroke in the hospital. Father Montillo was happy to know that he would see the Viscomi family there. He wanted to see some familiar faces.

43

Kelly and Kara drove through the giant gates of Calvary Cemetery. They drove past the giant Viscomi mausoleum. It was the first time that Kara really noticed it. Kelly drove around the corner and then stopped. Both she and Kara exited the car and walked over to a group of headstones that bore the name of Mahoney. They walked over to John Mahoney's grave. Kara stood in silence. She blessed herself and said a prayer for her father. Kelly stood in silence, looking at her watch. Mass would be starting at St. Lucy's right now and dinner was in progress at Claudia's house in Centerville. She would level with Kara about her father.

"Kara, there is much you don't know and haven't understood," started Kelly. "Your father was an up and coming force within Viscomi Construction. We were married and had our daughters and I was very happy. But your father was ambitious."

Kara interrupted her. "What has this got to do with anything?"

Kelly was abrupt. "Stop interrupting and I will tell you," continued Kelly. "Your father was ambitious and Viscomi Construction was and is a family-owned company." Kara was completely confused; she could not see where Kelly was going with this explanation. "Your father wanted a piece of the pie, and the only way to have it was to be part of the family," Kelly maintained.

"Okay," concluded Kara, "I guess that's where Teresa comes in?"

"Absolutely," affirmed Kelly.

"Your father focused on Teresa Viscomi Blake. He became obsessed with her, but she never looked his way. He left me at that time, and I didn't really understand it. I just knew that he wanted her, and I hated her for it. I will always hate her."

Kara didn't understand that. "That's not fair. She was in love with her husband—Robert, Robert, Robert. Dad was always jealous of Robert. Even when he died and Dad married Teresa, Robert was there between them."

"Your father wanted to be free when Teresa became free, and it couldn't look like he left me for her. She would have never gone for that, given her religious beliefs," Kelly speculated.

"But how could he know she would be free?" asked Kara.

"Kara, stop now. Your father arranged for her to be free. He planned Robert Blake's death by arranging for Robert's brakes to fail. Dr. Rhodes was there to take care of the rest." Kara was in shock. Tears streamed from her eyes. She gasped as though she would throw up. "Kara, give it a break. You wanted to know, now get a hold of your-self!" commanded Kelly.

"After our divorce and then Robert's death, John waited about eighteen months before approaching that little rich witch. He really wooed old Angelo, too. John knew that if Angelo approved of him that Angelo would push Teresa and him together. At the beginning, your father even tried to be nice to Tom and Naomi Blake, knowing that Teresa was very close to them. You know the rest. He married her."

"Okay, Mother," Kara said, trying to process all the information, "where does little Sarah come into this; and who is her father?"

"I was devastated about my breakup with your father and his re-marriage," continued Kelly. "I was on the rebound and started see-ing Carlo DeRoches. I had the unfortunate privilege of falling for another ambitious man, who was tied up with the Viscomi family and their construction company." Kelly was sobbing at this point. "After I became pregnant with his child, Sarah, Carlo convinced me that we needed to get something on John in order to have some power over him. When Teresa was visiting the Blakes on Nan-tucket, I got John drunk and seduced him. He believed that Sarah was his child. He felt guilty about Sarah not having two parents; so he and Teresa arranged for Sarah's adoption. Obviously, he could not tell Teresa or old man Viscomi that he believed Sarah to be his biological daughter."

Kara tried to make sense of the whole thing. Her head was swim-ming. She was putting it together now. "So, you and Carlo had this thing that enabled you to pull Dad's strings?"

"Right," answered Kelly. "Then Claudia's lawyer, John Swartz, let it slip to her that old Angelo was suspicious about Robert's death and the implication that she was in the whole thing with John. Little did he know that Claudia had her eye on Carlo, even though she didn't betray her husband physically. Carlo jumped the gun and arranged for Angelo Viscomi's death on the day he was to sign a new will."

"Oh, my!" exclaimed Kara. "Poor Teresa, this is all so monstrous."

Kelly leaned over and pulled some grass that was partially cover-ing John's headstone. "Your father realized that Carlo would eventu-ally move into old Angelo's bed and claim part of the company, upon marrying Claudia Viscomi. And when your father put together my re-lationship with Carlo, he realized that he was not Sarah's biological father. He was angry and threatened to expose Carlo's role in the death of Angelo Viscomi. However, Carlo did not inject him, nor did

Dr. Rhodes. One of the company's officers was the culprit. I just don't know which one."

Kara was sobbing. Through her tears she managed to ask one more question. "When did Dad find out about Sarah?"

"The last week of his life," answered Kelly.

Kara took control of herself. "Then who killed my father? Carlo?" asked Kara.

"No, I don't think so. There is someone in the company who is working with Carlo; but I don't know who. I think that this other guy did it on his own, because John put two and two together and wanted to protect Teresa from more trauma. Your father had to be killed because he stood in the way of Carlo's takeover of the company. Carlo did not want the plot exposed; he had too much riding on the takeover.

"So, Mother, why are you telling me now? Why are you telling me this?" pleaded Kara.

"Because, Kara, things are already in motion that will put Carlo on top and make him very powerful. Nothing will stop him."

Kara told her mother that they needed to tell Teresa about this. "Her whole world will be shattered, but she needs to know. She needs to protect herself from Carlo and the other guy." Kelly told her that it wasn't possible. "The chain reaction is about to happen and I will finally be with Carlo."

44

Mass was over at St. Lucy's Parish in Campbell, Ohio. The church sat on the corner across from the old Greek Hall that is usually rented for parties. The procession, with the statue of the Virgin Mary decorated in ribbons with money pinned to it, moved out of the front door. Father Montillo followed the men who carried the statue and intoned the Rosary. The congregation followed the priest, praying in turn.

Teresa was there with her children, Joe, Maggie, Frank and Sarah, Maria and Mario Testa, Mario Jr., Bobby Faccia, and Tony Foccata. As the group exited the church, they turned right to go around the block, still praying the Rosary.

When they were coming back around the block to the other side of the church, a gunshot rang out. Everyone scattered in panic. More shots rang out and Mario Testa Sr. lunged toward Teresa, just as he was hit by a bullet and collapsed onto the ground. Maria Testa screamed. Joe huddled with Teresa's children, as Frank blanketed his wife and children with his body. Bobby Faccia pulled his pistol, while looking around to ascertain from what direction the shots had come. He saw Tony Foccata at the old Greek Hall and ran over to him to ask if the shots were coming from the old Greek Hall. Tony did not know.

Sirens were blazing. The children were crying. There was mass confusion everywhere. Tony Foccata got Mario Jr. to run to his car and drive around the area to see if anyone was in a getaway mode. Bobby Faccia ran over to Mario Testa to see if he were okay. Frank hurried his wife, Sarah, the children, and others into the church. Joe did the same with Teresa and her children. The ambulance arrived for Mario; and his wife, Maria, went with him to the hospital. The Palmieri security guards verified that Mario Sr. would be okay and that only his shoulder was wounded.

Campbell city detectives arrived and began their investigation. Maggie was interviewed first and was later allowed to take the children back home to Paone. Frank and Sarah sent their children, little Angelo and Katie, with Maggie. When some of the stress leveled,

Teresa looked at Joe. "This was an attempt to kill me, wasn't it Joe?" asked Teresa.

"Yes, hon," Joe responded, "I think it was. Mario got in the way and saved your life. He got shot instead."

Teresa, Joe, and the rest were allowed to leave. Teresa's driver took them back to Paone where they joined Sarah and Frank. All of the children were very scared. Maggie attempted to divert their attention to a game. However, when the adults walked through the door, the children ran to them, crying and putting their arms around them.

The night grew darker and all were mentally and physically exhausted. Teresa tried to call her brother, Anthony, but there was no answer. "They must have gone to Sand Castle for the fireworks. I wish I could get in touch with them," said an anxious Teresa.

As day turned to dusk, Claudia's guests moved to Sand Castle for the fireworks. Claudia was in her element. Riggs directed the foot traffic around the house and away from the area that needed to be completed. All took their places to watch the fireworks that Claudia had purchased for their entertainment. The night air was cool by the sea. The stars were visible in the sky and it was a perfect night for fireworks.

The show began with a beautiful array of purple and white fireworks. The sound rang loudly through the air. After the second round of fireworks, Anthony looked down next to him and saw Claudia lying on the ground, her leg bleeding from a bullet wound. He quickly knelt to see if she were all right, when there was a piercing scream. On the ground lay Freddie Paolone, with a gun in his hand. Over him stood a Palmieri security guard.

Riggs called the police, while frightened people still huddled around their cars. The security guards did not allow anyone to leave. The ambulance arrived and then sped off with Claudia, who was still alive and alert. Riggs went into the house and phoned Paone. Joe answered the telephone and listened. After hanging up the phone, Joe informed the family of the shocking news he had just received. "Claudia has been shot at Sand Castle," he said; "but she is alive."

The stunned group huddled in a conference as Joe tried to call Carlo on his cellular phone.

Carlo was in a conference with Tony Foccata, when Kara and Kelly came through the door. Almost at the same moment, his cellular phone rang. "Hello, Carlo, this is Joe. There has been trouble both here and at Sand Castle."

"Yes, I know," acknowledged Carlo. "Tony and Mario Jr. just informed me about the incident. Is everyone okay?"

"Yes, Carlo, everyone here is okay, but Claudia was shot at Sand Castle."

"Is she all right?" asked Carlo.

"I don't know," Joe said. "You need to get there as soon as possible."

Kara stood back as Carlo informed the group about Claudia. Carlo also informed them that they would all fly to Hyannis in the next few hours. He then called and arranged to fly in the newly repaired corporate jet. He needed a direct flight there. Kelly said that she would go with him. She asked Kara to go, too.

"Okay, Mother," Kara relented. She was so caught up in the events that she couldn't think straight. Mario Jr. pulled her aside and told her of the attempted attack on Teresa and the wounding of his father who tried to protect her. He had called the hospital and talked with his mother, who said that his father was in good condition. His mother also told him that he should do whatever he needed to do—go to the Cape to help Claudia Viscomi DeRoches or stay in Youngstown. Since his father was all right, Mario decided to go to the Cape to help Claudia.

Kara changed her mind about going to the Cape and decided to go to Teresa. "I have to see if she is okay? Mother, did Carlo do all of this?"

"Go to your precious Teresa," spewed Kelly. "You are certainly your father's daughter." Kelly did not think her daughter would spill the beans to Teresa or the Viscomi family, but she was concerned. She dared not tell Carlo about her leveling with Kara about the plot to take over the company. If she had, Carlo would probably hurt Kara to keep her quiet. Kelly had to protect Kara. She loved her daughter.

The drivers arrived in the limousines to take the group to the airport. Kara told Mario Jr. that she would ride with him to see him off. The ride to the airport was brisk in pace. The motorcade pulled up to the front of the municipal airport. Tony Foccata, Kelly, Carlo, and the rest exited their cars and were shown to the appropriate gate for their plane. The corporate jet stood shining, waiting for clearance to take off. Mario Jr. turned and waved goodbye to Kara, who smiled through her tears as she waved back. She stood there as the plane was pushed back to take its place on the runway. Near her stood Bobby Faccia, who was staying with his boss, Mario Sr.

Suddenly, the plane stopped and a person came out on the runway. It was Frank Viscomi. He stood at the front of the plane. Stairs were brought back and Mario Jr. exited the jet. Frank put his arm around the young man, and they walked off the tarmac. "Your father needs you at this time. We don't want you going back to Hyannis. He's calling for you. You need to go to him," suggested Frank.

"But my mother told me it was all right to go ahead," responded Mario.

"Well, I'm in charge right now; and you are going back to see your father," demanded Frank.

Frank, Mario Jr., and Kara watched as the jet climbed into the sky. They turned and went to their respective cars. Kara went with Mario to the hospital and Frank returned to Paone. Just as Frank came through the door, Teresa answered the phone. She became paralyzed, numb, as she listened intently to the voice on the phone. She hung up the phone. Sarah, Joe, and Frank looked at her, wanting to hear whatever news there was.

"That was a call from Anthony. The FAA just informed him that the corporate jet exploded in mid-air. There are no survivors."

45

The dew on the grounds of Paone glistened the morning after the Feast of the Assumption. Teresa had spent a sleepless night, and went out of the house at 5:30 A.M. just to walk. The evening before, she had waited for Kara and Mario to come in from dinner—not to give Kara the bad news about her mother's death, but to isolate her from the latest tragedy. Teresa wanted to send Kara to bed for the night; and break the news the next morning. Alas, it was not to be. Mario Jr. and Kara heard about the explosion when they went to see Mario Sr. at the hospital after their dinner. Maria Testa had been overjoyed to see that her son was there and not on the plane. It was a miracle.

Kara had broken down in the hospital and sobbed uncontrollably when she learned that her mother had been killed. Mario Jr. tried to console her as he drove her back to Paone, treating her very tenderly. Teresa met them at the door and tried to comfort Kara. The effort was fruitless. The young woman was shattered. She was orphaned and nothing would ever be the same. Over and over, she talked on and on about needing to tell Teresa everything. Kara was in shock, and Teresa knew that Kara had things to say. However, Teresa was not sure that she was ready to hear them. She finally got Kara to her room and, against her usual social codes, allowed Mario to stay with her. Mario lay next to her as she cried herself to sleep.

Teresa was not prepared for the new day. She had an ominous feeling about what the day would bring. Walking through the wet dew, she perused the grounds, so rich and green. Paone had grandeur that was not comparable to any house in the Youngstown area. Roses were blooming everywhere; they had been Catherine's flowers. Her mother had loved flowers.

Teresa could hardly believe that she was here. Despite the remarriage of her father and despite the recognition of her brothers as the heirs-apparent, she was in control. She held the power within the company and was the owner of both Paone and the beloved, coveted Sand Castle.

She walked through the door and the cool air inside greeted her. The Midwestern summer day was already heating up outside. The children would soon want to take a dip in the pool. Sarah would have to supervise them. Teresa needed Maggie to enroll the children in St. Edward's Catholic School for the coming year. The children would need to be kept busy because she didn't want them to learn about the events of the previous evening. It was certainly difficult enough for them to witness the barrage at St. Lucy's Church. Teresa knew that she must reassure the children. Their world had already been tilted after John's murder. Now, their move back to Youngstown and the real possibility that someone was trying to murder their mother did not help to stabilize their lives.

As she entered the grand foyer, she heard Maggie scurrying around in order to organize and prepare the breakfast. Her sister-in-law, Sarah, had taken on a complete change of heart and was pitching in to help. Teresa was astounded at the change in Sarah, even if it were just for the day. She realized that she was in the midst of this intrigue and she was miraculously saved by Teresa's intervention. Sarah was grateful that she was here, living, and in the midst of her family.

Joe came over from the gatehouse. He saw Teresa and smiled. Teresa was exhausted and pale. Her hair was tied back in a ponytail; and her face, with no makeup, was drawn. Joe looked at her and hugged her. "It'll be okay, trust me, it'll work out," he said, trying to comfort her. Teresa, for her part, tried to have a staunch upper lip. But Joe's remark made her lip quiver, and she almost dissolved into tears. She waved him aside. "No, don't hug me right now. I need to get control or I'll never make it through the day."

Teresa settled down to Maggie's famous bacon, eggs, and fried potatoes breakfast. Joe dug in heartily. Frank came down and joined them. The three ate in silence. Frank pulled Sarah over to him as she scurried around and gave her a hug. She looked over at Teresa. "Teresa, I wish to God that I could help you. I'll take the kids into the kitchen and serve them breakfast there. We need to keep them away from this commotion."

"Thanks Sarah," Teresa uttered appreciatively. "We need to protect the children. They are so young and this stuff is so damn tough to deal with." Sarah was somewhat surprised. Teresa was always the lady; never had she used any curse word. This very minor infraction was certainly an indication that Teresa was on the edge.

Sarah went off to prepare breakfast for the children. Mario Jr. came downstairs and joined Teresa, Joe, and Frank at the table in the dining room. Mario helped himself to the food on the buffet and seated himself. He was quiet and thoughtful about the previous day's events. Mario was very grateful that he was alive. He sat in silence as Maggie poured a cup of coffee for him. The group had no need to speak; they were there in it together.

As they sat in silence, while finishing their breakfast, Teresa felt a hand on her shoulder and a kiss on her cheek. "Anthony!" she exclaimed, "I am so happy you are here. I needed you! You knew it and came."

Anthony beamed his wide warm smile and embraced his sister. "I asked Betty to stay at the Cape with Claudia, who has been heavily sedated. She doesn't know yet about Carlo and the others. I needed to get here and be with you." Joe got up and walked around the table to embrace his friend. Frank, in turn, headed toward his brother and saw Vincent Palmieri in the doorway.

"Come on in, the more the merrier. Misery loves company you know." Although Frank wasn't making sense, he certainly was understood by everyone present.

All remained seated as Anthony and Vincent helped themselves to breakfast. Just as they seated themselves, the great chiming doorbell rang. Maggie went through the foyer to see who was at the door. There stood Shannon Mahoney with her Uncle Sean, John's brother.

Marching into the room, with her uncle behind her, Shannon insisted on seeing her sister. Teresa told her that Kara had a difficult night and was still sleeping. "Perhaps you two could have a little breakfast before I go to wake her," suggested Teresa.

"Absolutely not. I do not want to spend any unnecessary time in this house. I want to get Kara out of here!" shouted the younger sister.

Teresa spoke in a soothing manner to calm her. "I'll do whatever I can to help you, Shannon."

"Oh, yeah! That's great. You and your family have taken everything from Kara and me, and now you want to help. Like I believe that."

Teresa felt somewhat wounded, but she tried to understand the girl's pain. She moved to touch Shannon, but the angry young woman recoiled. "Stay away from me, I've had enough. Get my sister," she commanded.

Maggie was about to tell Shannon to back off when Kara appeared, walking from the foot of the stairs in the foyer. "Enough! That's enough, Shannon," wailed the older sister. "It's time we all absorbed the truth. You need to know, Teresa. You, too, need to know. Where can we go?"

Teresa guided the whole group into the living room. There Kara sat between Teresa and Shannon. Anthony, Joe, Vincent Palmieri, and Frank came into the room and took their seats. Sean Mahoney positioned himself close to Shannon to offer support. Kara cried softly. She grasped Teresa's hands in hers, holding them like she would never let them go. Maggie closed the large double doors, after bringing a tray for coffee. Privacy was needed at this time.

Kara began to explain the previous day's confrontation with her mother. She began to speak and she repeated the revelations with great detail. Teresa sat spellbound, not wanting to hear what she already knew. The confirmation of John's treachery in Robert's murder was just as bad for her as was the initial revelation. The truth could not be held in secret anymore.

Teresa sat and quietly cried as Kara told her of Kelly Mahoney's revelations. As she listened, Shannon slipped her hand into her Uncle Sean's and squeezed hard. She sat motionless as in a trance, with stunning disbelief. How could she believe all of this? But this was Kara, and Kara would never make this up about their mother. Never.

When Kara was finished, she sat sobbing. Teresa embraced her. "Kara, oh Kara, you've been through so much. I am so sorry."

Kara pulled back and looked amazed. "How could you hold me and think of me, when so much has been taken from you? I don't understand."

Teresa looked at her tenderly. "Yes, I've lost a lot, but we all have. None of this is your fault. We've been part of a giant conspiracy that has altered each of us in various ways. There's no turning back now. Robert is gone, my father is gone, and John is gone. Nothing can change that."

Joe came and stood behind Teresa and gently massaged her shoulders, almost as a caress. Anthony was devastated. All one had to do was look at his face. He was completely and utterly destroyed. Teresa stood up and went over to him. He dissolved into tears as she held him. Sean Mahoney rose and took Shannon out of the room. Kara followed them to the front door.

"Please come with us," asked Sean. "You two girls need to be together," he continued.

"No, I am staying here right now," Kara protested. "You could stay with me, Shannon."

Shannon jerked her head. "No," she screeched, "I'll not stay here another minute." She ran off to the car. Sean shrugged his shoulders and ran after her. Kara watched as they drove off to Kelly's house on Fifth Avenue. Shannon wanted the comfort of the home in which she was raised, the home of her mother and father. It was familiar and it held the good part of the past, even though it was now being packed and vacated. The familiarity would surround Shannon and give her some momentary security.

Inside Paone, Frank sat in seething anger. "So, Carlo, Foccata, and Paolone helped to kill Papa in order to steal our birthright. Claudia stole our birthright and that shouldn't be." Ambling over to Teresa and Anthony, he gazed into their eyes with an icy reserve. "I'm going after Claudia. I am going to reclaim our birthright. She won't get away with this. I'm going to break that bitch."

46

The Viscomi family spent the remaining part of the day in peace at their Youngstown home. The location of the vast Paone estate allowed for privacy and solitude. Teresa asked Joe to arrange for a chartered jet to take them back to the Cape. Anthony called his wife, Betty, and inquired about Claudia. He was informed that Claudia had come out of her sedation and that her lawyer, John Swartz, had told her about the jet explosion and Carlo's death. She was very stoic. There was no typical screaming grief, no "crawling into the coffin" emotion. Her acceptance of the news was not predictable. Betty reported to Anthony that she had tried to comfort Claudia, but she resisted emotion and any expression of sympathy.

Teresa left Paone for about an hour to accompany Mario Jr. and Kara to visit Mario Sr. at the hospital. The jolly Maria Testa greeted Teresa with a hug. "Thank you for keeping my boy here, thank you."

Teresa hugged her and told her it was Frank who pulled Mario Jr. off the plane. "Frank knew that he should come to his mother and father. There is where he belonged."

After Kara and the younger Mario gave their greetings, they took Maria down to the hospital cafeteria for a bite to eat. Teresa sat with Mario Sr. and told him how Robert and her father had died. Mario was very emotional and cried. He was loyal to Angelo Viscomi, whom he also loved. Mario was very disturbed that his long time friend and associate, Tony Foccata, had a major role in the murder of Angelo. It was even more disturbing to Mario Sr. that it was probably Tony who injected Angelo with the fatal dose of bovine insulin.

Teresa put her arms around the old family friend and kissed him gently on the cheek. "I know that this has been difficult for you. To think that I married the man who had Robert killed! If I really dwelled on it, I probably could not go on. And I must go on for my three children. They deserve the life their fathers could not give them."

Teresa sat quietly as Mario calmed down. She held his hand as the recent pain injection took effect and he drifted off to sleep. Teresa sat holding his hand and thought of her future. She thought about protecting the children from the devastating information concerning their fathers and grandfather. Teresa thought about the Mahoney girls, Kara and Shannon, and how she might be able to help them. Then she thought about the company and the need to brainstorm with Anthony and Frank about the roles they all would play. The company also now had some key positions that needed to be filled. Carlo, Foccata, and Paolone were all gone. The Youngstown operation would be severely affected. Teresa sat in deep thought, holding Mario's hand.

Maria Testa and the younger two returned from the cafeteria. Mario Jr. was emotional upon seeing Teresa holding the hand of his sleeping father. That picture would be cemented in his mind forever, along with his loyalty to Teresa Viscomi.

Teresa stood when she realized that Maria had returned. She embraced Maria and said gently, "if there is anything you want, I will try to help you." They hugged and Teresa left for Paone to be with the rest of the family.

Driving into the grounds around the circular drive, Teresa parked at the main entrance. The house was ablaze with light. Entering the foyer, she caught a glimpse of Anthony entering the living room to join the other adults, Sarah, Frank, and Joe Cutruzzula. Teresa couldn't help herself as she called out to her brother, "You sure can tell that you don't own this house anymore. Would you want to pay this electricity bill?"

Anthony stopped in his tracks and turned to look at her with an expression of astonishment on his face. Then his face broke into a smile. "Oh, Sis, even in all of this, you haven't lost your sense of humor. I couldn't survive without you."

Both Teresa and Anthony entered the softly lit formal living room. Sarah, Frank, and Joe looked up and gave them warm greetings. Teresa called for Maggie to bring in some dessert and coffee for a family meeting. "Oh, Ter, not now, I'm not up to it," bellowed Frank. Sarah elbowed him and told him to be quiet. Joe looked in Teresa's eyes and saw real determination.

"Listen, Frank, this will be short and sweet, but it needs to be talked about, understand?" Teresa firmly stated. Frank meekly nodded his head.

After Maggie had brought the tray of desserts and Teresa poured the coffee, they were left in private behind the large double doors. "I want to talk with all of you about everything we just learned," Teresa started.

"Oh, Ter!" exclaimed Frank, "I can't, I just can't. Not right now."

Teresa responded very quickly. "I do not want to rehash the events. I want to talk about the outcome. I do not want my children to ever find out about this. They are vulnerable. To learn that Sarah's father,

182

by adoption, had the father of my young Anthony and Robert killed in order to marry me would be devastating. It would be too much. I hope that we can shield them at least until they are older, if not forever."

Anthony agreed. Frank and Sarah responded almost simultaneously, "Of course." The two looked at each other in surprise, smiled, and grasped hands like a young couple that had just started dating. Teresa noted some rekindling of affection there.

"There's one more thing," added Teresa. "I do not want Robert's parents, Tom and Naomi, to learn about this devastation. It would destroy them to learn that their only child was murdered and his widow had married the murderer. I don't think either could survive it." Anthony readily agreed. He and Joe were Robert's childhood buddies. They were like family to Tom and Naomi.

Frank was the only one to question the issue. "Don't you think they have the right to know. Robert was their only child. If it were my child, I would want to know."

Teresa rebuked Frank. "This is my call. They are my family. I want this Frank. Do you understand?"

"Okay," Frank responded, feeling properly chided.

Teresa then adjourned the family meeting, after telling everyone that they needed to prepare for the journey back to the Cape. Maggie had already packed and was showing the new maid where Teresa's and the children's things would go when they arrived from the York storage units. They would return to the Cape for the remaining weeks of the summer. The weeks would be hectic, as Sand Castle's renovation would soon be completed. Teresa had planned the summer's grand finale, the annual picnic. Teresa wanted it to be just like Angelo's and Catherine's Labor Day weekend picnic, a return to tradition and family solidarity.

47

Labor Day Weekend had finally arrived. It was Saturday morning and the move to Sand Castle in Osterville was to take place. Teresa and the children had spent the previous three days on Nantucket with Naomi and Tom. When Tom left for Boston to conduct some last minute business, Naomi traveled with Teresa and the children to the Cape. Tom would join Naomi at Sand Castle on Sunday for the picnic and leave for Youngstown with Maggie and the children on Labor Day in order to start school on Tuesday.

The Blakes had reassured Teresa that she should feel comfortable about taking a break and leaving the children in their care. They were happy to spend the time with their grandchildren, including little Sarah. Both Tom and Naomi considered little Sarah as their grandchild, even though their son was not her father. Teresa knew that the parents of her first husband loved her, and that fact had not changed with her second marriage to John. Not even John Mahoney's dislike for the Blakes could tear them from Teresa.

Teresa decided that she would remain at Sand Castle for three days after the picnic to enjoy some time in the house. After those few days, she and Joe would fly to Italy for a few weeks. Joe consented to go with her to Monte Paone, Calabria. Teresa would stay in the Viscomi house in the mountain top town. She had arranged for Joe to stay at his father's old home, just across the street from the Viscomi home. One could almost stick one's arm out the window and touch the other house across the street.

Teresa wanted to have a quiet beach vacation on the clear blue Ionian Sea. Down at Monte Paone Lido, they could spend some leisurely time on the beach. Perhaps a stop in Rome on the way home could be the grand finale of the vacation. Teresa could never tire of Rome.

Early in the morning, Joe dropped in to see Teresa. He wanted to catch up with her since her return to Hyannisport. She and the kids were eating one of Naomi's breakfasts. Maggie was over at Sand Castle, arranging for the move. All the clothes were being put in their appropriate places by the staff. Maggie would then return and go with the family to the cemetery to place flowers on Robert Blake's grave.

"Good morning everyone. Is everybody ready to celebrate the last hurrah of summer?" Joe teased.

Robert Jr. and young Anthony Blake were not amused. "Joe, that's mean. How would you like to leave the Cape and go where there is no ocean? I hate it," lamented Robert.

"Robert, it's okay. I'm going to be following you soon. I'm leaving the water for the first time in my life to move close to you guys in Youngstown. I hate it, too."

Just then Teresa chimed in smiling, "Oh, Joe, don't come to Youngstown. Stay here. No one is twisting your arm, are they?" Teresa smirked, her eyes dancing with delight.

"Joe, please don't listen to her," pleaded little Sarah. "Mommy, how could you tell him to stay here?"

Joe interrupted before Teresa could say a word. "Don't worry sweetie. Your meanie mother isn't going to stop me from being with you kids." Everyone laughed while little Sarah giggled.

Naomi told Joe to take a seat. She served him a healthy stack of pancakes and sausage. Teresa left her seat and poured him some coffee. "Gee, a guy could get used to all of this service," remarked a beaming Joe. "Don't get too satisfied, buster," warned Teresa, "you're not going to get this living on your own."

Naomi Blake chuckled and joined in on the banter. "Joe, don't let her tease you like that. Move in with her and the kids right now."

Teresa went white, and then burst into laughter. She put her hands around Naomi and squeezed. "I love you so much, don't ever change."

Naomi hugged her in return and said, "Teresa you are stuck with me for life."

Joe then informed Teresa about his plans for the day. "While you people are out moving into a plush mansion with every convenience and a private beach, I'll be driving to Boston on business. Anthony agreed with me about talking with the Palmieri brothers to evaluate any need for continued security."

Teresa gave Joe a pinch on the cheek. "I'm so glad. I think the danger should be over by now."

Joe agreed. "I believe you are correct, but I just want to be beyond doubt."

Naomi started clearing the kitchen, as she listened to the conversation. "You should stop in to see Tom today when you go up to Boston. Get him to take you out to dinner at a swanky place. He should foot the bill, too. After all, you're a son to both of us and you haven't been around for a long time."

Joe nodded his head and agreed. "You bet. I could use some time with a father. Tom is just the guy to talk to." Joe was thinking that

185

perhaps he could talk with Tom about his love for Teresa. Tom would understand, even though she had once been his son's wife.

Joe soon left and drove his Saab convertible out of Hyannisport, through Centerville to the Mid-Cape Highway and off to the bridge, Plymouth, Duxbury, and points north. He daydreamed all the way up to Boston. When he got there, he decided to stop in to see Tom, before his appointment with Vincent and Peter Palmieri. Joe reasoned that he could make arrangements with Tom to make sure he wasn't busy later in the day. He drove north as the wind blew briskly through his dark black, wavy hair. His black, wire-rimmed sunglasses shielded his dark brooding eyes from the glare of the bright hot sun. There would not be many more days like this one left in the year for this type of an outing in the car.

Meanwhile, back in the Hyannisport house, the children were being readied for the short trip to St. Francis Xavier Church's Cemetery. Maggie had returned from Sand Castle and offered to stay with little Sarah while the family went to place flowers on the grave. But Sarah wanted to go; she thought she was being left out. Naomi encouraged Teresa to allow Sarah to go. "She doesn't understand that Robert was the boys' father and not hers." Teresa agreed, and Maggie asked if she could go also. Teresa put her arms around Maggie and told her that she, more than any, had a right to go. Maggie had been with the Blakes since Robert was a young child. She helped raise him.

The family was divided into two groups for the trip in two Jeeps. Both of the vehicles were driven by Palmieri Security guards. Down Irving Avenue, they turned left onto Scudder at the Kennedy Compound, where the police guards were still posted. The cars made their way to Craigville Beach Road and around to Centerville. When they reached the cemetery, Teresa directed them to the section where Robert was buried.

Teresa and the other members of the group exited their vehicles and walked over to the grave. A plain marker, with a large cross, lay in the ground. It read, "Robert Thomas Blake." Teresa, Naomi, and the children placed roses that they had picked from the backyard on the grave near the headstone.

Teresa and the rest of the group stood in silence. Maggie took charge of the children and led them back to the Jeep. Teresa and Naomi remained at the gravesite, side-by-side. Teresa prayed for Robert and spoke to him in silence.

Walking from the grave, Teresa reflected on her life. Robert would always be with her and she would always visit his grave, but today was a milestone. She needed to move on. She had to move on, for the children, and for Joe.

Joe, already in Boston, looked for a place to park. The parking at Beacon Hill was at a premium and Joe didn't envy the residents of the area because on-street parking was difficult. He finally found a small spot in which he could back his little Saab. Jumping out of his car, he went to Tom Blake's door and rang the bell. A maid came to the door and told Joe that Mr. Blake was entertaining a few gentlemen. Joe brushed past her, saying that it really didn't matter, Tom always wanted to see him. Tom always said to interrupt him, nothing was too important to keep him from seeing a son.

Entering the front parlor, Joe stood frozen. He couldn't believe his eyes. Tom was indeed entertaining some gentlemen. There before him sat Tom Blake with Vincent Palmieri, Mario Testa Sr., and Frank Viscomi. "Oh! What are you doing here? Teresa expressly demanded that you leave Tom out of this." Joe was frantic.

Tom stood and moved toward Joe and hugged him. "It's all right, Joe. No one has done anything wrong. I invited them here."

"What do you mean, you invited them here?" asked a puzzled Joe.

"I invited them here to discuss a final report," explained Tom. "You see, I am the one who first hired Vincent Palmieri. I directed Vincent Palmieri to Angelo. I wanted to know about my son's death. Unfortunately, Angelo's participation in the investigation made the situation more complex. Those men, the ones who hurt Robert, also eliminated Angelo."

Joe was flabbergasted. "You have known all along? I just cannot fathom it all!"

Tom poured Joe a stiff scotch. "Drink up. When Angelo died, I felt that it was not quite on the up and up. So I asked Vincent to approach Anthony and inform him of the investigation. Anthony hired him, unbeknownst to him that Palmieri was also working for me. Anthony has no idea of my involvement."

Joe emptied his drink and asked for a refill. "Teresa wanted you to be protected; she loves you so much. There is no one in the world that means more to her than you and Naomi."

Tom nodded and responded, "I know, but I had to find out what happened to my only child, my son."

"Did you avenge him?" asked Joe.

"If you are asking if I killed John, the answer is no."

Frank cleared his throat and told Joe what he knew. "From what Vincent has dug up, we believe that Carlo and Foccata killed John. One reason was to cover up little Sarah's parentage. The other was to

187

move ahead and try to take over Viscomi Construction. John felt that Carlo and Kelly had betrayed him. He wanted to tell Claudia about their affair."

Tom then took over the story. "There is no doubt that Carlo, Foccata, Freddie Paolone, and John Mahoney were part of the plot to murder Robert." Tom sobbed and held his breath so that he wouldn't become more emotional.

"Frank, why did you pull Mario Jr. from the corporate jet? What did you know?" asked Joe.

Frank looked from Mario to Tom and back again. "Tom called me and told me that Mario Jr. was on the jet and that it would be best if I got him off immediately. He said that Mario's place was with his father."

Joe looked into Tom's eyes and met immediate understanding. He could verbalize no more questions. Tom knew that the plane would explode and he wanted to save Testa's son. Joe tried to take it all in. He slid out of his chair and stumbled to the door. Tom and Frank followed and asked him to come back inside. Joe waved them off. He had to get fresh air, he had to breathe, he had to get to his car and get out of there.

In Hyannisport, Naomi and the children were seated in their Jeep. Teresa and Maggie walked around the house. Teresa tried to drink it all in. Her eyes wide, she tried to block her emotions. She was leaving this place now for Sand Castle. She choked and brought one hand to her mouth to hold back the moans that would follow the tears brimming in her eyes. Maggie grabbed her other hand and walked with her out of the front door. "Come on Mrs. B, we're going home."

Driving up to Sand Castle, Teresa looked at the grandeur of the house, rising out of the plush, green lawn. The bright yellow cedar shingles made the home look exactly as it did years ago, when Angelo first brought his family there. That was the day that Teresa named it Sand Castle.

The Jeep stopped and the large black iron gates opened. The little caravan drove onto the grounds. Teresa asked the driver to stop for a minute, just to take in the sight. Here was a Sand Castle, rising from the earth, with grandeur and sophistication. It was exactly as it was the day Papa first brought them here. Teresa felt like a queen. Teresa Viscomi Blake Mahoney had arrived at her castle.

48

The smell of sauce permeated the air. On top of the six-burner, commercial-grade stove were two large pots of sauce, filled with meatballs and DiRusso sausage, brought from Youngstown. Teresa, Maggie, and Filomena, the new cook, had spent the morning preparing Teresa's special sauce. Today's dinner would mark a return to the traditional Italian feast for the evening after the Labor Day Picnic. Catherine Viscomi, in the past. had labored over the sauce as Teresa did this day. Catherine had preached over and over again the wisdom that she had learned from her own mother, Maria. She would say, "If you no have macchieroni, you no have nothing."

In the past, Teresa's mother would have a traditional New England clambake for lunch. Everything would be casual and the children would run down to the beach to swim and back again to the house to eat. The adults would eat and then settle into games of bocce or an Italian card game. There always would be time for anyone who wanted to go to the beach. The day was full of relatives, friends, company officials, and the Sand Castle staff, all enjoying a day of fun. The picnic on this day was the last hurrah of summer.

Teresa tried to recreate the old days, when her mother was the mistress of Sand Castle. Catherine's easy and informal style of entertaining made everyone feel at home. Everyone loved her and her easy brand of hospitality. Teresa was determined to recreate those good old days.

Riggs came into the kitchen and sat down. He was more casual and informal than he had ever been in the presence of Teresa. "Why, Riggs, you must be extremely tired after all this renovation," chuckled Teresa.

"Miss Teresa, I must confess that I am glad it is over," he answered.

"Well, we will take Paone more slowly than we did this house. I will be using a professional decorator there. We won't be returning it to its former appearance."

Riggs sighed, but did not respond to the remark. This had been an exciting yet draining project for him. Teresa and Riggs accomplished this without a decorator. They had restored the house to its former glory. It was truly magnificent.

Riggs jumped to his feet when one of the maids came into the kitchen to tell him the caterers had arrived. The luncheon would be clam chowder, steamers, chicken, potatoes, lobster, and corn on the cob. A special treat was ordered for the dessert, Boston cream pie. Little Anthony Blake and Joey Viscomi would be especially happy about that.

Guests were beginning to arrive. Maggie took over the organization of the caterers in order for Riggs to greet the guests. Teresa had changed into a casual summer dress for the family Mass that would be said by Father Montillo in the solarium. Anthony, Betty, and Joey would be there, along with Frank, Sarah, and their children. Joe had also agreed to come.

When the family began to arrive, Kara and Mario Testa Jr. came in the door. Teresa shrieked with delight. "I'm so glad you came. It will be really special now. Thank you so much." Teresa leaned over and kissed Kara on her cheek and hugged her in a tight clench. Letting go, she patted Mario on the back and asked about his parents.

"They're coming today," he informed her.

"Wonderful, I am so glad that your father has recuperated so well." Teresa was about to expound on her gratitude for Mario Sr. when he and Maria Testa came through the door. "Oh, Mario, thank God you are here."

Maria and Mario Sr. both encompassed Teresa in their arms. Maria exclaimed, "Miss Teresa, we are so happy to be with you here today."

"I think that this day is my real Thanksgiving," remarked Teresa. All of the family, Joe, and the Testas went into the solarium so that Father Montillo could begin the Mass. Riggs kept an eye on the caterers and allowed Maggie to join the family for Mass. He also greeted the additional guests.

Riggs stationed himself in the foyer and guided the new arrivals through the house to the grounds and refreshments. Several company officials arrived. Naomi Blake came down the stairs to the foyer upon Tom's arrival from Boston. She gave her husband a hug and showed him upstairs to their suite of rooms. Tom freshened up and decided to go down to the Library to relax and read the morning *Cape Cod Times*. Both Tom and Naomi were Episcopalians. Therefore, they felt no obligation to attend the Catholic Mass.

After Mass, the family dispersed. The children changed into their swimsuits and headed for the beach. A lifeguard had been hired to watch over the swimmers this day. The kids ran in and out of the water over to the grounds, and then back to the beach again. The grounds were soon filled with grownups, children, and a wonderful chaos.

Tom was still reading in the library when Frank Viscomi entered to sit and talk. Vincent and Peter Palmieri joined them. Tom was very concerned about Joe. He loved both Joe and Teresa's brother, Anthony, because they were Robert's best friends. They were like sons to him; but Joe was so disillusioned by the revelations of the day in Boston that Tom felt that he may not be able to mend their relationship. "And what will we say to Anthony about Joe's attitude?" Tom worried aloud.

"Nothing, because Anthony will never know," Joe answered as he surprised them upon entering the room. "I love Anthony, I love Teresa, and I love the kids. I would never hurt them and this might devastate them all. No, I will do my best to cover up this travesty."

Tom made an attempt to embrace Joe, but he quickly stepped aside. "Teresa has lost so much in life. I'm not about to open her life up to more heartache. She really loves you, Tom."

Just then Mario Testa Sr. stepped inside. "Joe, you have all of this wrong. There has been no wrong doing on the part of Mr. Blake. He just wanted my son to stay with me and Mr. Viscomi saw to it."

"You gentlemen must think that I am foolish and stupid. I know what has been going on here. I've known you, Tom, all of my life. I saw the truth in your face. I knew it instinctively. There is no justification for your actions, but I will not betray you. You took the law into your own hands."

Tom responded quickly, "Why Joe, the law didn't protect Robert or old Angelo. They would have never been avenged. My boy is in his grave and I will never truly enjoy life again. The only reward for me is to know that my daughter-in-law and grandchildren are safe."

With that, Joe looked at him with disbelief. His morals could not bend, even though he realized that Tom was right. He walked out the door to look for Anthony, Joey, Robert Jr., and little Anthony Blake. He was going to put this out of his mind and challenge the boys to a game of bocce.

The men in the library decided to disperse and join the crowd. Lunch was about to be served, and they wanted the day to go on as smoothly as possible. Tom Blake assured them that Joe would be okay, and he insisted that no one was to hurt Joe in anyway. Tom truly loved Joe and hoped that the schism would end.

As everyone convened on the lawn for lunch, Claudia Viscomi De-Roches made a grand entrance. She arrived on the arm of Sean Mahoney, with Shannon Mahoney bringing up the rear. Claudia, as usual, was overdressed. She walked into the crowd as though she were the Queen Mother, expecting all to bow and curtsey. Sean was very attentive and Shannon was very bashful.

Claudia marched right up to Teresa and said, "How nice of you to resurrect your mother's party in my old home. It certainly shows your

191

lack of style and taste. Why don't you show me around?" Teresa moved forward and told Claudia to follow her into the house. The other guests began eating. Teresa tried to keep her composure, remembering Claudia had just lost a husband. After all, she and Claudia had something in common. The second husband of each woman had murdered the first husband of his wife. It was emotionally devastating and beyond belief. Teresa would try to make her point compassionately.

Teresa took Claudia into the formal living room. The portrait of Angelo and Catherine Viscomi stared down at them from its place over the fireplace. They sat on the sofa, opposite each other. "Well, I see you put that old picture back up there. Couldn't wait, could you?" retorted Claudia.

"Actually, Claudia, I could not wait. I wanted to place the portrait in its rightful place. You see, this is where it belongs, because this was my mother's house. Every inch of the house was hers."

Claudia laughed haughtily. "You really are pitiful, Teresa. You can never erase me or the fact of me. I may not live in this house anymore, but I have a portion of the family money and company. You will never own that part of the company and never control it, despite your efforts. The family never really accepted me; but you all have to deal with me, and I will continue to make you aware that I am a reality. You will always have to deal with me." Claudia got up and left the room. When she reached the rear door, she turned to make one more remark to Teresa. "You really must develop a better style; you are so common!" With that, she walked out the door to Sean.

Teresa walked to the French doors and peered out through its windows. She looked on the gathering of people. She knew that she would have to always deal with Claudia. That was a fact. *Thank you Papa.* But Claudia was with John's brother, Sean Mahoney. Teresa had not bet on dealing with the two of them together. *What plan did they have to hurt her family? What planned intrigue would wreak havoc on the Viscomi family?* She continued to gaze at the group through the windows of the French doors. She made no move to go outside. Naomi came from the second floor and put her arm around Teresa, knowing that she needed comforting.

Outside, Tom Blake stopped his discussion with Frank and Mario Sr. He nodded in the direction of Claudia and Mahoney. Frank and Mario looked over at them, with obvious disdain.

Joe was aware of the group's attention on the new widow and her escort. Frank went over to his stepmother.

Joe and Teresa looked on from different areas—he outside, she inside. They watched Frank grab Claudia's arm in a rough manner. They watched as Sean intervened. A pushing match would have begun if Mario Testa Sr. had not wedged himself between the two and led Frank away. Bobby Faccia and Mario Jr. got the nod from the senior Testa. Both of the young men went over to Sean Mahoney and roughly ushered him to the front of the house, while Claudia protested.

Tom Blake went over to Claudia and suggested that she leave the party. He gently took her arm and sweet-talked her into the house. Teresa and Naomi stood back as they entered the door. "You are in terrible shock, dear Claudia. You need to rest, my dear. Go home and relax."

"I'll go home, Tom; I'll go home to my empty house. This should be my house. This is my house. This is the home I want, the one I deserve." She broke down in tears, sobbing on his shoulder.

"Claudia, it was not meant to be. This home belongs to the Viscomi family. You chose to move on when you married Carlo. You've got to let go. Treat yourself kindly."

"I'm treating myself kindly," Claudia responded. I'm buying the house in Centerville and I'm never going away." Teresa gasped as Tom led Claudia out of the front door and ushered her to the car, in which Sean Mahoney had been placed. They drove off to Centerville.

Tom came back into the house and walked over to Teresa and Naomi, who by now had been joined by Joe. Tom gently kissed his daughter-in-law on the cheek. "Don't worry, Teresa, I will not allow Claudia to cause any more confusion in your life. She may try to cause trouble, but she will meet her match in me."

"Oh, Grandpa!" exclaimed Teresa, "I know that Claudia is always going to be around. I thought we could make peace, but now I know that is not going to happen. I will need to be very wary of her and the menacing difficulty that she could create in our lives."

Joe tenderly led Teresa to the door. "Come on, Ter. You have guests. You need to act like the hostess that you are."

Teresa stopped and looked at Tom. "Grandpa, you are no match for Claudia. You just don't understand." Then she and Joe went out to talk with the guests.

Tom chuckled to himself, as he and Naomi went to join the others. Tom first went to Frank to discuss the confrontation with Claudia. "I think we need to talk a little later. Make sure Mario Testa is there for the discussion. We'll talk before the spaghetti dinner tonight."

Tom left to take a dip with his grandchildren and their cousins. Naomi settled into a large wicker chair to catch up on recent happenings with Maria Testa. Joe and Teresa strolled hand-in-hand over the grounds, greeting the guests and sharing pleasant conversation. Teresa noted Shannon's pleasant demeanor. "Maybe she'll realize that I really do care and want to help her and Kara," Teresa confided in Joe.

"Don't hold your breath," warned Joe. "Kara has Mario Jr. Shannon has no one. She is a loner. I hope she won't be drawn to Sean Mahoney and Claudia."

Teresa decided to put the confrontation at the back of her mind and enjoy the day that she had worked on for the entire summer. She and Joe walked down to the beach to sit in the sand and relax. There, at the beach, were Betty and Anthony, sitting on a blanket. They all sat together and reminisced about days gone by, when they were the children on Labor Day Weekend. They talked of the picnic and reminisced about Robert, Anthony, and Joe wrestling on the lawn, when they were children.

Teresa's mind drifted to the evening's plans. She hoped that all would be pleased with the biggest surprise of the evening—the fireworks. Despite Claudia, all was well. She now had her beloved home and security. The children would be happy here. There would be many new memories created. Catherine and Angelo would preside over their lives from their spot above the fireplace in the living room.

49

The clear blue turquoise water of the Ionian Sea gently rippled against the coarse sand on the beach. On the blanket, Teresa and Joe gazed out over the water, watching a group of boys scuba diving down to the bottom and bringing up squid in their nets. Monte Paone Lido was like no place on earth. It was a quiet September. Most of the vacationers had returned to the city to go on with life. Monte Paone Lido was a destination for Italians; it saw very few Americans. The Americans who did visit were descendants of Italian emigrants to America, like Teresa's parents and Joe's father.

The two people on the blanket didn't talk. They communicated in silence. Teresa reached out and held Joe's hand. The summer was over and many devastating secrets had been disclosed. Teresa needed this beach vacation to recover. She had grown closer to Joe. He was a good man and he was very protective of Teresa and her children. Teresa knew that Joe loved her, but she had resisted it. She had run from it. It was too close to Robert and it felt like a betrayal of him. But that was the past. John had made the difference. He showed her what life should not be. He showed her the ugly side of life. And now, Teresa knew how different the ugly was from the wonderful, the difference between John and Robert. Now she was ready for the beautiful because life was too short for the ugly. Now, Teresa was ready for Joe Cutruzzula.

Joe broke the silence, as Teresa held his hand. "This land is so beautiful. Why did our parents leave it to go to America?"

Teresa responded with a chuckle. "Perhaps they wanted to support their families and maybe eat!" Joe laughed and told her that she was right. With a smile on her face, Teresa continued. "They did end up on the Cape, which is a beautiful place. It's not quite like the sea here, but it is profoundly beautiful."

It was Joe's turn to laugh. "Yeah, but what about Youngstown?"

Teresa was serious with her reply. "Youngstown has very friendly people; but it's part of the Midwest, which is different from the East. Heck, it is very different from York, Pennsylvania. There are many warm people and Italian Americans there." Joe sighed in recognition of Teresa's truths. Her simple honesty was another reason that he loved her.

Driving back up the mountain to Monte Paone to freshen up for dinner, Teresa and Joe discussed the future. "Frank called last night," Teresa informed Joe. "Frank told me that Tom had contacted a friend at the Federal Aviation Administration to expedite the investigation of the plane's explosion. The FAA ruled that it was a malfunction of the plane's engines, which caught on fire."

All Joe could do was respond with an "Oh!" Teresa was surprised at his lack of words. "Well, Joe, isn't that wonderful? We can put this behind us and move on. What do you think?"

"I think that it was fortuitous that Tom Blake had a friend who could expedite the investigation," observed Joe.

"You're right," declared Teresa. "It certainly helped me. I'm so privileged to have Tom Blake as a father-in-law. He and Naomi are real family."

Joe drove up the winding hill to the old town. Nothing in the town was newer than four hundred-years-old. The winding road took them up the hill, past the cemetery. The cemetery was ornate and well manicured. Only a few generations were interred there. After a well-appointed amount of time, the graves were turned over and then new family members were interred in them. How different it was in America, where the graves are meant to last forever.

The couple drove slowly past the piazza to the old Immaculate Conception Church, which has existed for more than four hundred years. The interior of the church had been lovingly restored to museum quality. The statue of the town's patron saint, St. Francis Di Paolo, was encased in glass. Flash photography was prohibited inside the church.

Joe headed to the Viscomi house, where Teresa had arranged to stay. Her father had retained ownership of the house and the family continued to maintain it. The Cutruzzula house was directly across the street from the Viscomi house. The street was more like a single lane road. Teresa had also arranged for Joe to be a guest in this house, now owned by his cousin. Both she and Joe left the little car and entered their respective lodgings. They had arranged to meet and go to dinner down in Lido, around 7:00 P.M.

Teresa enjoyed being in Calabria. The little Viscomi house was rustic, furnished with antiques and comfortable, deep-cushioned furniture. Teresa was happy to be in the house and she was happy that Joe was across the street, sharing this time with her. She took her time to get ready for dinner. Joe had to disappoint his relatives because they had planned to entertain him. Joe promised that both he and Teresa would have dinner the next evening with them.

At 7:00 P.M., Joe and Teresa came out of their houses simultaneously. Joe put the top down on the little two-seater and drove slowly through the village. In the piazza, across from the church, the accordion player had begun to play some old Calabrese tunes. Older villagers sat on benches, listening to the music. Some gayer old-timers even danced a little, while others clapped their hands to the rhythm of the tune.

Teresa told Joe that after dinner she wanted to return to take part in the festivities and enjoy the music. Joe agreed that the evening would be perfect if they spent it on the piazza. Driving down the hill, they looked over the Ionian Sea that glistened from the reflection of the full moon. Teresa talked of Sand Castle and her plans to spend Thanksgiving there.

"We'll go there for the week of Thanksgiving and then we'll close the house until May. All the family will be there, and it will be wonderful. Frank's family, Anthony, Betty, and little Joey will all be there. Of course, Tom and Naomi will agree to come. Perhaps we'll even get Kara there. You'll be there, Joe, won't you?"

"Of course, Ter. Where else would I ever be?"

Joe and Teresa visit the Cutruzzula and Viscomi homes in Italy